VOYAGE OF THE STELLA

ALSO BY R. D. LAWRENCE

Wildlife in Canada (1966)

The Place in the Forest (1967)

Where the Water Lilies Grow (1968)

The Poison Makers (1969)

Cry Wild (1970)

Maple Syrup (1971)

Wildlife in North America: Mammals (1974)

Wildlife in North America: Birds (1974)

Paddy (1977)

The North Runner (1979)

Secret Go the Wolves (1980)

The Zoo That Never Was (1981)

VOYAGE of the STELLA

R·D·LAWRENCE

Holt, Rinehart and Winston   New York

Published by Holt, Rinehart and Winston, 383 Madison Avenue, New York, New York 10017.

Published simultaneously in Canada by Holt, Rinehart and Winston of Canada, Limited.

Library of Congress Cataloging in Publication Data

Lawrence, R. D., 1921-
Voyage of the Stella.

1. Voyages and travels—1951-. 2. Stella Maris
(Cabin cruiser) 3. Pacific coast (Canada)—Description
and travel. I. Title.
G477.L38 1982   910'.09164'33   81-6901
ISBN 0-03-058901-0   AACR2

First Edition
Designer: Susan Mitchell
Maps by Rafael Palacios
Printed in the United States of America
1 3 5 7 9 10 8 6 4 2

ISBN 0-03-058901-0

An age shall come with late years when Ocean shall loosen the chains of things, and the earth be laid open in vastness, and Tethys shall bear new worlds . . .

Lucius Annaeus Seneca
(4 B.C.–A.D. 65)

CONTENTS

Maps appear on pages ix, 5, 43, and 95.

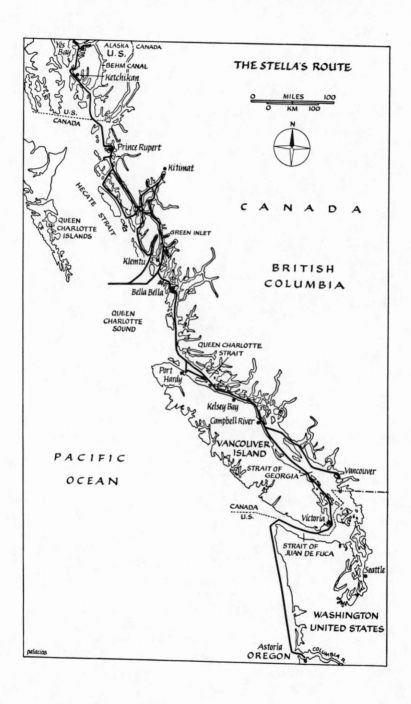

THE STELLA'S ROUTE

0   MILES   100
0   KM   100

N

ALASKA CANADA
U.S.
Yes Bay
BEHM CANAL
Ketchikan

U.S.
CANADA

Prince Rupert

Kitimat

C A N A D A

HECATE STRAIT

QUEEN CHARLOTTE ISLANDS

GREEN INLET

Klemtu

Bella Bella

BRITISH COLUMBIA

QUEEN CHARLOTTE SOUND

QUEEN CHARLOTTE STRAIT

Port Hardy

Kelsey Bay
Campbell River

VANCOUVER ISLAND

PACIFIC OCEAN

STRAIT OF GEORGIA

Vancouver

CANADA
U.S.

Victoria

STRAIT OF JUAN DE FUCA

Seattle

WASHINGTON
UNITED STATES

Astoria
OREGON

COLUMBIA R.

palacios

VOYAGE OF THE STELLA

THE STELLA MARIS

The deserted marina was quiet and dark, its docks and buildings shrouded by the penumbra of night. On shore, two naked bulbs glowed, each encircled by a halo of dampness in which a few early moths gyrated sluggishly. The lights from my own boat cast a small and feeble flush on the edge of the berth and were reflected like pale moonshine in the moving water to port. The date was March 13, 1972.

That morning I had taken delivery of my vessel and now, at 10:00 P.M., I was finishing preparations for a journey the main purposes of which were to explore the coasts and waters of the North Pacific's Inside Passage and to study the creatures that inhabit those latitudes. But as I contemplated the night from within the small cabin, I found myself wondering about the ostensible reasons behind my undertaking: Was I really motivated by exploratory and biological interests, or was I once again trying to escape the tragedy that had haunted me for three years? My intellect kept telling me I was, indeed, principally determined to observe and record the life and habitats that I was going to encounter, but at the same time my emotions nagged me, insisting I was running away from the past and seeking personal solace. Undoubtedly, both postulates contained some truth, but I could not then—and cannot even today—determine which had priority.

In this mood, I sat in the cabin and mulled over the circumstances that had brought me to Victoria, British Columbia's capital on Vancouver Island, where, sheltered within Oak Bay, the marina that housed my boat is located.

Like thistledown running before the wind, I had been pushed into aimless wandering by events that began at my farm in Ontario. On March 13, 1969, my life had been orderly and content; then, on the morning of the fourteenth, my wife, Joan, became ill. Her condition worsened steadily, but three weeks elapsed before the doctors established that she was bleeding inside her head. An aneurism, a little balloon, had thrust out of the branch of an artery in the middle brain, in an area that is inoperable. Joan died on June 7.

I will not dwell on the state of my emotions during the six months that followed my wife's death. After all, those who have lost a great love will know how it is at such a time, while those who have not will be unable to fully grasp the awesome depth of despair that envelopes the mind. Suffice it to say that each day became more and more unbearable and that I could not continue alone in a home and environment that had meant so much to both of us. I sold North Star Farm, in Uphill, Ontario. And I ran.

Instinctively, I made for the wilderness of British Columbia, to an area where in another time my wolf-dog Yukon* and I had found great contentment for more than a year. This was a mistake, for instead of rediscovering inner peace, I became even more depressed. Vandalism and human refuse made me rage at the injustice of a fate that could take Joan when she was only thirty-two and yet allow such depreda-

*See *The North Runner*, by R.D. Lawrence, Holt, Rinehart and Winston, New York, 1978.

tions to continue unchecked. This state of mind was not logical, of course, but that was how I felt.

During this journey, I was forced to kill a grizzly bear that had been previously wounded by buckshot fired from an aircraft. Even under normal circumstances I would have been upset and outraged by the utter cruelty of the hunters as well as by the need to put the bear out of its misery. But at such an emotional time, the killing of that bear—which actually charged me, forcing me to shoot it—had a disastrous effect on my emotions. Once again I ran, this time to another part of the wilderness.

In the early autumn of 1971 I accepted a job in a community in northern British Columbia, thinking that the involvement with work and people would help me attain some measure of emotional stability. Again, I was wrong. I quickly became bored. I lacked direction. Most of all, I lacked challenge. In short, I was going through the motions of living, but I didn't care about life itself.

This state of mind led to despondency, and as my depression progressed, memories of Joan and the farm came ever more frequently to mind. A week before Christmas I had a nightmare. In it, I was once more being charged by the grizzly. I saw myself lift the rifle and shoot again and again. Up to the moment of squeezing off the last bullet, the dream was as factual as the reality had been, but when I went to examine the carcass, I found myself staring into Joan's face, realizing that in some incomprehensible way I had been shooting at her instead of at the bear. She lay dead, her head shattered and bleeding, but from the neck down, the body stretched on the ground was that of the grizzly. Mercifully, I awakened at this point, but several moments passed before I could collect myself sufficiently to understand I had been dreaming. The time was 3:45 A.M. Before dawn came that day I knew I could no longer continue brooding over my sorrows. I needed a change, and quickly, or I would find myself in serious emotional difficulty. I had been dreading Christmas in the small town in which I lived; now I decided to take a holiday. I would go south—but where? After only a few moments of debate, I opted for Victoria, British Columbia's capital city on Vancouver Island. Why I made that particular choice I do not know. For the previous few weeks I had found myself thinking about the ocean with increasing regularity, and perhaps it was this consideration that determined my destination. Anyway, soon after eleven o'clock that morning, I was airborne and Vancouver-bound. That same evening, I was on board a ferry that was taking me to Victoria.

Upon my arrival, I did extravagant things. I dined sumptuously each evening, indulging my every gastronomic whim. My days were spent browsing through the many secondhand bookstores to be found in the small city, and I bought more than a few books as I checked through the piles of randomly placed volumes.

On the fourth day, I visited the British Columbia Provincial Museum, a small but fascinating place, which I enjoyed so much that I took to spending most of my time studying its exhibits, especially the oceanographic displays. There I met the curator, Dr. Bristow Foster, and it was he who unwittingly influenced my immediate future. Noting my interest in marine life, he introduced me to a visiting oceanographer from Ottawa who was engaged in writing a book on planktonic organisms. Bristow Foster also placed the museum's facilities at my disposal. And when he discovered that we shared a mutual admiration for John Steinbeck, Dr. Foster alerted me to a book written by the late Ed Rickets, a close friend of Steinbeck's who was the fictional "Doc" in *Cannery*

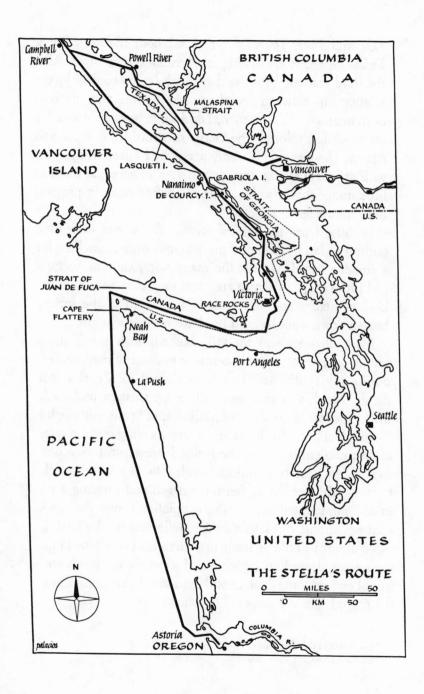

Campbell River

Powell River

BRITISH COLUMBIA
CANADA

TEXADA I.

MALASPINA
STRAIT

VANCOUVER
ISLAND

LASQUETI I.

GABRIOLA I.

Nanaimo
DE COURCY I.

Vancouver

STRAIT OF GEORGIA

CANADA
U.S.

STRAIT OF
JUAN DE FUCA

CANADA
U.S.

CAPE
FLATTERY

Neah
Bay

Victoria
RACE ROCKS

Port Angeles

La Push

Seattle

PACIFIC

OCEAN

WASHINGTON

UNITED STATES

THE STELLA'S ROUTE

0   MILES   50
0   KM   50

N

Astoria
OREGON

COLUMBIA R.

palacios

Row and *Sweet Thursday.** Rickets's book, *Between Pacific Tides*† proved so fascinating that I read it several times. After the third reading, stimulated as much by the book as by the relationship between Steinbeck and Rickets and my own deep interest in the two men, I decided to buy a boat and live on it while exploring the coasts of British Columbia and Alaska. Having arrived at my decision, I talked things over with an encouraging Bristow Foster, who gave me that last little nudge that is so often needed before one can progress from mere idea to action.

Because I am the sort of person who wastes little time putting a plan into effect, I immediately began searching for a suitable vessel, visiting the many salesrooms in Victoria and inspecting a variety of craft that ranged in price from the kind of luxury and size I could not afford to the sort of broken-down hulk I would not have wanted as a gift.

My preference was for sail, but although I had some sailing experience, it had been acquired many years earlier, during my youth, and had been limited to a twelve-foot dinghy fitted with only one sail, a toy used in protected, inshore waters off the coast of Mallorca, in Spain. Although I did not feel qualified to handle a larger sailing vessel on the often turbulent waters of the Inside Passage, on the second day of my search I almost decided to buy a beautiful, twenty-eight-foot sloop, Bermuda-rigged and carrying a jib in addition to the mainsail. The temptation to own this sleek boat was strong, but later that day, reflecting on the kind of explorations I would be likely to undertake, I concluded that such a vessel would draw too much water for my needs and would present some definite problems in solo handling along the rugged course I proposed to follow.

*The Viking Press, New York, 1954.
†Stanford University Press, Stanford, California, 1968.

The search was narrowed to powerboats. By now I knew almost exactly what I needed, so it didn't take long to find a suitable cruiser. It was twenty-four feet long, drawing three feet of water, with an eight-foot beam. This boat, with only twelve hours on the engine clock, was practically brand new. It was priced at nine thousand dollars, some four thousand dollars below list price. I went over the vessel carefully, noting that she had sufficient accommodations to sleep six persons (although I would have hesitated to carry five passengers in a boat of such proportions), was fitted with a 165-horsepower, inboard/outboard, gasoline-powered engine, and within the cabin was equipped with a two-burner, alcohol-fueled stove, a small icebox, a sink, and counter space. The rest of the cabin was given over to twin upholstered benches that flanked the main table, the whole making up into a double bunk. Midships on the port side, between the galley and the cockpit, was a small head—a walled space about one-and-a-half times the size of a shower stall—with a washbasin that, like the galley sink, was hooked up to the twenty-gallon freshwater storage tank and was operated by an individual hand pump. Forward, twin bunks to port and starboard hid a series of storage lockers beneath their padded surfaces—as did the cabin benches—and built into the bow was an additional locker for storing such things as rope, anchors, and chain. The cabin superstructure that rose above the bow deck was fitted with a large deadlight, a window that gave a panoramic view ahead.

The boat was an express cruiser. That is to say, the superstructure extended over the forward half of the after cockpit, the deckhead of which was raised above that of the cabin. As a result, the wheel and pilot's seat were also raised to offer a clear view through the cockpit windshield, which was well forward to allow space for a wide shelf that did double duty as chart table and general catchall, and on which the spherical, internally gimballed compass was mounted. In addition to the permanent shelter offered by the raised superstructure, the after part of the cockpit was totally enclosed by a removable canvas screen fitted with acetate windows to port, starboard, and aft. The six-cylinder engine was recessed in a well but was covered by a raised hatch that, fitted with padded cushions, served as a double bunk.

I spent two hours examining the cruiser, which was on shore on chocks. The more I looked and pried and probed, the more I liked the vessel, but, not wanting to appear too eager, I told the salesman I would have to think about it overnight and give him my decision in the morning. This was a barefaced lie—and I blush to admit it—because I had made up my mind within the first half-hour. I was going to buy this boat!

The next day the salesman and I did some horse trading. I offered to pay the asking price provided this included a 20-horsepower auxiliary outboard motor. We haggled for a time before the dealer finally agreed to the motor, but he balked at including a mounting bracket free of charge. In the end, knowing perfectly well that no buyer has ever gotten the better of a salesman, yet feeling that I had obtained a good deal, I capitulated, making out a check for a thousand dollars as down payment and agreeing to settle the outstanding balance by March 10, when I would accept delivery.

Christmas came and went. It was not the most memorable Yule of my life, but afterward, full of ideas and almost feverish with the desire to complete plans for my journey, I left Victoria for Vancouver. There, a few hours before taking a plane back to the north, I bought the twenty-four marine charts, which I would need in order to lay off a course from Victoria to Ketchikan, Alaska. Knowing it would take the balance of winter for me to complete all my plans and to locate and buy the many items necessary for my undertaking, I was suddenly anxious to get back. I looked forward to the task of laying off a main course through the Inside Passage and perhaps plotting secondary courses into many of the fascinating fjords and inlets along the way. In addition, I intended to bone up on navigation, for although I am somewhat expert at traveling through the wilderness guided by compass, map, stars, and sun, I knew from past experience that journeying over the surface of the ocean presents its own unique and challenging problems.

Returning from Vancouver on December 27, the first thing I did was to quit my job, giving four weeks' notice and regretting the need to give my employer so much time, for I now could hardly wait to get on with my preparations. For the next four weeks I worked all day at my job in the office and most of the night at home, laying out the main course and making lists of the provisions and equipment I would need on the voyage. This was a major job because a journey such as I was contemplating requires a great deal of careful planning if one is not to leave out some essential item or forget to allow for the vagaries of tide and currents in any one of the many locations that I would encounter en route.

After I left my job, I was able to devote all my energies to preparations for the trip. In this way the winter passed swiftly. When March arrived and it was time to return to Victoria, I suddenly realized that I had been much too busy to fret over my personal problems.

Now, on the eve of my journey, I found that I was once more stimulated and eager to face the challenges that lay before me. My emotional needs remained unfulfilled and I was aware that there would be bad times ahead, but by midnight, as I listened to the susurrus of the timeless ocean, I knew my energies and resolution had returned. Before turning in, I went on deck, noting that the sea was calm, the wind was lighter, and the boat basin was illuminated by a quarter-moon shining out of a cloudless sky. The next day I would go into Victoria to buy the last of my supplies and make final arrangements for the voyage.

I had taken possession of my boat after it was trailered to Oak Bay, where I had previously booked a berth. Here, accompanied by the salesman, who was clearly anxious to hand over the vessel and be on his way, I inspected the craft from stem to stern, starting the engine and running it for a time while checking to make sure that the new battery I had paid for had been installed and was fully charged. Satisfied that all was in order, I signed a release, allowing the salesman to leave. Then I set about stowing my belongings on board. These included my personal effects and equipment as well as a variety of foods and other supplies I had calculated would be necessary at the start of the journey. When everything had been put away and the boat's superstructure had been washed clean of the winter's grime, I felt it was time to go and buy the marine radio I would need for the journey.

I assumed that this purchase would be a simple matter, but I was soon to learn that in practice it is somewhat complicated. Canadian and international regulations require such equipment to be licensed as a ship station *before* it is actually purchased. In addition, the would-be operator must also obtain a license. In Canada, licenses come in two classes: one is called a Certificate of Proficiency in Radio Operation; the other is a Radiotelephone Operator's Restricted Certificate. The first piece of paper is earned when the applicant passes a technical examination; the second also requires a test, but this confines itself mainly to questions seeking to ensure that the applicant knows the right frequencies to call, is familiar with the rules governing radio procedures at sea (Canadian and international), and is able to send and receive correctly—which is another way of saying that an operator should know what to do if he or she is in trouble, and that the law takes a dim view of people who use obscenities on the air or frivolously clutter an already crowded ether. This certificate, not requiring any technical expertise, is the easiest and quickest to obtain, so I applied for it, despite the fact that I had once been trained as a radio operator. Armed with the piece of paper that made it legal for me to turn a knob, I next went to get the document that would bestow respectability on my boat, feeling somewhat like a prospective groom shopping for a marriage license. During this skirmish with the forces of bureaucracy, I learned that before I could obtain a ship station license, I had to register a call sign. Needing a name quickly, I chose *North Star*, but the unsmiling official rejected this immediately on the grounds that it would be confusing because the North Star is a navigational bearing. How about *Star of the North*, I suggested? No, that wouldn't do either. Okay, the *Stella Maris*, I offered for the third time. My inquisitor nodded solemnly. Thus my vessel became the *Star of the Sea*—which is, of course, the *North Star* . . .

Legalities attended to, I bought the previously selected 20-watt, 8-channel radio unit*, together with a whip antenna made of anodized aluminum to resist corrosion, and a

---

*Wattage ratings differ in Canada and the United States. In Canada radio sets are rated in accordance with the total radio frequency energy delivered to the antenna, but in the United States they are rated according to the power used by the final amplifier tube; this is generally two-and-a-half times the RF output power. Thus, 20 watts RF output in Canada is equal to 50 watts for the same set in the United States.

sheet-copper ground plate that was to be fastened to the hull, below the waterline, without which no marine radio is fully reliable.

After leaving the radio store, I went to buy a lifeboat, if such a grandiose name can be applied to the eight-foot, plastic dinghy I finally selected, one of those double-hulled little runabouts that make up for in portability what they lack in stability. I had no illusions about the orange-hued pygmy: If bad luck ever made it necessary to "abandon ship" in a rough sea in that cockleshell, I would be thoroughly wet and cold by the time I got to shore. Yet I was quite sure that the dinghy would eventually reach land, for it is virtually unsinkable. I selected it because of its practicality and, I hoped, safety, for there was no room on the superstructure of the *Stella* for storing a larger, more conventional lifeboat and no equipment with which to hoist and lower such a craft.

It was after five o'clock when I put the plastic shell into the back of the station wagon, too late to have the radio equipment installed at a nearby boat yard, but I managed to make an appointment for the next morning. Afterward, I drove back to Oak Bay, took my new purchases out of the car, and carried them on board. Then I cooked a meal. When my hastily prepared supper was consumed, I tidied up, preparing the *Stella* for the following day's work, when she would be hauled out of the water to have the copper plate fixed to her hull.

At ten o'clock that night, tired but content and taking pleasure from the gentle rocking of my vessel, I turned in.

UNEXPECTED JOURNEY

My first night's slumber on board the *Stella Maris* was restful
and undisturbed, but it was of short duration. The gulls saw
to that! Daybreak had arrived, but the sun was not yet visible
when the discordant calling of hundreds of gulls roused me
from a deep sleep. Sitting up in the bunk and looking
through the forward deadlight, I watched the swift, graceful
birds as they wheeled and dived and planed. For a time I
remained still, enjoying the performance. Then I began to
take stock of my surroundings, noting that even from a
distance of some thirty miles the peaks of the Olympic
Mountains in Washington were visible from my bunk, their
white crowns streaked by fingers of orange and daubed with
mauve and aquamarine. The view was commonplace
enough in those parts and somewhat marred by a small forest
of boat masts as well as by several buildings, yet the far
panorama caused me considerable excitement as a foretaste
of wonders yet to come. My enthusiasm was only slightly
dampened when I climbed out of my sleeping bag to find that
the temperature in the cabin was a chilly 45 degrees F. I put
the kettle on to boil; then, reluctantly, went into the head for
a cold sponge bath to the castanet accompaniment of my
teeth. There were distinct disadvantages to being aboard a
small vessel in March!

After breakfast, I faced the task of handling the *Stella* for the first time; but it was not until I had started the engine and, waiting for it to warm up, went on deck, that apprehension seized me. Surveying the obstacles around my boat, I noted that though the *Stella* was moored at the end of a line of similar craft and had clearance to starboard, she was going to have to go out astern into a narrow channel on the other side of which more powerboats were moored. There appeared to be only just enough room to maneuver, and no room at all for mistakes. Standing dockside at the stern of my vessel, she seemed longer than twenty-four feet, too long for me to tuck her blunt stern into that channel and swing her bow in a seaward direction. I began to get very nervous! Seeking to give myself confidence, I recalled the forty-foot rescue launch I once handled in the Mediterranean, but when I realized that twenty-five years had passed in the interim, I became even more apprehensive. Then I pulled myself together. The *Stella* had to be moved; and the longer I hesitated, the more tense I would become. I undid the mooring lines and climbed aboard to stand before the wheel.

With the control lever in stern drive and the power at idle, the *Stella* began to move slowly, inching away from the dock and showing herself acutely responsive to the helm. Characteristically, now that I was fully committed, my nervousness left me and I started to enjoy the experience. As graceful as one of the gulls swimming in the boat basin, my vessel backed fully into the channel, then moved dutifully ahead, settling down nicely with the engine running at 600 revolutions per minute (RPM). We threaded our way through flotillas of craft, turned to port into fairly open water, and some ten minutes later were nosing into the slipway at the boat works. As I turned off the ignition, I couldn't help giving the *Stella* a small, affectionate pat. I realized that she had already acquired a personality for me.

While the work was being done I drove to Victoria to buy an aneroid barometer and a small vane anemometer that registered wind direction and speed in knots per hour*. By noon I had finished shopping, but because the *Stella* would not be ready until 2:00 P.M., I went to a good restaurant and treated myself to a sumptuous shore lunch, thinking that I might not enjoy such luxury again until the autumn.

Under sunny skies, gliding at 1,200 RPMs on a flat-calm sea, the *Stella* and I headed away from land on a magnetic compass bearing of 35 degrees. We were being escorted by several dozen gulls, a screaming flock of opportunists who kept station astern, the position that experience has taught the clan to maintain in order to snatch the best pickings if garbage is tossed overboard. Dead ahead, twelve miles away in U.S. territory, lay San Juan Island with its fresh, green hills and small mountains gleaming in the sunlight, while the waters of Haro Strait cast back a thousand reflections that turned the ocean into a giant mirror.

After two miles, with Cadboro Point abeam to port, I altered course, now steering on a bearing of 52 degrees in order to clear Chatham Islands and Fulford Reef, beyond which we would head southward for two-and-a-half miles, turn westward, and eventually return to the marina in Victoria, for this was but a trial run, a journey undertaken to test the sailing capabilities of the *Stella* as well as those of her

*Beaufort Scale values (numbers indicate wind force, or speed, in knots): 0: calm; 1: 1 to 3; 2: 4 to 6; 3: 7 to 10; 4: 11 to 16; 5: 17 to 21; 6: 22 to 27; 7: 28 to 33; 8: 34 to 40; 9: 41 to 47; 10: 48 to 55; 11: 56 to 63; 12 to 17: 64 to 118, which express hurricane conditions. The scale was developed by Admiral Sir Francis Beaufort, of the British Navy, in 1806. Respectively, each number denotes wave height in feet as follows: zero; 1 to 3; 3 to 5; 5 to 8; 5 to 8; 5 to 8; 8 to 12; 8 to 12; 12 to 20; 20 to 40; 40 plus; mountainous and confused.

skipper. But it was also a pleasure cruise, a twelve-mile jaunt through waters that were relatively free of other shipping at this time of year, but in which many aquatic birds were to be seen. Indeed, as we were passing Fulford Reef, a pelagic cormorant winged up from the water and settled on the *Stella*'s bows, turning its back to me as it shook moisture from its feathers, then, with an impudent waggle of its long, blue-black tail, discharged a stream of feces on the clean deck. With that, the bird came about, looking directly at the windscreen, its red face and blue-green eyes aimed at me.

Once we were clear of the last rocks of the reef, I fed full power to the engine—as much to test the *Stella*'s acceleration as to dislodge the grubby passenger we had acquired. The *Stella* skimmed away like a dolphin, bow high, cleaving through the water while leaving a broad, frothy wake into which a number of gulls immediately dived, no doubt because the turbulence created had brought up minute larva and other life forms that did not escape the birds' keen predatory eyes. The cormorant sat stolidly where it had landed, remaining there like a scruffy figurehead until we once again hit cruising speed and were approaching Victoria.

One-and-a-half hours after leaving the marina, we were back in its neighborhood, having averaged a speed of exactly 8 knots. We were heading for the fuel wharf, to top up in readiness for the morning, when I planned to set out on our northward journey.

Having conned the *Stella* on a five-legged course over which my previously charted bearings proved completely accurate, and after putting the vessel through her paces and deliberately steering her through the turbulent wake of a large ferryboat making for the mainland, I was feeling quite cocky as I approached the gasoline wharf, full of confidence in myself and utterly convinced that I was navigating the best-behaved twenty-four-foot boat in the entire world. But alas, pride indeed "goeth before destruction and an haughty spirit before a fall"!

Approaching the wharf, I swung the *Stella* in what I was sure was a neat, even racy, turn, setting her bow nicely in line with the dock and at the last moment giving a stern thrust with the engine so she would glide against the line of old tires that acted as fenders on the wharf. I had timed it just right. The *Stella* checked her headway abruptly but maintained enough momentum to close the last five feet of distance and position herself gently against the dock. I put the gear lever into neutral, got off the pilot's seat, and threw the previously prepared stern line ashore, only then realizing that the pump attendant was not present but that a man in a business suit, obviously a visitor admiring the view and the many boats moored in the area, was standing some twenty-five yards away. As I went to scramble onto the dock to secure the stern line, the man waved and called out that he would secure it for me. I waved back, said thank-you, and threw the bow rope ashore. Then I turned, intending to switch off the engine.

I was going toward the control panel when I heard a shout from the shore. Looking around, I saw that the *Stella*'s bow was against the dock, but that her stern had moved about eight feet away and was still going, widening the gap alarmingly. She was making sternway! The Good Samaritan on the dock was holding the line and trying to pull the *Stella*'s tail back to the wharf. Astounded, I looked at the gearshift, sure that I had put in into neutral. I had. But the *Stella* kept on making sternway. In two strides, I reached the controls and switched off the engine, at the same time looking over my shoulder at the volunteer helper. Even as the motor stopped, the unfortunate man tripped on the loose rope lying on the wharf. He stumbled, tried to recover, stumbled again, and plunged crabwise into the water.

By the time I reached the side and stuck my head out, the *Stella* was some fifteen feet from the dock and the stranger was halfway between my boat and the wharf. He was still holding the rope and was, praise be, a good swimmer. I grabbed the boat hook and extended it over the side; he took hold of it in both hands and kicked as I started to bring him in. Moments later he stood in the cockpit, water streaming from his hair and clothing, a man of about my own age and height, darkly saturnine, part of his forehead and half of his right cheek severely scarred, seemingly from burns. With unbelievable cool, he smiled, extending his right hand.

"I'm John. What the hell happened?" he said as we shook hands.

He didn't wait for an answer. Instead, he brushed past me and entered the cabin, stopping in front of the table and starting to empty his pockets. Wallet, wristwatch, some papers, a soaked pack of Camel cigarettes, a butane lighter, a mushy bundle of Kleenex, keys . . . I stood there feeling foolish, gawking, but when my victim began undressing, I hurried to get a couple of large towels. He took them without a word, wrapped the smaller one around his head like a turban, stripped off shirt, shorts, shoes, and socks, and, stark naked, started to towel himself vigorously, his skin bristling with goose bumps as he shivered uncontrollably. Still toweling, he spoke again.

"We're about the same size, I reckon, so mebbe you can find me some dry duds?" He spoke quietly, a little smile on his lips—or was it a rictus brought on by the cold?

Gripped by a mixture of concern and amazement caused by this man's equanimity, I remained silent—dumbstruck, I guess—but went forward and hurried back with a full change of clothing, including a thick woolen sweater. In the cabin, John stood with the bath towel wrapped about his waist and the smaller towel draped over his shoulders like a cape. He was carefully spreading out his money and papers to dry. I noted that his goose bumps were gone but that he was still shivering slightly.

As he started to put on the flannel shirt I had brought, he looked down at his feet.

"Got any sneakers? Socks?"

When I returned with these items, John spoke again, his smile this time being readily recognizable as such.

"You know, one thing a man needs after a dunking in the sea is a good, strong cup of coffee, hot as hell. An' another thing he needs is a shot of something even stronger than the coffee!"

Up to this point I was aware that I had been behaving very stupidly, but now, reassured by this cool character and liking him for his easy grace—another man would have surfaced from the ocean spluttering insults at me, I am *quite* sure—I relaxed and introduced myself as I uncapped a bottle of Courvoisier brandy, found a tumbler, and half filled it with the fiery liquor. I handed the drink to John, decided that I, too, was in need of a little stimulus, and poured a more modest measure into another glass. When I looked up, I noted that my victim had downed half his drink and was lifting the glass for a second swallow, circumstances that bespoke volumes about my new companion's drinking prowess. No occasional tippler can ingest two ounces of brandy in one gulp without at least catching his breath! John calmly finished off the other two ounces in his tumbler and silently offered me the empty glass, nodding at the bottle. I poured the same again. This time he drank an ounce, smacked his lips, then sat down, pulling on socks and stuffing his feet into the canvas shoes I'd produced.

"Well, that's better! I'll tell you something, Ronny, that was sure as hell a *cold* bath you prepared for me!"

When people address me by the diminutive of my given

name, I react impolitely, but having dunked this man in water that was only about 40 degrees F., I could not bridle at the revolting nickname. Instead I restarted the engine and headed for the gasoline wharf again, this time watched by John and absolutely determined to make a good job of it. My approach was good and I copied my previous actions, except that as soon as the *Stella*'s forward way was checked, I switched off the engine. The boat glided nicely against the wharf and I climbed out with the stern rope and fastened it to the bollard. John tossed the bow line to me, and this, too, was quickly secured.

The absent wharf attendant had arrived in time to witness John's unplanned plunge and was greatly amused by the mishap. He showed his mirth as he dragged the hose over the dock and stuffed the nozzle into the main fuel tank inlet. Neither John nor I reacted with kindness to the gas jockey's humor. John voiced our mutual feelings.

"You think swimmin' at this time a year's so great, how would you like to take a dive in there?"

John did not receive an answer to his question, but the youth, who could have used a good bath, attended to his job without further clowning. When the fuel tank was full, the bill was paid, and the pump had thoroughly aired the bilges, we headed for the marina berth and the coffee I had promised my victim but which could not be made at the fuel wharf without fear of blowing everything sky high. Twenty minutes later we were once more moored to a dock, the kettle had been put on to boil and fresh brandy poured, but before indulging himself, John asked permission to look over the *Stella*, opining at the end of his inspection that I had bought a good boat. This, of course, called for a celebration.

Over coffee and more brandy than was good for either of us, we talked about ourselves. John revealed that he had earned his livelihood as a commercial fisherman for twelve years, quitting the sea after his boat blew up during a storm, when he was ten miles out from Charleston, in southern Oregon. That explained his burns. It was also the reason why he quit fishing and, after his recovery, turned to the more gentle if, he admitted, less exciting life of a salesman for a marine-equipment firm. By this time in our conversation dusk had arrived, and as John's clothes, hanging from an improvised line in the afterdeck well, were far from dry, I started to prepare a meal. As I was doing so, he asked me for my tool kit, saying that the mishap at the fuel wharf had occurred because the linkage from the gear lever to the engine was obviously loose. But, not to worry, he would fix it for me! At this news, I *did* worry. I was reluctant to accept his help, not because I doubted his knowledge or his competence but because he had by this time consumed a goodly amount of brandy. However, he would not be denied, so I presented him with the tools and he set to work, giving me a running commentary in a loud voice.

"There now," he finally announced. "That's got the little booger. There was a good inch of slack in the cable. Gimme a drink!"

John's last sentence marked the second stage of a memorable if unwise evening, a time of comradely tippling during which we became fast friends and even decided to combine our culinary talents by creating a sumptuous supper, a meal that would have proved excellent if we had not worked at cross purposes but which, by the time it was ready, neither one of us refused, despite its many shortcomings.

My erstwhile victim was divorced and always one step away from alimony payments, the money for which he often spent "havin' me a good time." He was, it seemed, something of a philanderer as well as a heavy drinker whose tolerance for alcohol was far higher than mine—but so was his recklessness. Knowing my own limits, I consumed one ounce to his two. Nevertheless, by the time we finished supper, I was already feeling the effects, and showing them on occasion, while John appeared to be as fresh and steady as a committed teetotaler. The meal and the brandy came to an end at almost precisely the same time, and whereas I was willing to let the drinking terminate at this point, John clamored for more. I had a forty-ounce bottle of gin, so now, between cups of coffee—which I insisted on—we consumed gin and orange juice, a combination that my friend referred to as an orange blossom.

At midnight, feeling that one more drink would cause me to disgrace myself in the head, I convinced him to accompany me for a second meal in a nearby café.

The one we chose was operated by a woman in her mid-fifties who was of ample proportions, stridently loud of voice, and as tough as a longshoreman. Maud was her name, and she had the habit of slapping people on the back with a hand the size and weight of a cast-iron skillet. But she was a friendly soul.

Maud was a cat lover. She had ten of the felines at home and two in the café, one of which had in recent weeks delivered herself of a litter of seven kittens. Even Maud felt that nineteen was too many cats, and she was now seeking owners for the small-fry. To prove her point, she bustled into the back of her eatery and returned bearing in her great hands a morsel of gray-blue fur that had the longest ears I have ever seen on a member of this species, green eyes, and an appealing look that neither John nor I could resist. There and then we decided to adopt the little thing, and this gave Maud so much happiness that she locked up the café (we were the only customers by then, anyway, for it was almost 2:00 A.M.)

and found a bottle of rye whiskey. The drinks she poured for us were almost as generous as her figure, and this devil-may-care spontaneity immediately won John's heart. While I sipped very slowly, Maud and John drank toasts to themselves, to the kitten, to the sea, and to each other's departed spouses, who were so honored not because they were missed, but because they were *gone.*

The kitten awakened me at 6:30 A.M. by sitting on my face. I had a headache and I was tired, not having gone to bed until four o'clock. Otherwise, I was in better shape than I deserved to be after a long night of libation, but the memory of John's and my farewells caused me to feel distinctly uneasy as I put the small cat on the deck.

John and I had left Maud's place at 3:30 A.M., the kitten reposing in my arms as we strolled toward the marina and then stopped by a pay phone so John could call a taxi to take him back to his hotel. Waiting for the cab, we argued mildly over possession of the little feline. Both of us wanted it, so we settled the matter with the toss of a coin. John, I was now thankful to recall, had won. Afterward, we stood dockside chatting and John told me that he planned to leave Victoria right after breakfast that same day, taking a ferry to Port Angeles and there renting a car to drive to Astoria. For these reasons he said he would come to the marina at eight o'clock to return my clothes and collect his own. Then he asked me if I would keep the kitten overnight because he didn't think he could get it into the hotel. That was when I uttered the words that were now causing me anxiety.

As the taxi was pulling up and we were about to say good-bye, I suddenly felt guilty about John's plunge into the Pacific and was gripped by an intense desire to make up for the mishap. Would he, I asked, like me to take him home on board the *Stella*? His instant and enthusiastic acceptance of the invitation determined the matter then and there. Entering the taxi, he said he'd be seeing me "bright and early."

Now, rising from the bunk, I fed the kitten a saucer of milk, washed myself, consumed two large glasses of orange juice, and made coffee before swallowing two aspirins and going to the cockpit to begin preparations for the journey. Suddenly I realized that I had no charts to cover the waters south of Cape Flattery. This was a nuisance and would delay our departure for an hour while I went into the city to get them. Moments later I forgot all about the charts when I discovered that the kitten had defecated on top of the engine hatch. When I had cleaned up the mess and was about to have some coffee, I noticed that the little feline had done the same thing again, this time beside the sink counter! It was not the most auspicious beginning of a voyage that would see me navigating a new boat in foreign waters along a totally unplanned route and during what promised to be a day of rain and wind. My uneasiness increased. I could not help regretting the rash invitation.

It happened that I was born at sea during a storm in the Bay of Biscay in Spanish territorial waters after a fetal journey of some six thousand miles from Cape Town, South Africa, and I was raised by the Mediterranean Sea. So the oceans hold no terrors for me. Yet I afford them great respect. Hitherto, I had always sought to prepare myself in every way possible before venturing out to sea in a small vessel, such preparation invariably including considerable research of the waters over which I intended to navigate. I had done no less while planning my proposed northward journey and had learned that the western shoreline of the United States is subject to more wave shock than any other coastal region in the world, a circumstance engineered by the prevailing winds and by the enormous expanse of water that lies between Asia and North America. Navigating the boisterous yet relatively protected waters of the Inside Passage to Alaska would undoubtedly pose many challenges, but I had the feeling that none of these would compare in magnitude to the turbulence the *Stella* would have to endure while butting her way along the Washington coast to Astoria—and back! I felt personally unprepared to tackle the voyage that I had thoughtlessly suggested, even though the research I had done during the winter included the entire Pacific seaboard of Central and North America. The fact was that I had concentrated most of my attention on the waters I would encounter on the northward trip, absorbing only casually the details relating to the southern regions. But I *had* committed myself, and therefore I had to reconcile myself to the voyage.

Later, sitting in the cabin drinking coffee and eating two boiled eggs, I began to warm to the prospect of taking the *Stella* on a south heading. I had never been to Oregon, and Astoria is a place that had interested me for many years because it was the site of John Jacob Astor's fur-trading fort; first established in 1811, when the sailing ship *Tonquin* entered the Columbia River, it was a tiny enclave of civilization in an otherwise untamed region. Thinking about these things while looking through the cabin deadlight at the overcast skies, it occurred to me that I had been seeking a challenge ever since last autumn, when I came out of the British Columbia interior. A joust with the open Pacific in March was surely a worthy windmill at which to tilt! Astoria lies at a latitude of 46°11′30″; Ketchikan is located at a latitude of 55°20′35″. As the proverbial crow might fly, the straight-line distance between the two U.S. communities is 549 nautical miles, but only time could tell me how much sea I would have to navigate before the *Stella* reached the Alaskan town. Apart from the fact that no boat pursues a straight course when following the contours of a coastline, I had already planned on making a number of detours en route. Now, the very first, and probably the longest, of these side trips was to be unplanned.

My thoughts were interrupted by the kitten, upon whom I had earlier bestowed a name: Poopdeck. He came to me, mewling, and started crawling up my leg, undoubtedly knowing that I had forgiven his sins. Indeed, I was already becoming attached to Poopdeck. Curled up on my lap, the kitten began to purr loudly, his splayed front paws kneading my pant leg while I sipped coffee and puffed on my pipe.

Just before eight o'clock I heard the sound of an automobile approaching the dock. It was John. He looked well scrubbed and glowing with health, and he was rudely boisterous. As the cab driver removed his cases from the trunk, John turned to face the *Stella*, waved, and yelled a ribald greeting that caused me to wince at the volume of the call as well as the vulgarity of the words—until I recalled that I was the sole occupant of the marina at that season. I answered him in kind, but in a more subdued voice, reflecting meanwhile that my friend's interior plumbing must have been manufactured out of stainless steel lined with asbestos. If ever a man deserved a hangover, it was John; but here he was, cheerful, rowdy, and obviously not in pain. He was dressed in fashionably cut jeans that must have cost three times the amount I paid for my own less svelte but more comfortable brand, an equally chic dark blue pea jacket with golden insignias on the lapels, a flame red toque on his head, and expensive boating shoes on his feet. Hefting his two cases, my unrepentant friend came galloping over the board-walk that led to the *Stella*'s berth and, reaching the side, dumped his bags noisily into the afterdeck well, before clattering over the side with more élan than grace. I stood holding Poopdeck and grinning, despite my tender head. John slapped me on the back with cheerful but definitely inconsiderate abandon.

"Man! That was some wingding last night!" he said loudly by way of greeting, at the same time reaching forward and taking Poopdeck from my hands.

I poured coffee and we sat in the cabin discussing the journey, checking the tides, and listening to the weather forecast, which promised rain and winds up to Force 4. We decided to leave as soon as our mugs were empty, John waving away my desire to go ashore for charts with assurances that he knew the coastline so well he could navigate it blindfolded, a claim I did not dispute for fear he would actually seek to prove it by demonstration!

Writing in the log at 10:15 that morning I noted that the *Stella*, piloted by John, was passing Race Rocks to port and Edith Hook, outside Port Angeles, to starboard, making 10 knots at 2,000 RPMs and heading on a magnetic bearing of 214 degrees: ". . . seas moderate, waves cresting to four feet; wind out of the west at 9 knots (Force 3). Skies heavily overcast. No rain. Distance traveled from Victoria: 16 miles."

We had been at sea for one-and-a-half hours, making our cautious way from the marina until we cleared the reefs in the area of Gonzales Point, Victoria. We then increased RPMs and turned on our present bearing as we drew abeam of Trial Island. It was obvious that John was a competent sailor and by now I fully accepted his knowledge of these waters, yet I was still worried about my northbound journey, when I would have to return this way on my own. For that reason, I tried to keep track of the bearings and landmarks by which my companion was steering, but I gave up the attempt soon after we passed Race Rocks when John boldly conned the *Stella* right across the traffic separation zone that is marked on the charts as one-way shipping lanes through the Strait of Juan de Fuca. The chart I had been using to this point ended just west of Race Rocks, but the separation zone was noted on it, accompanied by this warning: "One-way traffic lanes overprinted on this chart are RECOMMEND-ED for use by all vessels traveling between the points involved. They have been designed to aid in the prevention of collisions in the Strait of Juan de Fuca waters, but are not intended in any way to supersede or to alter the applicable Rules of the Road."

This meant that it was permissible to use either lane, but in face of the capitalized recommendation, I, as a tyro in these latitudes, would have headed the *Stella* along the westward, or outbound, route, which lay in Canadian waters. However, I didn't argue with John when he said that so long as the weather remained reasonable and visibility stayed as good as it was then, he would cross the international boundary into U.S. waters and then navigate just far enough offshore to stay clear of rocks and shoals.

Earlier, we had discussed gasoline logistics and decided to put in to Neah Bay for refueling because from that part of the northwest coast of Washington to La Push, some fifty miles south, on the western shores of the state, fuel would be unobtainable. Originally the *Stella* had been fitted with a single 72-gallon gasoline tank, but the first owner had installed an auxiliary 30-gallon tank, bringing the total to 102 gallons. According to the maker's specifications, the *Stella* was said to use about 5 gallons of gasoline an hour while cruising at 1,800 RPMs under calm sea conditions. This was estimated to produce a speed of 12 knots an hour, thus giving a ratio of 5 gallons of fuel per 12 miles traveled *under ideal conditions.* As the future was to show, these statistics were quite realistic; but, as anyone who has navigated these waters will know, ideal cruising conditions are the exception rather than the rule. This meant that it was just about impossible to estimate the exact fuel demands made on the *Stella* by rough seas and high winds. In theory, given calm weather, the *Stella* could cruise for 20.4 hours and cover 244.8 nautical miles in that time, but only a fool would gauge his fuel consumption as finely as that. The distance between Victoria and La Push, along the course set by John, is approximately 115 miles, well within the *Stella's* range. Nevertheless, it was wise to keep the tanks topped up, a practice I maintained during the months that followed.

Because of the likelihood of foul weather, John gave more power to the *Stella* after our stop at Neah Bay, seeking to cover as much distance as possible before conditions worsened, for he wanted to reach the shelter of La Push during daylight. Now he set a course around Cape Flattery that took us between Tatoosh Island and the westernmost tip of the cape, an area of water that is full of rocks, but over which we ran without difficulty at high tide because of the boat's shallow draught and the helmsman's experience.

Soon after we rounded the headland, John pointed to a tall, rugged pillar of rock rising straight out of the water for about 150 feet, a column lying a little more than a mile south of Tatoosh Island.

"That's de Fuca's Pillar," he informed me.

It so happens that I have always been greatly interested in the doings of the original navigators of the New World and I was familiar with the history of this particular and singular landmark, which was unknown to my sailor friend. While the *Stella* lunged through the water at 2,400 RPMs, I told

John about the rather fascinating events that culminated in the charting of this part of the Pacific coast.

Today, it is easy to forget that navigators employed by the Spanish had already explored much of the northwest coast of North America during the sixteenth and seventeenth centuries, as is evidenced by the many Hispanic names still found on modern charts, from California to Alaska. The Strait of Juan de Fuca is a case in point. In 1592, de Fuca, a Greek whose real name was Valerianos Apostolos, was ordered by the viceroy of Mexico to explore the northwest waters. He did so to such good effect that he found the strait that now bears his name, navigating it for a considerable distance and at the same time noting, and plotting, the distinctive rock pillar that rises just off the tip of the cape. Inasmuch as the sciences of navigation and charting were then still in their infancy (by today's standards), it is not surprising that the old sailor got his latitudes mixed up, showing the entrance to the strait as lying between the forty-seventh and forty-eighth parallels, a position that caused later mariners to doubt the existence of any such opening between the state of Washington and Vancouver Island.

Captain James Cook, who named Cape Flattery in March 1778, completely overlooked the opening during extremely foul weather, which is not to be wondered at when it is considered that de Fuca was almost one full degree off in his calculations. Cook evidently hunted for the opening when still some sixty nautical miles south of it, and by the time he neared his goal he failed to see it because of a storm that had plagued him for several days. For almost two hundred years geographers had scoffed at de Fuca's pretentious claims, but in 1781, Captain William Barkley, master of the fur-trading ship *Imperial Eagle*, noted the 150-foot pillar of rock and, following de Fuca's directions but ignoring his given latitudes, found the entrance to the strait. Nearly four hundred years after its discovery, de Fuca's Pillar remains a marker for navigators, an extraordinary piece of natural sculpture that has been resisting the pounding of the Pacific Ocean since time immemorial.

By 4:30 that afternoon the weather had worsened. It began to rain heavily and the wind veered to blow out of the northwest, increasing to Force 5. The *Stella* was just passing to starboard of Sea Lion Rock, a marker that John said was eight miles from La Push. This was good news. The heavy cloud cover, the moisture, and the lateness of the hour combined to reduce visibility to no more than 150 yards. I would have preferred to reduce speed because the *Stella* was now pitching and tossing violently, but John insisted on maintaining the RPMs. The entrance to La Push is tricky and he wanted to negotiate the channel as early as possible, before darkness set in.

Just how tricky this passage was I learned about an hour later, when we turned around the gloomy bulk of James Island and entered a narrow inlet, picking our way, running lights on, through the gloom. On the starboard beam was a thin, curving neck of land; abeam to port was a wide sandbank crowned by a 350-yard-long rock dyke that traveled parallel to our course. Practically feeling our way and with the engine just above the idle, we eventually came alongside a small jetty within a well-protected basin. Here we were visited by a U.S. customs agent who thought us something of a nuisance because he had been about to go home for supper. But he was friendly and casual, giving my papers a cursory examination, having a quick look around the *Stella*, and asking me how long I planned to remain in the United States. Leaving us, he warned that the weather would probably be worse by morning, a lugubrious forecast that was not confirmed by the radio, which predicted that the rain would stop during the night and the wind would moderate.

La Push is some 120 miles north of Astoria, which was a good day's sail from our present position, so we decided to get up early and leave as soon as it was light enough to navigate safely—provided that the customs agent was wrong in his forecast! John, who had piloted the *Stella* most of the way from Victoria, had formed a high opinion of her seaworthiness, maintaining that she could "handle herself" in anything up to a Force 8 wind, praise indeed from a professional seaman who had sailed these waters for so many years. Nevertheless, I silently promised the *Stella* that I would not allow her to venture out of harbor in weather more severe than Force 6. That was the magic number above which I would not untie her mooring lines, having absolutely no intention of voluntarily risking myself or my vessel in a Force 8 storm, with winds of up to forty miles an hour! Of course, it would be another matter if we were unlucky enough to get caught in a sudden blow of such strength, so it was comforting to consider John's opinion; but even so, in that event, I would unhesitatingly head for the nearest shelter. I enjoy challenges, but masochism forms no part of my makeup!

At five the next morning we were up and having breakfast, delighted to find that the cloud cover had moved away overnight. The wind was strong outside the harbor, but the radio reported it as Force 5 and informed us that it was expected to moderate to Force 3 later in the day. Waiting for a little more daylight, we sat in the cabin drinking coffee and discussing my return journey. John wanted me to stay in Astoria for a few days so he could "show me a good time," but I felt he had already showed me as good a time as I could handle and I insisted that my schedule would not permit me to accept his kind offer. But I did agree to meet him ashore and have dinner with him after he took Poopdeck and his luggage home and picked up a couple of charts for me, the first of which would show the coast from the Columbia River to Destruction Island, the second from Destruction Island to Amphitrite Point, on the west coast of Vancouver Island.

When the *Stella* left the shelter of James Island at 6:15 A.M., the northwest wind hit her broad on the starboard quarter, or, as John said, "slapped her on the right cheek." Ahead, the waves crested to about five feet, most of them decorated with whitecaps and throwing off clouds of spray, but the boat handled well at cruising speed, despite a tendency to roll rather more than was comfortable.

In daylight and with good visibility, I realized that the distance between the mouth of La Push harbor and the jetty at which we had moored was something less than a thousand yards. It had seemed much more than that as we threaded our way in through last evening's murk. I also became aware that the coast in these latitudes is filled with rocks and reefs, forming a jagged belt outward from the shoreline more than a mile wide in places and about forty miles long, stretching from Cape Flattery to Destruction Island, just north of the forty-seventh parallel.

John, enjoying himself at the wheel, told me with a grin that there were more rocks to be found per lineal mile in these waters than anywhere else along the coasts of Washington and Oregon. I don't know whether this is true or not, but there was no denying that the shore looked damnably inhospitable, a fact that caused me considerable uneasiness when I remembered that I would be coming this way again on my own. With the kind of familiarity that breeds contempt, John disregarded the hazards that lay to port of the *Stella*, taking pride in them instead and, I am sure, deriving a little pleasure from my discomfiture. I may be doing him an injustice, but I felt at the time—and I still do—that soon after we cleared the shelter of James Island he deliberately conned the *Stella* between a rocky eminence known as Quillayute Needle and an area filled with black granite fangs and small islands that lies between La Push and Teahwhit Head. Later, when I came back this way armed with charts, I learned that eleven fathoms of water lay between the *Stella's* keel and destruction, but at the time, I reacted as John expected, sitting silent and tense in the port seat and staring at the spume and spray that constantly shot up from the reefs and rocks that appeared to lie almost in the boat's course. Meanwhile, John kept grinning, enjoying himself greatly.

By the time we reached Destruction Island, the wind had moderated to Force 3, but the clear skies had begun to cloud over. My navigator fed more power to the engine, setting the control at 2,800 RPMs. The *Stella* lunged through the water at an estimated 12 knots, a rate we maintained for some ten hours, when Cape Disappointment appeared fine on the port bow. An hour after sighting the cape, we were moored at a wharf in Astoria.

John gathered his things, called a cab from a shoreside phone booth, and then stood chatting with me at the dock, while waiting for the taxi. We agreed to meet later at a restaurant in the downtown section of the city, a place I was to find by means of a map that my friend drew on the back of an envelope. He still wanted me to stay in Astoria for a few days, but I was anxious to start back and did not want to delay any further; nor was I overly eager to spend any more time drinking, a task at which the Oregonian had proved so adept!

We met as planned, and the evening passed quickly. We

enjoyed an excellent meal, during which I confined myself to one drink and some wine. Afterward, we hesitated outside the restaurant, each somehow reluctant to say good-bye but embarrassed by his emotions. We had become fast friends during the few days of our relationship, and although it was obvious that our friendship could not continue beyond this evening, we both regretted the fact. We shook hands firmly and our eyes met. We turned away in unison, John heading for home, I strolling thoughtfully toward the waterfront. Our chances of ever meeting again were remote.

Later, as I neared the Columbia River, I noted that a fairly strong breeze was whipping up whitecaps beyond the *Stella's* mooring. Despite this, I felt that we could safely leave our shelter in the morning if the westerly did not increase overnight. And since there was no point in fretting about tomorrow's weather, I spent little time debating the matter. At 10:00 P.M. I made coffee, drank a mugful, then turned in, sleeping soundly until the alarm awakened me at 4:30.

Since I had taken on fuel before going out with John the night before, I now breakfasted, cleaned up, and, with visibility reasonably good, pulled away from the dock. I ran a course through the brackish water that fills the estuary of the Columbia River, making good way despite the continuing rain. The wind was blowing out of the west at 15 knots, but because the Columbia River basin is more than three miles wide and remarkably free of obstructions, the *Stella* showed a clean pair of heels as she aimed her sharp bows at a point between Clatsop Spit and Cape Disappointment. A little more than an hour after leaving Astoria, we were on a homebound bearing and maintaining speed against a sea that was making five-foot waves.

By noon, the weather had worsened. Now we were encountering heavier waves, and the wind had increased to

Force 5. Slowly, the blow picked up momentum, the ocean became more turbulent, the rain heavier. I had hoped to reach Neah Bay before stopping for the night, but approaching La Push at 3:45 that afternoon, I entered the shelter of its harbor. After taking on fuel, I had an early supper and turned in.

ANCHORS AWEIGH!

The Pacific Ocean was the color of molten pewter, its surface made turbulent by a Force 6 wind that blew steadily from the northwest at a speed of some 25 knots. Seaward, to the limits of vision, the whitecaps that formed on each spiraling wave were continuously being converted into spindrift. Flotsam plucked from shore, or wrenched upward from the bottom, appeared and disappeared fitfully, at one moment surfing on the crest of a roller, at the next plunging beneath the agitated waters. Landward, six-foot waves dashed against the rocks of Umatilla Reef, bursting into irregular spouts that were felled by the wind before they could climb to their full height; each collapse set up its own frothy backwash that met the incoming seas, argued a little, then was absorbed amid a trail of yellowish, gyrating spume.

Standing at the wheel of the *Stella Maris* while peering fixedly through the windshield that was being stroked in vain by twin wiper blades, it seemed to me that the whole world was gray and *wet*. Lead-hued clouds sat overhead as though determined to remain forever in these latitudes, their gross underbellies releasing torrents of rain over land and sea, an incessant watering that had continued unabated for two days and nights; the craggy coast of northwestern Washington was cloaked by a diluvial curtain that created darkling shapes out of the usually cheerful evergreens that grow so profusely in this region, investing the shoreline with a forbidding and alien personality. Even the ubiquitous gulls were grounded, and now, at 8:30 in the morning, clusters of them could be seen huddled on the rock ledges of a tiny island that lay off the boat's starboard beam. Above the islet, Cape Avala butted into the ocean, a brooding mass loosely wrapped in a shroud of moisture that sought to hide the shape of the promontory. As the *Stella* came abeam of the surly cape, I changed to a new bearing, heading the boat on a course that would clear the tip of Cape Flattery before entering the Strait of Juan de Fuca.

The weather would have offered minor inconvenience to the skipper of a large vessel, but to the pilot of a twenty-four-foot powerboat, the seas and the wind-lashed rain were at times frightening opponents. Encountering the *Stella* broad on the port bow, continuous waves sweeping in from the open Pacific sought to push her off course, while the backwash from the nearby coast exerted an almost equally strong pressure against the starboard side. These conditions made steering difficult, the problem compounded by my need to keep a tight grip on the wheel and an especially sharp lookout ahead, to port, and to starboard, scanning each upheaval of sea for runaway tree trunks, those hazards to navigation that are one of the endproducts of the abundant logging operations found along coastal waters of the north-western United States and Canada. Twice during the preceding two hours I had been forced to wrench the *Stella* off course to avoid colliding with suddenly appearing logs, timbers eighteen inches in diameter and at least as long as my boat, which, half-submerged even in calm water, now traveled just under the disturbed surface, rising suddenly on the crest of a roller just ahead of the boat.

As I came abeam of the last rocks of Umatilla Reef, with

some two hours to go before reaching the Strait of Juan de Fuca, I switched on the marine radio and was heartened when the announcer forecasted moderating winds accompanied by light drizzle. I would have preferred to hear that there was sunshine in the offing, but inasmuch as this was March 17, I supposed that rain was almost inevitable in these latitudes. The main thing was that the weatherman was calling for a Force 2 wind; this, according to Beaufort Scale, promised a light breeze, its velocity no more than 4 to 6 knots, with wavelets that had smooth crests and did not break.

Several times during the course of this journey, the Pacific had managed to intimidate me to the point where I was almost ready to give up the entire enterprise, to sell the boat and confine myself to land-based exploration of the shore waters. The funk was evanescent, undoubtedly triggered by the ferocity of the storm and my own emotional insecurity, but it was intense while it lasted. And yet, each time the *Stella Maris* rode serenely over the roughest water, or responded swiftly to the wheel to avoid the logs, my fright left me and I felt glad to be undertaking this adventure.

The primordial qualities of the ocean never fail to reach into my spiritual being, to touch some secret place in my heart, and to cause me exhilaration, even during times when monstrous upheavals of the surface remind me of my own insignificance. Always there is wonder to be found in the sea. Gazing into placid water, down through layers of translucent green, I am lost in contemplation of unfathomable mystery; riding lead-gray waves in a small craft, I marvel at the wit of man the boat-builder, who has managed to venture out in his contraptions into the most ancient and violent of all natural worlds.

When the ocean speaks, I listen; and I hear the beat of my

own self keeping time with the rhythm of Life, for here I once began, a minuscule particle of organic flotsam that rode the currents and winds, eventually outgrowing its medium to walk upright on land. From its shallows at shoreline to its most awesome deeps, the ocean remains the great enigma of creation. Now, as the Pacific trounced the *Stella*, and as I watched the perpetual motion of the water, I found solace. Quite suddenly, the future beckoned excitingly; and the past, especially the time since I had left Ontario, could no longer oppress me.

Some thirty-six hours had elapsed since I said good-bye to John in Astoria and although I was tempted to believe that the rain would last forever, I now faced the journey, and my commitment to the task ahead, in a completely different frame of mind. I knew at that moment that I would never again become discouraged by the elements, just as I knew that there undoubtedly would be times ahead when I would again feel fear; but it would be a healthy kind of fright, a challenge to be met and conquered. Today, with Canadian waters a scant two hours' sailing time away from our present position, I felt that all I had to worry about were the maverick logs that seemed bent on our destruction. I had been keeping a sharp eye on the anemometer, until I realized that since there was nothing I could do about it if the wind increased beyond Force 6, it would be better to ignore the spinning instrument, and to stop worrying about it. I thus accepted with equanimity the fact that we had already passed the point of no return to La Push and that there was no shelter to be found this side of Neah Bay, on the north shore of Cape Flattery. Having reached this conclusion, I began to experience a sense of oneness with the *Stella*, as though she were a part of me, an extension of myself that was anxious to help me defeat the elemental forces which surrounded us, though why it is that men become so attached to their ships is beyond my full understanding. I had developed a similar relationship with the Chestnut canoe that carried me over so many lakes and rivers, a sense of comradeship enriched by definite feelings of affection. Perhaps it is that all men must love *something*; and that, when alone—as I was now and had been before my meeting with Joan—they cannot be emotionally whole unless they are able to give expression to their need, the presumption being that a surrogate love is better than no love at all. Whatever the reason, I found myself becoming emotionally attached to the *Stella Maris*.

Our backs turned to de Fuca's Pillar, which stood indomitable under the assault of the waves and wind and was surrounded by spindrift and cloud, we steered wide of Tatoosh Island and Duntze Rock; then, turning sharply to starboard on a bearing of 96 degrees, we started to make better progress. The wind was at the *Stella*'s stern and she was moving with the tide along the inbound traffic lane.

Land was in sight on both the port and starboard sides. Washington's craggy coast was no more than three miles away, Vancouver Island's shoreline, made indistinct by the rain, being some eight miles to the north. No doubt because of this, I felt more confident and less tense, despite the turbulent seas and the incessant downpour. We were making better time, and even though it was still necessary to keep a sharp watch for logs, I knew now that, provided I did my share of the work, I could rely on the *Stella* to take me safely to port.

With about an hour of murky daylight to spare, we at last reached Victoria, and the *Stella Maris* snuggled up to her old berth in the Oak Bay marina. It had been a good journey.

Some seventy-two hours after returning to Victoria from Oregon, the *Stella Maris* lay idle in a little bay at the south end of De Courcy Island, part of a group of five isles that stretch like beads in a necklace between Pylades and Stuart channels, about eight miles south of Nanaimo. Secured by bow and stern anchors, the boat danced gently atop two fathoms of water, her white hull mirrored on a surface that was only slightly disturbed by the incoming tide. It was four o'clock in the afternoon and I was about to go below to tidy up the charts and check the fuel and oil levels, but first I allowed myself a few moments in which to inspect our surroundings.

The day had been glorious, and although the sun was now low over the western side of Vancouver Island, it still highlighted much of the land and sea, creating uncountable reflections that sparkled with the intensity of crystal, a constantly changing display that contrasted dramatically with the heavy etchings observable among the trees and beyond the north faces of the rocks. The sky was mostly blue, but flotillas of white cloudlets scudded slowly southward. Beyond the opening between De Courcy and Ruxton islands, Pylades Channel looked as though it had been covered by a vast sheet of steel, presenting a seemingly solid surface which now and then produced brief glimmers of the sky; but the sea in our bay and beyond its mouth offered a true aquamarine tint, its waters calm and translucent except for occasional dimples made by the questing mouths of small fish, perhaps herrings. As I watched, a big salmon jumped, its graceful silver body clearly evident for a fraction of time, the splash made by its return to the ocean magnified by the stillness that dominated the afternoon; the circles it left behind traveled slowly in ever-widening rings until they lost their momentum and were absorbed by the flat sea.

The bay that sheltered us is shaped like a horseshoe. It is about 200 yards wide and about 150 yards deep, its total

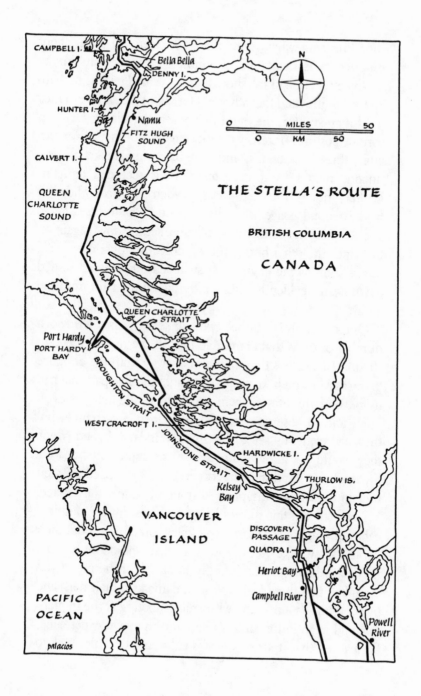

CAMPBELL I.

Bella Bella

DENNY I.

HUNTER I.

Namu

FITZ HUGH
SOUND

CALVERT I.

QUEEN
CHARLOTTE
SOUND

THE STELLA'S ROUTE

BRITISH COLUMBIA

CANADA

N

O   MILES   50
O   KM   50

QUEEN CHARLOTTE
STRAIT

Port Hardy
PORT HARDY
BAY

BROUGHTON STRAIT

WEST CRACROFT I.

JOHNSTONE STRAIT

HARDWICKE I.

THURLOW IS.

Kelsey
Bay

VANCOUVER

ISLAND

DISCOVERY
PASSAGE

QUADRA I.

Heriot Bay

Campbell River

PACIFIC

OCEAN

Powell
River

palacios

shoreline somewhat more than 500 feet. Of this, about nine-tenths is composed of inhospitable rock, but in the northwest section of the shore there is a small beach, perhaps 50 feet of fine sand that advances for about the same distance until it encounters the forest that covers the island. Here, in various postures of rest, were clustered a number of western gulls, three cormorants, and nine harlequin ducks, all now unconcerned by our invasion of their secluded domain. Earlier, they had reacted uneasily when the *Stella* glided in from Ruxton Passage, the gulls and four of the ducks rising to circle the bay for some minutes before setting down again on the sand, the other birds strutting nervously over the beach; but as soon as the engine was switched off, they all settled down again, evidently resting after taking their fill from the ocean.

Our arrival also disturbed two hair seals at ease on one of a number of rocks that are visible just off the northern end of Ruxton Island, less than half a mile away from the entrance to the bay in which we proposed to anchor. The pair watched us for some minutes, allowing me to focus the fieldglasses on them and to observe every detail of their appearance, but they had evidently set an invisible boundary beyond which they would not allow themselves to be approached. As the *Stella* closed the distance between us, they slipped off their rock in unison and disappeared smoothly under the surface.

I had studied this species last year, when I was living in a cabin on Vancouver Island, so I knew something about their habits. They are extremely wary animals, no doubt because they have been so unmercifully hunted by fishermen (who complain that these seals do much damage to their nets) and by shoreline "sportsmen" who enjoy shooting at the inoffensive and beautiful creatures. Yet, from my own experience, I'd learned that if an observer is calm and does not seek to approach them too closely, they will at least tolerate human presence.

Hair seals (*Phoca vitulina linnaeus*), or harbor seals, as they are often called, are variously colored, their coats composed of stiff outer hairs about a half-inch long over an "undervest" of fine, curly down. Their background color ranges from creamy fawn to dark brown; superimposed on this are irregular brown spots, similar to the rosettes of a leopard but not as distinct. The animals have rounded heads and no distinguishable ears, the auricular aperture, or *meatus*, being almost hidden within the fur and located immediately behind the large, limpid eyes. They have black-lined noses and long facial whiskers, a combination of characteristics that causes hair seals to resemble large, friendly dogs. Earlier, before setting the bow anchor, I had scanned the area outside our shelter and focused my glasses on the rocks of Ruxton Island, but the seals had evidently hauled themselves out of the water in another locality. There was still no sign of them now.

As I was about to go below, a bald eagle glided above, traveling from north to south with that wonderful grace so characteristic of these great birds. It was about a hundred feet up, its lithe movements observable by the naked eye. I watched until it disappeared beyond the trees of Ruxton Island, then returned to the cockpit to complete my chores.

It didn't take me long to tidy up, and, as there was still time to do some exploring before evening, I went topside and unlashed the dinghy, wondering how it would behave on this, its first trial. I had no doubts at all about its portability; in two minutes I had unlashed it and put it over the side, securing its painter to the *Stella*'s after rail, beside the stern ladder. When this was done, I went below again to get my fishing rod and to gather up half a dozen glass specimen jars, which I packed in a haversack, for apart from testing the dinghy, I was going to try for a small salmon for supper, and, if there was enough daylight left afterward, I wanted to collect some shoreline life forms for later study.

The little runabout bobbed and danced erratically while I was getting into it, but once I was settled on the built-in seat, it became stable and proved to be easily handled, responding willingly to the small oars with which it came equipped. In moments I sculled to the mouth of the bay and there I let the dinghy drift, fastening an inch-long orange spoon to the fishing line and casting into some five fathoms of water. Retrieving the lure, I noticed that it was being followed by a small rockfish near whose domain among a patch of bull kelp the spoon had passed. Casting again, this time farther away from the kelp, I retrieved without noticeable result. But only three casts later the spoon was checked in midretrieve; I had caught my supper. It was an eleven-inch grilse, or young coho salmon, in its second year of growth. I killed it quickly by striking it over the brain with a small club carried for that purpose; then I wrapped it in a wet cloth and dismantled the rod and line.

I never fish for sport, only for sustenance. For this reason I generally use small lures and habitually cast in fairly shallow water so as to avoid the big fish, for I abhor waste. Any fish heavier than two pounds is too large for me to consume during the time its meat will remain fresh, and when I occasionally do hook a big one despite my precautions, I always liberate it immediately.

The taking of any living thing in the name of sport or as a trophy is, in my view, a practice of questionable morality. By the same token, I find myself in disagreement with those who would have us all become strict vegetarians. I will kill for food when I cannot get what I need at a store and I will kill in self-defense or to end the suffering of an animal injured beyond salvation; but I do not take pleasure in the act and I usually feel guilty afterward.

I am occasionally scolded by conservationists when they learn that I fish and hunt as the need arises, and I am often verbally abused by the "fun slayers" when I criticize sport and trophy hunting. The former cry "Shame!" because they argue that I am causing intense suffering, while the latter accuse me of being a bleeding heart, insisting that mammals suffer hardly at all and that fish are insensitive to pain.

When thus chided by the conservationists I explain that in hunting mammals or birds (which I do rarely now), I have always made a practice of killing with the first shot, never raising a gun until I am within accurate shooting range; indeed, I have often gone hungry rather than risk wounding an animal. As to fishing, I explain that by seeking to take small fish that are soon removed from the water and killed quickly, I am not torturing my prey. Then I try to deal with the concept of pain.

Those who believe that animals feel unendurable pain are as mistaken as those who contend that they feel hardly any pain at all and that cold-blooded creatures are totally insensitive to it. The truth lies somewhere between the two assertions.

All animals that have nervous systems can feel pain, and fish are no exception. But pain experienced by modern-day humans is almost invariably magnified by anticipatory fear. That is to say, we tend to overreact when we are hurt, or even when we contemplate the possibility of being hurt. Animals do not anticipate in this way, and so they are not prone to magnify pain out of actual proportion—many of them even appear able to block out pain altogether after its initial onslaught (a characteristic largely lost to humans but one still demonstrated on occasion).

Life has always been the endproduct of death, at least as far as nature is concerned: dead matter, whether ingested as nourishment or decomposed as soil nutrient is always the stuff of life in the wilderness. The hunter kills out of need within the scheme of nature, and sparingly; the hunted themselves consume living matter, be they grazers or browsers. Man, in those places where civilization cannot reach, is often forced to become a natural consumer. Since his digestive tract is unable to assimilate the cellulose in the majority of green plants available in the wild, he must on occasion take animal prey. But man diminishes himself if he kills wantonly, if he takes pleasure in his kills, or if he feels no respect for the animal that necessity has caused him to slay.

Landing on the beach after catching the salmon, I prepared the specimen jars. I was going to look for small organisms that could be taken alive, studied at leisure, and released again within their proper habitat. To this end, I first put some sand in each jar, forming a suitable bottom on top of which I placed one or two small rocks, bits of shell, and pieces of seaweed before filling the container to the three-quarter mark with seawater. I wasn't looking for any specific organisms, intending to take one or more representatives of whatever species I discovered until all the jars held at least one sample.

This was to be the first of many such collecting trips, the object of which was to glean as much information as possible about the life forms that inhabit the tidal waters of the northwest coast of North America. I was not seeking to copy the work done by Ed Rickets and others, whose knowledge of marine biology dwarfed my own, nor did I expect to emerge from this voyage as an expert in the field of marine life. At best, I hoped to add a little to the humble store of information that I already possessed and to observe firsthand at least some of the organisms I had hitherto studied only in books. To presume to do more than this during a few months of exploration with limited resources would be the height of arrogance and, worse, would seriously interrupt the processes of reason and observation by cluttering the mind with a sense of mission, the kind of commitment that causes too many observers to search only for specific things and to be blind to all but that which they want to see.

Herman Melville, writing more than a century ago, said in *Moby Dick* that there is "one knows not what sweet mystery about this sea, whose gently awful stirrings seem to speak of some hidden soul beneath." It was this *soul* that I hoped to glimpse during the course of my journey, the undefinable life-spirit that is manifest throughout all the seas and oceans of the world; to find it, I knew that I needed to seek the acquaintance of as many oceanic organisms as possible without thought of priorities or selective classification. I wanted to observe, touch, relate with, and seek to understand all those individual organisms that a combination of luck and diligent searching might bring to my notice.

Looking for beach and tide pool specimens was only one aspect of my quest. By living atop its surface, smelling its fragrance, and experiencing its many moods by night and day, I sought to cultivate a sense of unity with the ocean and to become, by means of the *Stella Maris*, a part of the marine environment. As Polaris was my lodestar, so my sturdy boat was my power; she was now as much a part of me as I was a part of her. In like vein, the land that rose out of the deeps could also offer inklings of the oceanic soul, for the coastal world is greatly influenced by the sea, which in its turn is influenced by the terrestrial landscape. But even these things were not enough, I had concluded while planning this voyage during the cold weeks of winter. I had to go down into the ocean, swim under the surface, dive to the bottom aided by the scuba equipment I had purchased, employing the skin-diving skills developed as a child and, later, the aqualung techniques learned off the coasts of Spain and North Africa.

The journey to and from Astoria had already given me a little more knowledge of the sea; later, when the weather was warmer, I would experience the mood of the netherworld of the Pacific. For now, I had to be content with collecting some of the many humble creatures that abounded in the shallows, in tidal pools, and even under the sand of the beaches. It was therefore with a sense of excitement that I began my search that afternoon, working almost feverishly for somewhat longer than an hour, until the light began to fade. On my return to the *Stella*, I took stock of my finds: two chitons, one three-inch clingfish, a larval shrimp, one eelpout, and two jellyfish. I had also collected some bladderwrack seaweed and a bull-kelp float to which some two feet of stem adhered. Carefully setting all the specimens on top of the engine hatch cover, I entered the cabin to prepare supper.

At 6:30, after clearing the table and washing the dishes, I slipped into a warm coat and went on deck to sit for a time in quiet contemplation of the gathering darkness and the gradually appearing stars; pale at first, each new arrival slowly increased its refulgence in tempo with the ebbing light and the strengthening darkness. I watched them as they appeared, some in solitary splendor, others in companionable clusters that twinkled green and ruby when viewed through the fieldglasses. There was going to be a quarter-moon, but it was not due to appear for another two or three hours yet. And this pleased me, for I derive great enjoyment from star-watching against the blue-black background of a cloudless sky, especially when I can scan the heavens at dusk and observe the splendid arrival of night, counting meteors, identifying individual stars and constellations, while allowing my inner being to roam through the far reaches of space.

Polaris, which has so often guided me through the darkened wilds of Canada, hung almost directly above the *Stella*, escorted as usual by Ursa Minor and Beta Cassiopeia, which is the chronometer of night that revolves around the North Star, counterclockwise, and completes a full circle every twenty-four hours. Ursa Major showed clear and bright, its two pointers, Dubhe and Merak, aiming at Polaris. They all came to greet the *Stella* and me: Draco, Andromeda, Lacerta, Cepheus, Perseus; my favorite cluster, the Corona Borealis, occupying its allotted space between Hercules and Bootes. Countless stars, some clear and sparkling, others noticeable only as faint, luminescent dots in far space, were arrayed above my head.

The March chill sent me below after an hour, but just before seeking shelter in the cabin I paused for some moments to observe the land and the water, listening for night sounds and noting the reflection of the stars on the pellucid and calm surface. The ocean, as usual, was speaking, but in its quietest voice. It susurrated on the beach, whispered outside the bay, scolded the rocks that sought to interrupt its peaceful soliloquies. Somewhere near the western shoreline a sleepy duck quacked softly; from the vicinity of Ruxton Island a hair seal barked, uttering a series of high, doglike yelps, and then was still.

For the next four hours I studied the organisms I had brought on board, starting with the chitons, or sea cradles, which belong to a primitive class of mollusks, the Amphineura. More than a hundred species of these snaillike animals inhabit the west coast of North America and some seven hundred different species have been classified throughout the world. Ranging in length from one inch to the giant brick-red gumboot chiton, which is thirteen inches long, this elongated relative of the octopus and squid wears a shell composed of eight overlapping plates that causes it to look somewhat like a small armadillo, or perhaps like a giant wood louse. All of the different species are light-sensitive and tend to feed at night, usually spending the daylight hours adhering like limpets to the underside of rocks. Most chitons are vegetarians, some are carnivores, while yet others prefer a mixed diet. They crawl by means of a foot, rather like clams and snails, feeding as they move. Under the shells, around the body, chitons have a mantle, or girdle, the rear end of which is equipped with breathing gills, but they have no eyes and their heads are so small that they are hardly evident. From beneath, the small but well-defined round mouth can be clearly seen; this is equipped with a radula, a sort of ribbonlike tongue covered with sharp projections, like a file, which is used to break down the food. The two specimens I was observing belonged to the species *Katarina tunicata*, or leather chiton, so-called because most of the shell is covered by a brown, leatherlike sheath. In these animals the girdle is black and the muscled foot is pale orange. Chitons are also known as sea cradles because they tend to curl up when disturbed and, viewed from below at such times, they resemble small cradles or baskets. One of the specimens I had taken from the rocks was two-and-a-half inches long, the other was three-and-a-quarter inches in length. Both curled up when I pried them from the small rocks on which they were sheltering from the light, but after a few minutes, when I returned them to their miniature sea world within the jar, they settled again, sucking themselves onto the rocks. I put them back on the engine hatch, away from the cabin's battery-powered light.

The next specimen was a flathead clingfish, *Gobiesox maenandricus*, a four-inch individual with a large, broad head, a humped back, and a flattened body. The most remarkable feature of this species is a powerful sucking disc by which the fish can attach themselves to the undersides of rocks and boulders. A collector must actually slide them off if they are not to be squeezed to death by careless fingers working too strongly against the suction. Colored variously from olive brown to almost cherry red and further decorated by netlike shadings of dull orange, clingfish can swim swiftly in order to avoid enemies or to capture small prey; and they can blend easily into almost any marine background because of their body markings and hues. These fish are easy enough to catch when adhered to a rock, however, since they evidently feel quite safe when so attached. The one I was examining did not appear to be unduly distressed by the handling it had received earlier, and when I placed it on the palm of my hand, it promptly adhered itself to my skin. Back in the jar, it darted down and sucked itself onto its rock.

The tiny blackbelly eelpout, *Lycodopsis pacifica*, I had captured in a small rock pool, had at first fooled me, causing me to believe it was a larval eel that I had discovered. The species, when mature, attains a length of up to eighteen inches, but the one darting about in the jar, sharing its temporary quarters with the shrimp larva, was a veritable baby, scarcely an inch in length and about three-eighths of an inch in girth at the head, its widest point. It had quite large, feathery-looking pectoral fins and a tapering body surmounted by one continuous fin that began just behind the head and ended ventrally at its cloaca. The front part of the dorsal fin was decorated by a conspicuous black spot. As its name implies, the underbelly was jet black. Altogether this is a curious little fish that feeds on marine worms, crustaceans, small bivalves (clams, oysters, and others), and starfish. Since they have been taken in water as deep as two hundred fathoms, and because their eyes are located high up on either side of the head, it is likely that these fish are born in the shoreline shallows and later migrate downward, feeding on bottom organisms and needing upward vision to alert them to the presence of prey animals or to the approach of enemies. But the little fellow I was watching was a long way from the deep ocean.

The three-eighth-inch crustacean that shared the eelpout's quarters was quite readily identified as a shrimp, but I could not tell to which species it belonged. Indeed, I had captured it accidentally when I scooped out the eelpout together with some seaweed and sand. I became aware of the minute shrimp only after it emerged from its hiding place in the weed. In like vein, I had unknowingly captured a very small blue crab, also an infant and hardly bigger than the shrimp.

The jellyfish, each about the size of a quarter, belonged to the species *Aurelia labiata*, or moon jellies, animals that when full grown can attain a diameter of ten inches. Disc-shaped and quite transparent, they are distinguished by four U-shaped gonads, or sex glands, that show through the tissue and are arranged rather like a four-leaf clover. Jellyfish belong to the class Scyphozoa (from the Greek: *skyphos*, meaning cup-shaped, and *zoion*, meaning animal). Moon jellies have four narrow arms that surround the mouth and hang below the disclike body, the edge of which has sixteen equally spaced indentations from which radiate a fringe of small, stinging tentacles. Except for the U-shaped reproductive organs, which can be either yellowish brown, orange, or purple, these organisms are colorless.

All jellyfish swim by pulsating their delicate bodies, although they are almost always at the mercy of tides and waves, unable to move forcefully or rapidly at will. These predators rely on the stinging cells in their tentacles to subdue animals that accidentally brush against them. When this happens, the jellyfish becomes alerted by a simple set of nerves and its tentacles entrap the prey and sting it to death, after which the food is drawn through the mouth and into a four-lobed stomach.

At certain times during the summer moon jellyfish are exceptionally abundant, sometimes completely covering the surface water in bays such as the one in which the *Stella* lay at anchor. At this stage they breed, discharging their eggs into the water, after which the majority are washed up on shore, where they die. The fertilized egg becomes a polyp, a little swimming organism that soon settles itself on some solid object where it develops into a tubelike growth that slowly changes its appearance, growing downward from its anchoring rock like a stack of tiny saucers glued together and suspended from one end. When hatching time arrives, the last "saucer" in the stack develops tentacles and breaks away, a minute jellyfish. In this fashion, one by one, thirty or more small jellyfish emerge from the original egg, each in turn, from the bottom up. As one breaks away, the next in line takes its place and completes development, males and females evolving from the same hanging stack.

I knew quite a lot about jellyfish even as a child, for the Mediterranean is host to a large variety of species, most of which, I do believe, managed to inflict an excruciating sting on me at one time or another. I used to collect them alive in jars, watch them for a time, and then return them to the sea; and I used to observe dead specimens washed up on the beach, noting that the strong sun quickly evaporated the moisture from their bodies, leaving behind a small amount of dried-up tissue that resembled its original shape not at all. The moon jellies I was now examining, however, did not yet have the power to cause pain, for when I poked them with an experimental finger, I felt no stings even though their tentacles were clearly activated.

Following my usual practice, I made quick notations while observing each animal—reminders, really, which I'd use later to develop more complete reports. With my task concluded, I put the jars back in the haversack and climbed down the stern ladder and into the dinghy. The quarter-moon and the star-filled sky gave just enough light to see by as I rowed to the beach, but I needed a flashlight to pick my way to the rocks, where I released all the captives and emptied the jars, washing them out with seawater. Afterward I sat on the beach, my back to the forest, watching the bay and the firmament and listening to the sounds of the night. Then I returned to the *Stella* and hauled the dinghy back on board, lashing it in place on the extended cabin top before checking both anchors to make sure they were holding. I planned to leave at first light in the morning, so I was going to turn in early; but before doing so, I completed the log, noting that the tide was beginning to ebb and that the night continued clear.

I was awakened at 1:30 A.M. by the accelerated rocking of the *Stella* and the sound of waves slapping against her hull. I crawled out of the bunk to go topside dressed only in shorts. The sky was now partly overcast and a brisk wind had sprung up, blowing from east-southeast right into our little bay; the anemometer recorded a speed of 7 knots, placing it at the low scale of Force 3. The water, responding, was making waves that crested glassily to about three feet. After checking the anchors and finding them secure, I decided to go back to bed, relying on the movement of the *Stella* to wake me if the wind increased its velocity. I was tired, so it took me only minutes to fall back to sleep. But I didn't rest for very long!

It was about 2:45 when I was awakened again, and this time I knew by the violent motion of the *Stella* that the wind was blowing a lot harder. It even caused me to stagger as I jumped out of bed and, without stopping to dress, ran into the cockpit and then on deck. The boat was dancing like a cork. The moon, still visible in a sky that was now partly cloudy, allowed me to see that the *Stella* was turned broadside to the waves, something she could not have done unless the bow anchor had been dragged out of the bottom. Taking hold of the rope and giving it a pull, I felt the slack, thus confirming that the anchor had pulled free. I started to haul it in, thinking that I might yet manage to reset it and force the bow back so it would face the incoming seas. As I pulled, I looked around, noting that the outgoing tide had revealed an array of vicious rocks that lay threatening in the east half of the bay. Working quickly, it didn't take me long to get all the rope aboard and to recapture the errant hook, though by the time I hauled it on deck I was shivering from the cold. Naked but for my flimsy shorts, I decided I had better hurry below, start the engine, and, while it was warming up, dress myself in dry clothes. I still believed I could salvage the situation. But just as the big Volvo fired, the *Stella* shuddered and her stern swung around, aiming for the rocks. The second anchor had let go!

During moments of stress such as I was then experiencing, events seem to move so swiftly and the body's adrenaline floods so profusely that there is neither the opportunity nor the desire to assess with conscious deliberation the calamity that threatens. Because of these things, I reacted *subcon*-sciously, realizing immediately that unless I put the engine into gear and took the helm, the *Stella* would be pounded to pieces on the ferocious rocks that lay astern, no more than fifty yards away. With no time to dress, I took the helm, set the throttle at 800 RPMs, and put the lever into the ahead position, turning the wheel to starboard as hard as I could. I felt nothing beyond an all-consuming desire to *get the hell out of there*, that very thought phrasing itself within my mind. The *Stella*'s bow turned sharply and the rocks receded, but as I was about to correct the steering to set the boat on course for the opening, the engine stalled, its cessation coinciding with a sudden jerk of the stern section. With horrifying clarity I knew that the remaining anchor rope, which I had hoped to drag out as we went, had wound itself around the propeller, stalling the engine. This revelation was quickly followed by a despairing conclusion: We'd had it!

I do not know for how many seconds I sat at the controls as though paralyzed, my mind a complete blank. It couldn't have been long, because when I came to my senses, I noted with relief that the *Stella* had turned right around, evidently under the momentum of the last revolutions of the screw and guided by the starboard wheel I had not had time to correct before the engine stalled. Initially, I was simply glad that we were no longer drifting toward the rocks, but concern returned quickly when I realized that the boat was now heading directly toward the small beach, on which a log, twenty inches in diameter, was rolling.

Powered by wind and waves, the *Stella Maris* now ran swiftly toward the sand; and the log! I watched helplessly at first, but as it became mathematically certain that we were going to run aground, I left the pilot's seat and made a dive for the boat hook, unzipping the starboard screen and seeking to slow our momentum by leaning far over the gunwale. In vain did I try to plant the metal end of the boat hook into the swiftly rising bottom. Feeling like an inefficient picador astride a balky horse in a Spanish bullring, I repeatedly stuck my "lance" into the sand, but the momentum of the boat thrust it back at me, and I was forced to pull it out, swing it around, and try again. Before I really knew what was happening, the *Stella*'s bow rose as her stem came into contact with the log, which acted like a roller, allowing her to ride up until there was enough weight resting on the keel to check her forward movement. I felt relief again, thankful that we were beached rather than being pounded to pieces on the rocks.

I soon realized that our predicament was still serious, though. The incoming waves struck the *Stella* on the port side, causing her to roll at a steep angle, but the backwash from shore, striking her starboard beam, tossed her the other way just as steeply. From left to right she went, a mad teeter-tottering that buffeted my ribs as I tried in vain to push us off. Time and again I felt the gunwale slam into my side, but alarm had made me almost completely insensitive to pain and I continued to work like a madman in an effort to get us clear. Whether or not I might have succeeded I cannot say, because in the middle of it all, as I was about to exchange the boat hook for an oar, common sense came to my rescue and I stopped behaving like a fool, pausing instead to think things out.

The *Stella* was not yet coming to harm. Rolling back and forth on her small point of contact with the log, most of her length was afloat—from a point beyond amidships to the stern—so that time and again she was tilted in the opposite direction before her hull could hit the log. Eventually, the abrasive tree trunk would grind into her keel, rasping away the tough fiberglass out of which her entire hull had been molded, but I didn't believe such damage was imminent. On the other hand, if she *did* come off the log while the propeller was still fouled, there would be no way of controlling her without the power of the engine.

It must be understood that though I had managed to recapture a measure of composure, my mental processes were not yet functioning at peak efficiency or else I would not have interrupted myself when I suddenly began to shiver uncontrollably to enter the cabin and dress immediately. But that's just what I did, climbing into jeans, slipping on a thick, woolen jersey, and stuffing my feet into canvas boating shoes.

I felt better on my return to the constantly rocking cockpit. But although I was by no means warm, in my anxiety to get the *Stella* afloat and under power, I dismissed the matter of clothing as no longer being of consequence. Instead, I applied myself once again to our problem and came to the only logical conclusion: I'd have to go over the side and cut away the rope that fouled the propeller.

My hunting knife was hanging from its belt behind the pilot's seat. It seemed to be trying to avoid me as it swung like a pendulum with the violent motion of the boat, but I caught it on one of its wings and withdrew it from its sheath. Now, robotlike, my brain responded to its single command.

I don't remember climbing over the side, but I do recall, vividly, the shock my system received when it was suddenly immersed in the water. I had landed off-balance and while I fought to stay on my feet the *Stella* reared toward me, striking a sharp blow to the side of my head. The collision evoked a hollow, booming sound audible above the noise of wind and ocean. I suppose it must have hurt, but I wasn't conscious of any pain until some hours later when I felt the tender bump. At that moment, my greatest preoccupation centered upon the need to cling to the boat's smooth and unstable hull as I staggered toward the stern.

In moments the water was up to my chest, the waves breaking over my head; then I was completely submerged and found I could make better progress while beneath the pounding breakers. Holding my breath, I at last was able to touch the engine leg and to hold on to it while I took a quick gulp of air, knife held in my left hand. Underneath again, I switched the blade to my right hand immediately after I touched the coils that were wrapped around the propeller shaft. I cut the rope, having enough presence of mind to hold on to the free end with my left hand. Now I put the knife between my teeth and began to unwind the half-inch nylon line from the stalled screw. Twice I was forced to rise for air, almost losing my grip on the anchor rope, which was floating on the surface for at least half its length. After what seemed like an eternity, my lungs shrieking for oxygen, I felt the short length of rope come free, and I literally shot up to the surface.

Taking a deep breath while stuffing the severed line into my waistband so that it would not again pose a threat, I grasped the trailing rope in both hands and walked into the sea until the waves rolled right over me and my body's buoyancy threatened to knock me off my feet. My intent was to cut off as much of the trailing line as possible, sacrificing the anchor but ensuring that the floating rope would not again become entangled with the screw. Balancing precariously, I slashed through the nylon, blessing my habit of maintaining a razor edge on all my cutting tools.

Having swallowed a couple of good mouthfuls of water, I gasped as I struggled to shore, trailing the line behind me and no doubt looking like a poorly caricatured Medusa rising out of the deep to turn the world to stone. Beside the log, knee-deep and streaming water, I tossed the cut rope, some twenty-five feet in all, onto the *Stella's* bow before scrambling after it, an action something like trying to sit a saddle strapped to a bucking bronco.

Inside the cockpit once more, chilled to the marrow, I clung to the wheel and turned to face the stern, anxious to see if it was in water deep enough to allow me to restart the engine. The afterdeck appeared to be rising and falling, though I couldn't be sure because of the violent rocking of the hull.

I decided to take a chance, recalling that a safety device would prevent the Volvo from firing unless the skeg was clear of the bottom. I turned the key. The motor fired and immediately settled into a steady beat, but since it had to warm up, I grabbed the oar and tried once again, in vain, to push us off. I gave up in disgust and staggered back to the controls to put the engine in stern drive. At full revolutions, it did nothing but create an enormous patch of froth that spread around us and even washed up on the beach. There was only one thing left to do: Climb overboard and try to *push* the *Stella* off.

I returned the throttle to idle, made certain that the gear lever was in neutral, and stumbled over to the starboard side, taking hold of the gunwale and waiting until the waves canted us in that direction. I jumped out, landing short of the log but managing to reach the bow without difficulty.

At first, all my best efforts were useless, but as I became desperate, and angry, the adrenaline flowed. I dug my feet into the sand, bent low to get my shoulder under the bow, then heaved upward and pushed at the same time, every muscle quivering with the strain. Nothing. I kept up the pressure. There was a pounding in my skull and I could feel the veins on my forehead and face becoming engorged with blood. But as I felt the *Stella* move, just a little, I somehow found the strength to push and lift all the harder. Suddenly, with an audible hiss, the *Stella* slithered backward and off the slimy log all in a rush, floating clear at last.

The abrupt lack of resistance caused me to fall forward, stumbling over the thrice-cursed tree trunk and falling facedown on the surface. Frantic with anxiety lest the *Stella* be pushed back on shore, I leaped up, waded as quickly as possible through the roiled sea, and jumped for her bow, grasping the rail with both hands. For some seconds I just hung there, my feet kicking against the water until, heaving convulsively, I was able to hitch myself high enough to get one elbow over the railing. A moment later the other elbow was securely anchored, but now I realized that the *Stella* was traveling backward, *under power*. John had not, after all, fixed the slack cable. Thank God for rubber-soled boating shoes! Without them I would not have been able to gain enough purchase against the smooth, wet hull to allow me to climb over the chrome railing. But I managed. I even succeeded in clinging to the deck when the *Stella* gave a quick heave and tried to toss me overboard while she continued to go astern, aiming herself at the same rocks that had threatened us earlier. Staggering to the superstructure, I eased myself along the catwalk that ran alongside the cabin and gained the open screen, reaching the wheel before the *Stella* could back herself into the rocks.

As I turned the helm to port with one hand, I slapped the gear lever into the ahead position with the other, then crammed on the power. The gods were with us that night, or perhaps miracles do happen, for the *Stella* avoided all obstacles and charged like a greyhound toward the opening of the bay. And it was certainly her doing, not mine. I couldn't see a thing until we were clear of the shadows of land and turning into the turbulence of Ruxton Passage.

The cloud cover was intermittent and the moon, each

time it emerged, was just bright enough to allow me to see ahead if I hung out over the side. But I was soaking wet and so cold that my hands were becoming numb, and I knew that unless I could leave the wheel and get into dry clothes I would soon become hypothermic, perhaps to the point of collapse. I now realized that it had been foolish of me to get dressed earlier. If my mind had been functioning normally, I would have prepared dry clothing in the cockpit, ready to put on when the *Stella* was again afloat and out of danger. But then I remembered that without the boating shoes I might never have managed to get on board again. . . . I gave up pointlessly remonstrating with myself and formulated a plan instead.

Stuart Channel, into which we were heading, is about two miles wide and clear of rocks between De Courcy Island and Vancouver Island, its depth thirty-five fathoms. I would hold on until we reached open water, but then I was going to set the power at idle, tie down the wheel, and go change my garments. Fifteen minutes later that is what I did, remembering John's plunge into the icy water and feeling a lot more sympathy for him now than I had at the time. Peeling off clothing as I ran inside the cabin, I got some towels and began drying myself vigorously. Then I dressed my lower half and collected shirt, parka, and gloves before wrapping a towel around my head and running back to the helm. Steadying the boat's course occasionally, I finished dressing, still shivering but already starting to feel better. On impulse, when again fully, and dryly, attired, I went to get the bottle of brandy and returned with it to the wheel, which I then unlashed. I was again in control of the *Stella*! I took two swigs of the fiery liquor straight from the bottle, and as the warmth flooded through my shriveled body, I felt recovered enough to take the Courvoisier back to my cabin, leaving the

Stella to bob and curtsy at will while I gathered up my pipe, matches, tobacco, and watch. It was 3:30 in the morning and the tide was still ebbing.

For about an hour I cruised in the deep water of Stuart Channel, waiting for more light and keeping a lookout for runaway logs, none of which, fortunately, came our way. My reason for stalling in the same area had to do with Dodd Narrows, the opening between Mudge Island and Joan Point, a strip of water some two hundred yards wide, through which the ebb tide rushes at 8 knots. I did not want to negotiate this passage in darkness, although it was not exactly daylight when I eventually conned the *Stella* through. As we bucked the outgoing tide, our stern buffeted by the Force 4 wind, I had the impression that the entrance was trying to close in on us. Once we were clear of this dogleg channel, the bulk of Gabriola Island loomed inhospitably on the starboard beam and the smelly discharge from a pulp mill near Nanaimo assailed my nostrils; I could see the chimneys but not the discharge. The odor—once described to me by an overly enthusiastic advocate of "progress" as being the sweet smell of success!—convinced me to keep going right past Nanaimo and to run for Campbell River, some eighty miles north and well within range of my present fuel reserves.

By the time the *Stella* was abeam of Malaspina Point, on Gabriola Island and opposite Nanaimo, I had reason to change my mind about proceeding directly to Campbell River. The wind increased its velocity and changed direction radically, blowing now from the west. The marine weather station was issuing continuous small-craft warnings for the Strait of Georgia; one powerboat was missing and all vessels were asked to keep a lookout for her. North of Nanaimo, beyond Neck Point, the blow was worse, the seas higher. Adding to my concern, my side was hurting abominably, so much so that after I gently probed along the eighth and ninth ribs, I became convinced that both bones were fractured. I knew this coast from the previous year and so I was aware that some twelve miles north lay a safe and snug marina on the west side of Cottam Point, in Northwest Bay. I would make a run for it.

Reducing power because the *Stella* was bucking the big rollers, I was distracted by the roar of airplane motors. Leaning out of the cockpit and looking up, I saw an aircraft from the Canadian Armed Forces Search and Rescue Centre in Vancouver; it was buzzing me, undoubtedly because its pilot thought that the *Stella* might be the missing boat. As the twin-engine plane roared over, then banked to starboard, apparently preparing to make another pass, I grabbed the five-cell flashlight from the chart shelf and leaned out again, flashing two *L*s, the signal that all is well. Three times I flashed dot-dash-dot-dot, dot-dash-dot-dot, but whether my signal was received by the crew or not, I cannot say. However, the plane did turn again, this time heading on a north bearing. Meanwhile, the seas continued high and the wind was strong, although its velocity did not increase. A half-hour later the same rescue aircraft, coming south now, buzzed me again, but I simply stuck head and shoulders out of the cockpit and waved, giving the thumbs-up sign. They left me alone, probably wondering what kind of maniac would be plodding northward in the face of such weather.

By ten o'clock that morning the *Stella* was moored at the Northwest Bay marina and I was ashore, having a cup of coffee with the owner. The wind had risen to Force 7 and I was most happy to remain idle until the storm tired itself out. By evening, though the gale had slackened somewhat, it was still blowing at about 20 knots.

I sat in the cabin after supper completing the log, noting

that my own neglect had probably been responsible for the slipping of the anchors: I had forgotten to buy a couple of lengths of chain with which to weigh down the anchor stock and make it easier for the flukes to dig in. Which goes to show that one can never think of absolutely everything. I had spent the winter making lists of everything I thought I would need on the journey, but I had quite forgotten to include the chain. The local marina had none, but now that I was moored to the dock, I wasn't worried. I knew I could get what I needed in Campbell River.

4

SEA MONSTER

It was a reluctant traveler who climbed painfully onto the dock at 5:45 the next morning! I had been up for half an hour, but despite coffee, orange juice, and two aspirins, I felt dreadful, as though I had been run over by something large and heavy.

Upon rising, I had examined my side. From armpit to hip, extending laterally from a point just to the right of the spine and reaching almost to the breastbone, my flesh was an angry red that already showed signs of purpling. Both my legs were also bruised and scraped, and my head hurt where the *Stella* had clouted it, especially when I probed the lump with exploratory fingers. At first I was of two minds: Stay and rest? Or go? I was practically certain that at least one of my ribs was fractured, but since the day dawned fine, with clear skies and a breeze that registered only 4 knots, I elected to go, planning to stop and seek medical attention at Campbell River.

Moving was a sweet-sour experience. It hurt, but it helped, provided I didn't make any sudden gestures. Little by little I limbered up, and by the time I went dockside, I found I could get about quite well, except when some inadvertent movement insulted my ribs and caused them to reply. I had taken on fuel the night before, so, after two cups of coffee laced with brandy, I slipped the mooring lines and conned the *Stella* out of Northwest Bay, past Mistaken Island, and into the Strait of Georgia, where I steered on a bearing of 264 degrees magnetic. The sea was choppy, but sitting on the well-padded pilot's seat and keeping the revs down, I felt no serious discomfort. So we passed Parksville, and Qualicum Beach, then turned on a new bearing to run between Hornby and Denman islands into Lambert Channel, midway through which we altered course again to clear Cape Lazo and Comox. Experimentally, I accelerated to 2,000 RPMs and the *Stella*, bless her, cut through the waves cleanly, dancing just a little and rolling not at all.

I had previously decided that most of my serious studies were going to be undertaken above latitude 52° in regions where I would encounter few people and a great many more life forms, so this run off the east coast of Vancouver Island, while pleasant on a day like we were enjoying, was nothing more than travel time, necessary miles that had to be covered before we reached the waters and coastline that really interested me. My charts, already plotted, called for stops at Campbell River, Kelsey Bay, and Port Hardy, from which last community, the most northerly on the east coast of the island, we would cross Queen Charlotte Strait and enter the Inside Passage.

By midmorning the wind had dropped to 3 knots, and I gave more power to the *Stella*. We were running through an area of deep water that was clear of other shipping, so I tied down the wheel and entered the cabin to pour coffee from the thermos, again lacing the brew with a little brandy. Sipping from the mug, I sat at the wheel, leaving it tied down, and watched through fieldglasses about twenty hair seals disporting themselves on the rocks and shoals of Seal Islets some two miles off the port bow. Because they were a little too far away to study clearly, I finished my coffee and went forward, opened the hatch that gave access to the bow, and carefully eased my head and shoulders through it. I inspected the coast around Cape Lazo before forcing my protesting bones and muscles to climb all the way out. Then I inspected the *Stella*. She looked rather scruffy. She was in need of a good scrub down, mud-daubed, splattered with the droppings of gulls and cormorants, and bearing the marks of her struggles in the shallows of De Courcy Bay in the form of pieces of seaweed that were stuck to her deck and the cabin's sides. But to me she still looked rakish and functional. She was a good vessel. The *Stella* had proved herself to be tough and reliable, and I had no doubts whatsoever about her ability to take me to journey's end, and back.

At noon we were moored at the government dock in Campbell River, and soon afterward I arranged for a mechanic to come aboard and adjust the errant gear selector so that the *Stella* would never again go astray when she was supposed to be standing at idle. When the mechanic finished his work—it only took fifteen minutes—I paid him twenty dollars, locked up the cabin and forward hatch, and set out for the local hospital.

Strolling, enjoying the sunshine, but experiencing considerable discomfort, I stopped now and then to rest and to look at some of the boats drawn up on shore at various marinas in the waterfront area. There were many sleek sailboats and flotillas of powerboats, some small and humble, others grand and sumptuous, expensive playthings not yet to be risked on the spring waters of Discovery Passage, which, under the influence of strong southerly or southeasterly winds, produces heavy races during flood tides at its entrance off Cape Mudge and again off Race Point, nine miles west, conditions that cause the tidal rip to travel at speeds between 5 and 8 knots.

Looking back at one point, I became conscious of the fact that my *Stella* looked rather bedraggled when compared to some of those grand cruisers, many of which were being washed and shined by their nattily dressed owners. But my little boat was honorably stained, and she looked as though she was proud of her blemishes. I was certainly not ashamed of her!

Still within sight of the *Stella*, I noticed a group of beautiful people clustered around several equally beautiful power cruisers that were having their bottoms lovingly wiped by marina attendants. The four men wore yachting club blazers, and the two women in their midst were attired in pantsuits and sported gaudy but expensive scarves on their glossy heads. They were looking at me and at my boat, their expressions critical, clearly testifying that their owners viewed us as quite unsavory interlopers. There was a comedian in the crowd, a man in his mid-thirties carefully bedecked in blue blazer complete with club insignia, a silk cravat around his throat, and on his head a resplendent "captain's" cap; this ensemble was somewhat marred by a sagging stomach, which dropped pendulously to cover the waist of his cream flannel pants. As I approached, but before I was near enough to hear the words spoken, the life-and-soul-of-the-party nudged two of his companions and made some very witty remark that caused them all to have a good laugh.

I have already noted that the *Stella* was in need of a cleanup, as was I. Unshaven and as travel-stained as my boat, no doubt my face registered some of the stresses to which my person had recently been subjected. I didn't really mind being the butt of their jokes, but when I was near enough to hear every word that was uttered, the comedian made a comment that did manage to irk me, not because of the words themselves but because of the volume at which he delivered them, obviously for my benefit. Such displays of bad manners always annoy me, whether I am the butt of them or not.

"Hey!" said the fat man, again nudging one of his companions. "Here comes the guy that empties the head holding tanks!"

I was in the act of passing the group, about four feet to the right of them. I was not in the best of moods, being tired, hurt, and impatient because I was losing time on this trip to the hospital. Slowing my stride and waiting for their exaggerated laughter to end, I replied: "If I *was*, Mac, you'd be the very first thing that I'd suck up the hose!"

Silence greeted my words; the inane grins were wiped off like chalk marks under an eraser. I walked on, giving them my nastiest look, a fixed stare from under heavy, black eyebrows that topped a face cloaked in equally black bristles.

As I drew past them, I heard another voice whisper a warning: "Jesus Christ, Charlie. *Shut up!* Look at the big knife!"

Until that moment I had completely forgotten that I was still girded by the belt from which the hunting knife was suspended in its sheath. As knives go, it isn't enormous, but it isn't small, either. It is ten-and-three-quarter inches long, with a six-inch blade that is one-and-one-eighth inches wide at the hilt and then flares to an inch and a half before curving to the point. I don't think of it as a weapon but as a tool, and I wear it constantly when I am in the wilderness, a practice I fell into easily while journeying aboard the *Stella*. I had forgotten to take it off, as I am so accustomed to its weight that I am more apt to notice its absence than its presence. When it is not needed, I wear it over my right buttock.

Its influence on the group was clearly greater than the

effect of my words and my good humor was quite restored. Nevertheless, it occurred to me that it wouldn't be such a good idea to walk through town and into the hospital with the knife suspended over my backside, so when I saw several sheets of discarded newspaper just outside the docks, I stopped to collect them and wrapped up the knife and belt. I carried the innocent-looking package into the hospital.

After a two-hour wait, I was at last ushered into the presence of an intern, another fastidious soul, who proved reluctant to touch me after I'd peeled the wrappings from my torso. I was a bit rank, insofar as it had been a while since I'd washed properly (unless one counted my two prolonged baths in the ocean), but after I identified myself and explained my mode of travel, he began probing, evidently feeling that a scruffy patient who was the owner of an expensive boat, and a *researcher* to boot, was better than a patient who was broke or a bum, a bit of sophistry that did not endear the boy doctor to me. I had reason to dislike him even further when he pressed hard on my ribs, deriving more medical knowledge from my instant cry of pain than from the unnecessarily harsh palpation; he also learned a few unscientific words! But, no diagnosis can be complete nowadays without X-rays, so I spent another three-quarters of an hour while the pictures were taken and developed and while the child medico was attending to other patients (or drinking coffee). In the end, my own unpracticed diagnosis was confirmed. Ribs eight and nine had sustained fractures. Now I was wrapped in adhesive tape—wide, very sticky stuff that was slapped on from spine to sternum and felt like a straitjacket.

Back on board the *Stella*, I realized that my run to Kelsey Bay would have to be postponed until the morning, for it was now after four o'clock. I hadn't eaten breakfast or lunch, so I went ashore and bought a couple of six-foot lengths of chain and another anchor to replace the lost one, then found a restaurant where I enjoyed a large and leisurely meal.

The next morning I delayed departure from Campbell River so I'd be able to run through Discovery Passage at slack water. We left at 9:30, soon clearing Race Point and the narrows that lie a few miles beyond it, where Maud Island and Wilfred Point face each other across less than a half-mile of water. The day was fine and the wind hardly moved the anemometer's vanes, allowing the *Stella* to make 14 knots at 2,500 RPMs, a speed that got us to Kelsey Bay just after one o'clock. Since it was so early, I considered going on to Port Hardy, but because the adhesive was causing my ribs to hurt almost continuously, I opted for discretion rather than valor. Instead, I spent the afternoon gull-watching, now and then strolling ashore and talking with some of the commercial fishermen whose trawlers were moored nearby. After supper I sprawled on the bunk and read *Between Pacific Tides*.

At dawn the next day the *Stella* again set her sharp nose in a west-northwesterly direction, sailing in an orderly way along another one of those traffic separation zones, this one stretching for only about six miles along Johnstone Strait, between Hardwicke and Vancouver islands. We encountered some other vessels in these latitudes, mostly fish trawlers but also several tugs towing enormous iron barges that were crammed untidily with logs; from one of these floating containers I watched three thirty-foot tree trunks fall into the water.

As a look at a chart will show, this region of British Columbia is simply packed with islands of all shapes and sizes, a veritable sailor's paradise, and it tempted me greatly. The scenery is simply breathtaking, especially on a sunny day. I took a great many photographs as the *Stella* worked her way up Johnstone Strait, past Cormorant Island, where the little village of Alert Bay sits picturesquely on the west shore, and then threaded her way through Haddington Passage, with its many rocks, before entering Broughton Strait. It was a very inviting area indeed, and I might have tarried thereabouts, exploring some of the many accessible inlets and bays, but for the pain in my side.

Some time later the *Stella* cleared the westernmost point of Malcolm Island and entered Queen Charlotte Strait, running well within sight of the east coast of Vancouver Island, a coastline that attracts many waterfowl. Cormorants were there aplenty, of course, and a variety of ducks and loons, particularly arctic loons, sleek and beautiful birds somewhat smaller than the so-called common species. At this time of the year the arctics were still dressed in their winter plumage, garments more somber than their breeding finery; even so, their streamlined shapes, decorative white throats and fronts, and dark backs, coupled with their consummate mastery of the waters, made the fisher birds worthy of note.

Leaving the waterfowl astern, the *Stella* made a 90-degree turn to port, aiming her bow at Port Hardy, which is sheltered at the end of a long bay of the same name.

This was to be a brief stop, solely for the purpose of taking on fuel, for in view of the weather, which was perfect, and the time, 9:00 A.M., I planned to cross to the mainland and make for Namu, a distance of about seventy-five nautical miles.

At the fuel wharf I checked the oil while the attendant pumped forty gallons into the main tank. Then, switching on the electric bilge pump to clear any fumes that might have accumulated, I went ashore, paid the bill, and waited a few minutes before again turning on the engine. The *Stella* now swung about and retraced her course on a reciprocal bearing, soon arriving at our former position and reentering Queen Charlotte Strait. From here, somewhat less than half a mile north of Masterman Island, we proceeded almost due north for eight miles until we reached a point about a mile off the mainland shore, when we turned on a new heading.

At 1:10 P.M., thirty-two miles from Port Hardy, we cleared Queen Charlotte Strait and entered Queen Charlotte Sound, Cape Caution abeam to starboard and the open Pacific, stretching for some four thousand miles all the way to Japan, lying off our port side, a vast expanse of green-blue water that was clearly in a benign mood this day. Long, even swells came rolling toward shore, oil-smooth, translucent, each a replica of the others except for the hues elicited by the sunlight and the sky. Rising to perhaps eighteen inches, the gentle rollers glowed and shimmered, sometimes as green as the ocean, at other times light aquamarine blue streaked with gold and silver; not a bit of froth was visible as they came marching in from the horizon, encountered the *Stella* and caused her to bob like a toy duck in a bathtub, then continued their stately progress toward shore.

I cut back the RPMs, wishing to experience this truly peaceful sea, to enjoy the quiet and the space. What a contrast existed between the sun-drenched, gigantic ocean and the rugged land, with its tall peaks, each wearing a mantle of pristine snow and sparkling under the golden rays! I kept turning to port and to starboard, fixing the image of the sea in my mind and then turning to gaze in awe at the splendor of the Coast Mountains. At one point, a bald eagle rose from the edge of the distant shore, climbing effortlessly, a toy bird at the distance but easily recognizable, its white head and tail attracting the light. Soon afterward, with startling suddenness, hundreds of herrings burst out of the ocean, some of them rising several feet, a spray of motile silver that hung suspended for an infinitesimal fraction of time, then disappeared again. I suspected that a single large fish had charged the school, capturing a victim or two before giving up the hunt; otherwise, and especially if a number of predators had been involved, the herrings would have continued to jump out of the sea as they sought to escape.

The *Stella* was making 4 or 5 knots, idling along placidly, encountering the swells abaft the port beam, being lifted gently up one side and then sliding down the other. She rolled only slightly, pitching somewhat every time she climbed a roller and then set her bow for the descent, but her movements were measured and not at all unpleasant. I even forgot about my tender bones.

Consulting the chart after taking a bearing on a T-shaped promontory that jutted abruptly into the water, I noted that we had run about three miles since passing Cape Caution. We were now at a latitude of 51°11′48″ and a longitude of 127°49′36″, the point of land that had served as a mark being identified as Neck Ness—perhaps because some imaginative soul had believed that its outline on a chart resembled the famous Scottish monster? Still holding the fieldglasses, I left the wheel to look at the ocean, thrusting head and shoulders through the unzipped screen to see more clearly. Visibility was excellent, and the horizon line showed like a thin ribbon of well-polished silver as I swept the glasses from left to right before scanning the water closer to the *Stella*. About to return to the helm, I noticed an indistinct, apparently lengthy object poised momentarily on a swell, but it disappeared before I could focus on it. Twice more it came into view, but I could not identify it. I dropped the glasses while keeping my gaze riveted to the same patch of water, seeking to estimate the distance between us and guessing it to be two or three miles, too far for the naked eye to detect more than an occasional shadow that appeared and disappeared fitfully. Using the binoculars again, I saw nothing but sea at first. Then the amorphous apparition returned to view and again hovered momentarily before dropping out of sight. Was it a piece of wreckage, I wondered.

Curiosity impelled me to take the *Stella* off course and feed more power to the engine. I made a sharp turn in an attempt to advance on the mysterious object in as straight a line as possible. When I judged that we were headed directly for it, I checked the compass. We were running on a bearing of 260 degrees. At 3,000 RPMs the *Stella* was making some 15 knots, riding easily across the swells, meeting them almost head-on, her bottom slapping rather noisily against each upheaval. I lifted the glasses periodically, but the bouncing motion we were experiencing made it impossible to focus. After about five minutes, estimating that we had halved the distance, I slowed down, cutting the revs to just above idle and going forward to climb through the hatch and stand on deck. What the fieldglasses brought to my eyes was quite beyond belief. I lowered the lenses and shook my head to banish the ridiculous impression I had just received while telling myself I had been influenced by Neck Ness's connotations of the fabled monster. I looked again. Sure enough, about a mile away, floating on the surface and riding with the swells, was a serpentine creature that appeared to be about fifty feet long, from the dorsal section of which four distinct humps protruded. Impossible! But impossible or not, the creature was there, right before my astonished gaze. And it moved, wriggling sideways now and then so that its protruding humps changed angle and height, the forward two rising while the hindmost pair dropped. The *Stella* crept closer. Again I brought the creature into focus, realizing now that it occasionally moved ahead and that the second and fourth of its humps appeared to be sculling. When less than a mile separated us, I put the gear into neutral, removed the standard lens from the camera, and fitted in its place a 250mm telephoto. In the viewfinder, against a 35mm screen, the "monster" looked like a small piece of driftwood, even through the magnifying lens. I wasted two frames, regardless, before returning the camera to the chart shelf. After that I remained undecided. Truth to tell, I felt apprehensive. Nothing I had ever seen or read about could account for that gigantic, serpentlike creature, which was at least twice as long as the *Stella* and of unknown girth. I was even tempted to return to our original heading, foregoing the chance of identifying it. But curiosity defeated caution. I put the *Stella* in gear, gave her power, and kept on going, turning to steer a course that would take us closer to the creature.

I timed our progress. According to my log, we traveled for one minute and twenty-six seconds before the mystery was solved. Just as I had it nicely in focus, the single creature divided itself into two, one half advancing to swim alongside the other, each now showing characteristic, telltale shark fins. But what fins! The dorsals were shaped like true triangles and appeared to be more than two feet high; the caudal fins, or tails, did not stick up as much, but at least twelve inches showed above the surface in each instance. We were now about three hundred yards away, close enough for me to identify the two basking sharks even without the glasses. One of them appeared to be about the size of the *Stella*; the other was larger, perhaps thirty feet long. I really wanted pictures of these huge selachians.

Quickly I changed lenses, going back to the standard, 50mm, f:1.8. Camera in hand, I gave a little more power to the engine and waited with growing excitement as we drew closer and closer to the behemoths. When we got within 150 yards, I put the motor at idle and dashed forward; but as I emerged from the hatch, both sharks dived at the same time, a clean, downward thrust at a shallow angle that hardly disturbed the surface. For a second or two I saw their indistinct outlines under the water, enormous, aqueous shadows that all too soon sank into the deep. Confound it!

I stooged around the area, keeping a sharp eye on our surroundings in the hope that the sharks would rise again. Ten minutes later they did, but now at least a thousand yards away, out to sea. They were swimming due west at a good clip, submerged except for the tips of their big dorsal fins, visible only when they rose with a swell. Terribly disappointed, I reluctantly turned the *Stella* toward the mainland, sensing that the big fish would prove difficult to approach and knowing that we could not afford a long chase if we hoped to reach Namu before dark.

The basking shark, *Cetorhinus maximus*, is the second largest fish in the world, exceeded only by the whale shark, a veritable giant that can attain a length of sixty-five feet. Both species feed exclusively on minute plankton organisms and are therefore harmless—unless a careless sailor gets in the way and is smashed by their powerful tails.

Basking sharks grow to a reported length of forty-five feet and weigh many thousands of pounds (one thirty-foot specimen was almost five tons). They feed by swimming beneath the surface of plankton-rich waters with their mouths wide open. They strain the water by means of five long gills set on each side of the body, retaining the larvae, eggs, and other tiny organisms scooped up in this way. The gills are equipped with long rakers that trap the solids found in the sea but allow the water to escape, a technique also employed by the whale shark. But the basker has another unusual attribute; it is able to remain motionless on the surface for hours at a time, a habit it often displays and which accounts for its name.

Unlike true fish, sharks do not possess swim bladders, those elongated, balloonlike containers that fish can fill or empty at will so as to rise, sink, or, by attaining neutral buoyancy, remain suspended under the surface at any depth. Lacking these flotation devices, most selachians must keep moving or sink, but the basking shark manages in some way to rest on the surface, perhaps by working its long pectoral fins much as a human treads water. I cannot be sure, but as I examined the two sharks through the fieldglasses, it seemed to me that they were moving their pectorals and that the water around them was slightly agitated as a result.

These fish are gregarious. They gather in groups of several dozen at times and are evidently inclined to swim in tandem, the head of one just behind the dorsal fin of another, presenting in profile the strange, humped shape that caused me to believe I had discovered a genuine sea monster some fifty feet long.

About an hour after our meeting with the sharks, we had an encounter of a different kind. The *Stella* was preparing to enter South Passage, a six-mile opening between Calvert Island and Kelp Head that leads into Fitz Hugh Sound, when three killer whales rose to the surface less than half a mile away, almost directly in line with our bow. These fascinating and much-maligned mammals were high on my research list, so I hurriedly reached for the camera and altered course slightly, hoping to approach the pod closely enough to secure a good photograph. But fate seemed to be teasing me that afternoon. First it offered me two tantalizing sightings, and then it snatched them away with unseemly haste. The whales, one twenty-footer and two smaller animals, sounded within a minute of rising, leaving behind an area of disturbed water over which the thin vapor of three spouts hung for some seconds before dissipating. I had seen the big whale spout, its vented breath rising explosively out of the single blowhole and spreading almost immediately, drifting backward. In vain I scanned the water with the glasses, but the orcas did not return to the surface.

We resumed our journey, but I sulked like a spoiled child, feeling I'd been cheated, no longer lost in the wonders of the country through which we were navigating; the tall, white-clad mountains, the interesting inlets and bays, the birds. I fed more power to the *Stella* and devoted myself to navigation, occasionally scanning the chart. My nasty mood did not leave me until we docked at Namu at 5:30 P.M.

Namu is a predominantly Kwakiutl Indian community on the mainland, just south of the fifty-second parallel. Directly opposite, some six miles across Fitz Hugh Sound, is Hunter Island, a craggy, inlet-riddled isle some seventeen miles long by nine miles wide, the southerly end of which coincides with the start of the Inside Passage. Above Namu rises a range of mountains by the same name. The village boasts a post office, a store, a cannery, and telephone service, making it a veritable outpost of civilization between deep sea and wild land.

Within minutes of arrival the *Stella* attracted a small crowd of curious but shy children, sultry-eyed youngsters with fine features who gazed silently at the boat and her owner and responded with small, embarrassed smiles when they were spoken to. I had purchased two pounds of candies for just such encounters, and I now bribed my way into their good graces by distributing this largess, two to each but three to a little enchantress who totally captured my heart with her impish smile. As usual, a group of dogs came too, scruffy sled dogs of uncertain ancestry, some small and thin, others huge beasts of proud mien and bold temperament. One of these, a blue-eyed thug with only one ear, dared to try to steal the wee girl's candies; but before I could interfere, the angelic three-year-old turned into a small virago, striking the hulking dog on the nose with a puny fist, causing him to dart away with a howl of alarm. A bigger child, a boy of about seven, followed the animal, advancing on him threateningly and uttering some formidable curses in peculiarly accented English. These kids could take good care of themselves! They also had a keen eye for business.

This same boy, who appeared to be both the eldest and the leader of the group of ten, eyed the *Stella* critically, allowing his gaze to roam all over her before looking at me once, then quickly averting his big eyes.

"Boat's got plenty crap. . . ."

His statement was clearly the preamble to something else. I nodded agreement, keeping silent as I watched the other children, noting an expectant look on each face. The leader, staring at Whirlwind Bay, just outside Namu's harbor, spoke again.

"You want we should clean that boat?"

"How much?"

"Five bucks. An' we clean *good*."

Knowing something about entrepreneurial child-leaders, I sensed that the fee would not be equally distributed after the job was done, so I made a proposal of my own.

"I'll tell you what," I offered. "Five bucks is okay, but I'll pay you in change, right? I'll give fifty cents to *each* of you." (It happened that I had acquired a pocketful of loose change—at least five dollars' worth—for I have the habit of always using bills and unwittingly collecting a lot of silver and copper.)

The nine passive members of this Kwakiutl task force

grinned from ear to ear at my suggestion, even the tiny princess. But the boss-boy was not all that knocked out by the scheme. He fidgeted for a while, looking distinctly uncomfortable.

"Mebbe not all these kids work as hard as me, you know?" he finally said.

To settle the matter fairly, for in truth the three-year-old girl appeared too small to work at all, I made a second proposal.

"Okay, you organize the work party and I'll give you a buck for yourself and fifty cents for each of the others."

There was general agreement, but I had the feeling that in the end the leader might still get a little more than his fair share of the money. However, hardly was the matter of fee settled than the whole troop darted on board, so enthusiastic that they began "sweeping" the Stella's dirty deck with their hands, cormorant droppings and all. I stopped them, got two plastic pails and a supply of rags, filled the buckets with seawater, and let them go to it. They worked like little Trojans for half an hour and did an excellent job. As a bonus, after I paid them, I dished out six candies to each of them—well, the tiny girl got eight, but no one except me was really counting. It was dusk when the happy band went ashore and disappeared into the gloom.

Alone again, I made supper, very conscious of my ribs and especially of the adhesive that bound them. It pulled painfully no matter how I sought to arrange myself, causing me to believe that it had been applied incorrectly. On the whole, I wasn't feeling very well. In addition to my aching ribs I was also uncomfortably conscious of my right knee, which had been injured—and healed—some time ago but which still causes difficulties under certain circumstances. Climbing up the bow of the Stella after I pushed her off the beach had subjected the knee to some rough treatment. Now it was swollen and quite painful—nothing to get alarmed about, for I knew from past experience that it would get better on its own after a few days of rest, but a troublesome thing when added to the ache in my side. I was also tired.

Thinking about these problems after supper, I concluded that it would be wise to rest up for a week or so, and to this end I began studying the chart, looking for a quiet place in which to anchor and vegetate until I felt fit enough to continue the journey. There were so many spots to pick from that my final choice was dictated more by whimsy than anything else. Kwatna Inlet was my choice. The entrance to this long and relatively narrow anchorage is located in Burke Channel, equidistant from Namu and Bella Coola. On paper it promised excellent shelter in any weather, and being bounded on three sides by mountainous wilderness, it offered an opportunity to study land as well as marine life.

Having settled the matter, I plotted an initial course up Burke Channel, then put away the chart and went to bed. But I couldn't sleep; the pain in my side was being constantly aggravated by the confounded corset I was wearing. After two hours of wide-awake discomfort and utter exasperation, I got up, determined to remove the bands of tape that were making the injury feel worse than it had before they were applied. Working awkwardly and mostly with my left hand because the right was only capable of providing minimal assistance once I peeled back the adhesive to a point immediately underneath my armpit, I eventually found myself stymied. I just couldn't reach far enough around my own body to free the rest of the bands. But I was encouraged to go on when I found that removal of even half the tape afforded immediate relief. What to do now? After a few minutes of thought, I went to the tackle box and cut off a couple of yards of heavy, steel fishing line, tying one end tightly around the loose, bunched adhesive, then fastening the other to the handle of the head door. This done, I rotated my body, pulling away as I did so. The tape came off. It hurt, eliciting protests from the ribs and removing some patches of skin in the process, but I soon felt a good deal better.

I next anointed chest, side, and back with cooking oil to remove the sticky residue, and after wiping myself clean, I secured a three-inch bandage entirely around my torso; this held the fractured ribs firmly in place but allowed me to move without exerting a pull on my flesh, an occurrence that hitherto had immediately communicated itself to the cracked bones. On a previous occasion I'd also fractured two ribs, but on the *left* side of my body, and was at that time equally well trussed with the same kind of confounded tape (it too was removed and replaced by an elastic binding), so I must presume that medical science has good reasons for recommending such treatment, but from my lowly viewpoint I cannot for the life of me determine what these may be. All I know is that tape hurts, an elastic bandage does not—and each of the four ribs mended nicely despite my unscientific treatment. Anyway, the immediate result of this unskilled meddling was that I went to bed and immediately fell asleep.

The remains of a hair seal were floating midway along a narrow bay that lies on the south side of Kwatna Inlet, almost opposite the Burke Channel entrance. It had been a small animal, but whether male or female I could not tell. All that was left of it was the rather chewed head, part of the chest, and about half the back, the severed edges ragged and already bled almost white after an indeterminate number of days in the sea. I had spotted it soon after I conned the *Stella* into the natural harbor, and on closer investigation discovered that although it was not putrefying, it was far from fresh, emitting a rather sour odor. The gulls, of course, had found the remains; several dozen were feeding on it before our arrival disturbed them. It was, in fact, the swooping, screaming gulls that had drawn my attention to the unfortunate animal in the first place. It was impossible to establish the cause of death or dismemberment. The seal could as easily have been killed by an orca as by a grizzly that had managed to surprise the seal while it basked on a rock, for the big bears are extremely fast when stalking prey. It could also have died of sickness, or been shot, its body drifting and becoming food for fish and birds.

At first I had considered anchoring in the fingerlike bay, but on finding that its shores were rather steep and rocky and its mouth was almost immediately opposite the inlet's entrance, I turned the *Stella* right around and steered her into the inlet proper, a wider but fairly narrow body of water that was about five miles long. At its very end, the shore sloped more comfortably and the spit of land that formed the inlet offered excellent shelter from the wind. Here I set one anchor, off the bow, but I doubly secured the vessel by joining two one-hundred-foot lengths of rope, one end of which was attached to the *Stella*, the other to a tree on the immediate shore, leaving plenty of slack line in between to allow for the rise and fall of the tides.

By 1:00 P.M. the *Stella* was securely moored and I had set up the tent on a level piece of shore. I had even managed to catch a small fish, a chum, or dog salmon (*Oncorhynchus keta*), sixteen inches long, a species that spawns as far away as Teslin Lake, in the Yukon Territory, and travels some two thousand miles inland to get there. As is my usual practice when camped on shore, I discarded the inedible parts of the fish in plain sight on a rock near the shoreline some two hundred feet away, in this way ensuring that while even such things as guts and head are not wasted, they will serve a second useful purpose by allowing me an occasional opportunity to sight the creatures that come to eat the leftovers. I fully expected that the gulls would find the food quickly, but they were evidently too busy feeding off the seal to bother with this small bait. Later, though, when the mouth-watering aroma of frying salmon wafted inshore on the breeze, another sort of guest was drawn to the scene. I heard the crashing sounds of its movement some five minutes before the nearby bushes began to shake. But the animal didn't emerge at once; it stood quietly, unseen, taking stock of the situation. Guessing that it was a grizzly and remembering the Damdochax Lake calamity, I quietly entered the tent to get the Winchester, setting it down near to hand and placing five cartridges in my shirt pocket. I wasn't expecting trouble, but grizzlies are too unpredictable to trust fully, so I wanted to see this one, to assess its temper, before extending the hand of friendship.

It certainly was a patient creature! Four minutes and forty-six seconds by stopwatch timing it stood immobile and silent; then I heard it begin to rise on its hind legs. It looked rather comical when it at last came into view with only its head sticking up above the shrubbery, its meaty, black nose quivering while its muzzle moved first in the direction of the salmon's remains and then in my direction, its small and myopic eyes seeking to determine what manner of being was filling the wilderness with such delicious odors. I ignored it, eating my meal straight out of the frying pan, occasionally sipping a not-so-cold but most welcome beer. Presently, when my neighbor decided I was harmless, its head disappeared as it dropped back to all fours; soon afterward it strolled into view. It was a blond bear, young, probably two years old, and weighing something less than two hundred pounds, I guessed. I could hear it snuffling as it ambled with seemingly clumsy gait toward the offering on the rock. In a trice the whole lot was gobbled up and the smooth rock licked clean. Now the grizzly looked at me again and I saw it was a male. Not wanting to encourage him to come too close to my camp, I spoke, wishing him a good day and suggesting that there was lots of room in this country for the two of us. Evidently he agreed, because he turned his head away and walked to the shoreline, surprising me by taking a few laps of salt water before about-facing and disappearing into the bushes from where he had emerged.

My ribs felt a lot better now that they were decently held together by the elastic bandage, but I elected to sleep in the more comfortable bunk on board rather than on the hard floor of the tent. I was also anxious to ensure that the *Stella* was well anchored, the events at De Courcy Island still very fresh in my memory. Taking all edibles with me, I closed up the tent in late evening and rowed back to the *Stella*. I sat on deck until I began to feel chilly.

Thus began what I later referred to as my lazy time. I idled considerably, pampering my ribs and knee and doing only those things that appealed to me. I had bought three five-gallon containers for additional supplies of fresh water, so I had thirty-five gallons on hand when we arrived at Kwatna Inlet. By washing with seawater and shaving every other day with fresh water, I knew I would not run short, even if my daily dip in the ocean was at times an overly refreshing experience. The *Stella*, behaving herself, swung occasionally and rose and fell with the tide but remained more or less in one place. After the third night, I took to sleeping on shore, pandering to my ribs with an air mattress and a blanket spread over the sleeping bag.

It was a good rest period, during which I explored the land

within a dozen miles around the inlet, met a total of seven grizzlies whose only concern was to go about their own affairs—the young blond one became a fairly regular visitor who accepted the tidbits I put out for him every evening without becoming a nuisance—and I collected, studied, and afterward liberated a variety of tide pool and shallows organisms. At last, on a beautiful morning in mid-April, I struck the tent, carried all my belongings back on board, and, after freeing the *Stella*, left this haven.

CROSSCURRENTS

Running through Milbanke Sound in a small boat during an outflowing tide and under the influence of long Pacific swells is an experience not soon to be forgotten, even when the day is sunny and the wind light; but when the weather is wet and Force 4 winds blow out of the west while tidal bores rush seaward, the crossing is awe-inspiring, eliciting fear and exhilaration at one and the same time. As a passenger on the big ferries that ply the waters between Kelsey Bay and Prince Rupert, I had felt the effects of this unruly stretch of water several times before this morning, so I knew that it could be rough; but walking the heaving decks of a vessel that weighs thousands of tons or leaning against its rail to watch the big rollers from a height of twenty-five feet cannot begin to compare with the sensations and emotions experienced when the same passage is made in a twenty-four-foot cruiser.

Sitting at the helm of the *Stella*, I was acutely conscious of the turbulence that made mountains out of the waves and fashioned whirlpools from the currents. By leaning out over the gunwale, I could actually touch the sea with hardly a stretch of my arm; spindrift constantly hit the windscreen, and sullen, leaden water burst over the bow each time we ran down a seven-foot roller. These conditions prevailed in our most immediate vicinity—indeed, our very presence created them.

Our surroundings were quite different. Heavy swells came in from the open sea and battered the *Stella* at the same time that the outflow rushed to meet us at angles varying from fine on the port, to fine on the starboard bow, causing the boat to move drunkenly, wagging her stern to left and right, pitching her length continuously, and rolling quite steeply to port and starboard. In the cabin, things were adrift: cans of food out of the galley locker, dishes in the sink, other items left unsecured due to my oversight, all rolled and clanked and rattled, adding their percussive notes to the threnodic composition created by the wind as it whistled against the radio mast, howled around the superstructure, and wailed under the dinghy. The skies were filled with swollen clouds spewing strings of lashing rain and jagged black rocks thrust themselves into view at periodic intervals along the starboard shore. As if these things were not in themselves sufficient to daunt us, the rip was intent on putting further obstacles in the *Stella*'s path. Numerous runaway logs rose threateningly at intervals; it seemed as though they were stalking us, approaching unseen until they suddenly appeared atop a swell or rose almost vertically from the vortex of a whirlpool.

There were other kinds of flotsam as well, including a number of trees, complete with their top branches; these had been plucked from shore by the rains and spring floods and were led by great tangles of roots—Gorgonian heads that could sink us with one blow. Compared to these, the assorted pieces of wood, empty containers, and broken branches that regularly bobbed up to the surface were puny obstacles. Yet they too had to be avoided.

Milbanke Sound lies between latitudes 52°10′00″ and 52°16′12″, running west-northwest between longitudes 128°31′00″ and 128°40′00″; these positions coincide in the southeast with the tip of Wurtele Island and in the northwest with the end of Price Island, the diagonal distance between the two points measuring nine nautical miles. This is the entrance to the sound, an area of water fully exposed to the Pacific, across the vast face of which the West Wind Drift sweeps with spectacular majesty until it spends itself against the land. Here, in the northeast part of the great ocean, this drift, the so-called Japan Current, results largely from those forces exerted by the prevailing westerlies, which drive the seas from Asia to North America at a leisurely rate of some 3 knots during calm weather, but at considerably more impressive speeds when Favonius takes a deep breath and expels it forcefully over the water. The current produced by the drift becomes divided some four hundred miles off the west coast of Vancouver Island. Part of it flows north to end in the Gulf of Alaska, while the other part runs south to California and Mexico. But the place where the waters separate, the paths that they follow, and the speed at which they travel vary from season to season and in accordance with the intensity of the winds. Coming as it does from semitropical latitudes, this water is warm and thus largely responsible for the more moderate but wet climate that dominates along the coasts of Washington, British Columbia, and Alaska. It is also responsible for the occasional appearance of southern fishes in these waters, including pompano, barracuda, tuna, and, on fortunately rare occasions, even great white sharks, to name but a few of the visitors.

Northeast of the main entrance to Milbanke Sound lie Seaforth and Mathieson channels, the latter obstructed by two islands—Lake and Lady Douglas—which cause the tidal waters to divide, creating Moss Passage. North of here the Inside Passage is split by Sarah and Swindle islands, and these, because of their locations and configurations, have fashioned a veritable network of channels, passages, and inlets. During outgoing flows, the waters are compressed and forced to run through long, narrow outlets, building up speed until they are eventually disgorged into the sound to confront the long-distance swells. And inasmuch as tides in these latitudes can attain a height of twenty-four feet, the volume of water expelled and the pressure of its discharge are enormous.

On days when the Pacific Ocean is quiet, there is still more than enough turbulence to be encountered in the sound during the main rush of the outflow, but when boisterous westerlies whip up the swells far out in the open sea, the meeting between rollers and tidal bores produces sufficient disturbances to cause even the big Alaska ferries to dance. But the *Stella* wasn't just dancing—she was performing acrobatics! Her unpredictable movements kept me so busy gripping the wheel and searching for obstacles that I had no time to dwell on the fear I'd suffered when we first nosed out of Seaforth Channel and felt the brunt of the upheavals.

At one moment the boat hung poised on the crest of a big roller and all I could see was the leaden sky; seconds later she climbed over the top and nosed down into a veritable hole. Now, from my position in the cockpit, only great, solid-looking walls of dark water were visible. Down and down we went, as though we wouldn't stop until we crashed on the rocky bottom, but then the *Stella* shuddered slightly, her nose began to lift, and some sky crept into view above the rim of the cup into which we had slithered. Up and up came the bow, revealing more sky, some quick glimpses of land, until at last we were again climbing a swell; three-quarters of the way up, the *Stella* would pause, as if resting for what was to follow. Then she'd surf, running with the roller until her bow and midships section overbalanced us and we nosed down to repeat the same maneuver, again and again.

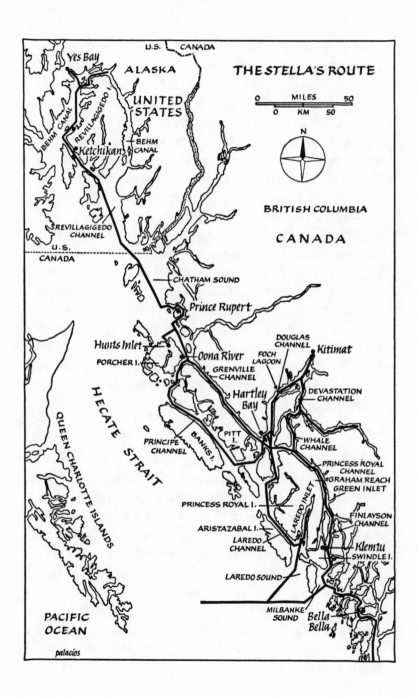

At first my immediate thoughts had centered on the engine. I prayed it wouldn't fail us just here. Later, confident that the Volvo meant to go on beating its rhythmic way through the ocean, I began to curse the wheel, or, more particularly, its designers, who had sacrificed efficiency for the sake of shiny frivolity, hoping that such magpie attraction would induce fair-weather sailors to covet the pretty thing. It was highly chromed, and therefore slippery, and four thin, round spokes emerged from its center at ninety-degree angles but did not protrude outside of the circumference to offer reliable handgrips. I had cursed this slithery wheel during our return from Astoria but now I thrice-cursed it, for I had to grip it so tightly that after half an hour my hands ached from the effort and my fingers were becoming devoid of feeling, forcing me to waggle them at regular intervals and to thus interrupt, no matter how fractionally, my concentration. This was to prove the *Stella*'s only weakness, and I never did blame *her* for it. But that crossing made me resolve to bind the chrome with some nonslip material as soon as we reached a peaceful anchorage.

Insofar as common sense and consultation with the charts and tide tables will readily convince small-boat owners to stay clear of Milbanke Sound during the kind of conditions we were experiencing, it may be wondered what we were doing there. Why was I deliberately running this gauntlet of swell and rip when I should have known enough to avoid it? The fact is that I *did* know better, but my desire to make the crossing was stronger than my apprehension of the sea and weather. If it is possible for the human organism to feel disgust, anger, and sadness all at the same time, then such an emotional triumvirate was the cause of our risking the wrath of the elements.

We had left Kwatna Inlet soon after first light under cloudy skies and light wind, the weather being apparently undecided although the marine forecast called for rising westerlies and rain. I had at first hesitated to proceed northward, but on finding that we had lots of fuel, I reasoned that if the weather deteriorated we could put in at Bella Bella, some forty miles away, and remain moored there until conditions improved; so I elected not to return to Namu. Instead, we turned sharply to starboard after clearing the mouth of Burke Channel and ran on a 330-degree bearing up Fisher Channel through a sea that was somewhat choppy but by no means unpleasant. As we made headway the cloud cover increased and the wind freshened, yet the going remained good until we turned to port and entered Lama Passage to run between Hunter and Denny islands. Now it started to rain fairly hard. I switched on the wipers just as we passed abeam of a fish trawler whose occupants tooted a greeting and waved.

Half an hour later, as we ran with Hunter Channel on our port beam and turned to starboard to head northward along Lama Passage, the anemometer registered a blow of 9 knots, or Force 3. Waves crested to three or four feet, occasionally breaking and making whitecaps; the rain became heavier. Bella Bella was about four miles away, so I decided to seek shelter there and spend at least some of the idle time buying needed stores and stretching my legs on shore.

We tied up at the wharf just after nine o'clock. I ordered fuel, went dockside while the tanks were being filled, and was soon in conversation with a tall, tough-looking man whose face was badly scarred and whose left eye appeared to be sightless. He was a Norwegian, a onetime commercial fisherman from Stavanger who had migrated to Canada during the sixties. Friendly and obviously familiar with these waters, Thor, as he introduced himself, confirmed that I would be wise to stay put for the day. He said the weather was going to get worse but was expected to moderate during late afternoon or evening. He especially warned against entering Milbanke Sound and running against the tide, which was even then falling, pointing to his scars and telling me he had received the injuries two years earlier when a runaway log had risen out of the waters of Milbanke and crashed through the windshield of his boat, one edge of it hitting him in the face before it slid back into the ocean. He had managed to struggle back to port and was rushed to the hospital, but he remained scarred for life and his left eye was practically useless, retaining only 20 percent of its vision. Had I been planning to continue northward before meeting Thor, I would have changed my mind after listening to his horror story and seeing the effects of his meeting with one of those dangerous timbers. As it was, I explained my intentions and we talked about other things for a time. Later, my acquaintance directed me to a nearby café and said he would join me there after he finished up a few chores at the docks. Coffee and a second breakfast that I didn't have to cook myself became instantly appealing, so when I had settled the bill for the fuel and moved the *Stella* to another berth, I went ashore, found the café and entered it.

The place was divided into two sections. The front room was long and fairly narrow, containing a counter and stools; the back room was large and somewhat bare, but about fifteen round tables, a sufficient number of chairs, and an oil heater managed to fill it reasonably well. It certainly wasn't elegant, but it would do. I noticed that all but one of the tables were occupied by natives, perhaps a dozen men. They eyed me rather sullenly, most of them drinking wine or rye whiskey from bottles only marginally concealed by the paper bags from which the necks of each container protruded. All of the men had coffee cups before them, for the café did not have a liquor license, but those customers were not there for the java!

Ignoring the looks, I sat at the unoccupied table, my back to the wall—a precautionary habit developed after half a lifetime of experience with not-so-nice places—and I ordered bacon and eggs and coffee when the waitress arrived to minister to my needs. My presence had immediately inhibited conversation, but now some desultory talk resumed while I was subjected to almost continuous scrutiny. Five minutes after my order was taken, the food arrived and I was pleasantly surprised to find that the coffee was excellent. I began my meal.

I was still eating when an extremely drunken Indian staggered through the doorway and stopped in front of me. He was short, of poor physique, and dressed in jeans, boots, an old parka, and a T-shirt on the stained front of which was emblazoned in crimson letters: RED POWER. Swaying, he glared at me, mumbling words I did not understand. I ignored him, conscious of the silence that had followed his approach to my table and aware that the other occupants of the room, none as drunk as the newcomer but all nevertheless considerably inebriated, were now looking at me expectantly, in anticipation of trouble.

Getting no response, Red Power leaned dirt-encrusted hands on my table and spoke louder and I suppose clearer, because this time I understood him.

"Shove off!"

At that I looked up, meeting his angry eyes. The air of hostile expectancy filled the room. A brawl was in the making. What to do? I didn't want any trouble, but unless I did *something*, trouble I was going to get. Apart from the two women at the front counter, I was the only white in the place, and, since I was obviously a stranger, it was clear that the occupants of the room were more than willing to join the hazing initiated by their tribal brother. I had three choices: I could continue to ignore the man and hope things would settle down; I could get up and leave; or I could deal with him in kind. The first choice, I was sure, would aggravate rather than pacify the troublemaker. The second choice went very much against the grain—I had been minding my own business and there is enough *macho* in me to forbid such ignominious retreat. That left choice number three.

I spoke quietly, but my voice could be heard throughout the room: "Go to hell!" He straightened, taking his hands off the table, and made as though he was going to turn away, but before actually doing so he glanced around the room. He must have sensed encouragement from the eyes that greeted his, for he mouthed some vulgarities, leaned forward to grab a bottle of ketchup that was on my table, and raised it, undoubtedly meaning to strike me with it. I am a peace-loving man and not given to brawling, but I have definite regard for the security of my person. I didn't want to hurt this importuning drunk, yet I could not allow him to break a bottle of ketchup over my head. He was slow, no doubt inhibited by the alcohol he had consumed, and since I am blessed with excellent reflexes, I had time to think about my defense, to calculate my moves. Seeking to inflict the least amount of damage, I rose, drawing back my right arm as I did so. Before his own extended arm could descend with the bottle, I delivered a good blow to his forehead with my open hand, making contact with its heel, my fingers folded at the second knuckles so as to stiffen the palm. Such a blow offers two advantages. It has the power to knock down without inflicting serious injury, and it is painless to the deliverer, presenting no risk of broken knuckles. My antagonist staggered back two steps, the bottle of ketchup flying out of his hand as he collapsed full-length on the floor. As I expected, he remained conscious but dazed, the kind of bemused condition that dulls the reflexes and tends to subdue anger. *He* no longer worried me, but the others did. I turned to face the room, seeing hostility in the gaze of every man present —and feeling considerable discomfort in the area of my broken ribs! Two ticks of time passed as I swiveled my knife belt with deliberate ostentation, ensuring that the gesture was not lost upon my audience. Several of the men who had been in the act of rising, now sat down. So did I. Assuming a cool I was far from feeling, I returned to my meal, watching the drunk as he picked himself up off the floor and turned toward the exit, not a word escaping him. A moment later he staggered out, and before I had cleaned my plate Thor arrived. The little drama was ended, yet it left me with extremely mixed emotions.

I discussed the affair with my companion, who said he regretted that he had not been present because he would have dearly loved to wipe the floor with all those present. The fact that he spoke in a loud voice and swept the room with contempt-filled eyes told its own story. None of the natives responded to his bare-faced challenge. He explained his anger, telling me that drunkenness was the number one problem in the community and that many natives were so debauched and troublesome that brawls were a daily occurrence.

When we left the café and parted company, I went to buy my supplies, noticing that all but three natives out of more than two dozen that I saw were seriously intoxicated. At ten in the morning! Dockside the story was the same. Four natives, including the man I had "argued" with in the café, stood about fifty paces from the *Stella*, all of them swaying; they were passing a whiskey bottle from mouth to mouth but didn't seem inclined to start more trouble. This is when I became disgusted. It was also the moment that I decided to leave Bella Bella, a community that had triggered too many unpleasant emotions in me.

Confrontations stemming from political, racial, or religious ideologies have in one way or another dominated my entire life, or, at least, that part of it that is within reach of memory: first in Spain, when I was eight years old and already familiar with the street-fighting and bombings that led to the abdication of Alfonso XIII in April 1931. The confrontation then was between monarchists and republicans; the latter succeeded, but not for very long! Three years later there was more street-fighting and bombings, so that one always needed a white handkerchief in the pocket to wave as a sign of neutrality during bloody altercations, even when walking to and from school.

Sitting in streetcars was dangerous, and one learned to place oneself as near the exit as possible in readiness for those occasions when a flaming bottle of gas mixed with tar came crashing through a window. With the rise of Hitler, Mussolini, and the Spanish Falangists, adherents of the fascist doctrines, my school was divided: many of my classmates espoused the dictatorial causes and our friendship was broken; one of my brothers marched with a Falangist *centurria*, a term coined from the legions of Rome, who were formed in groups of a hundred, each in the charge of a centurion. Abyssinia (now Ethiopia) was invaded by Mussolini's armies, and mustard gas was used; the two factions in Spain intensified their hatred of one another.

Before these events, as a small boy of a Protestant family in a Catholic country, I was involved in religious confrontations, at school, at home, among my Spanish mother's relatives, until I felt that I was neither one thing nor the other and I gave allegiance to neither faction. In July 1936, two months before my fifteenth birthday, the Spanish civil war began; this was the most horrible confrontation of them all. Friends became enemies, brother sought to kill brother, and one million people died. By 1939, nine days before my eighteenth birthday, the great global confrontation went into high gear and I was calloused and cynical, believing in nothing but my own ability to stay alive and fanatically determined to oppose dictatorship. I was by then so accustomed to confrontations of one kind or another that I accepted them with equanimity: they were a way of life and I navigated through them much as I was now steering the *Stella* across Milbanke Sound. Bigotry and racial intolerance no longer angered me, even when I was the recipient of them. Except for one occasion. That *did* leave a mark. It was in August 1944, and I was in an English hospital, wounded, some twelve hours after being carried out of the fighting. Unshaven, exhausted, and in pain, I was not responsive when a nurse awakened me at five in the morning and, placing a basin beside my bed while waving a razor, ordered me to "get decent." She was examining my chart as she spoke, and when I said I didn't feel like shaving just then, she reacted angrily.

"Well! There's a war on, you know! You *foreigners* should go back where you came from if you're not prepared to keep *our* standards!"

Her outburst was beyond belief. It generated such anger within me that her words are still fresh in my memory thirty-six years later. It was not the stupidity of her remarks about the war addressed to a man who had a great deal of firsthand experience of it—such idiotic words were often spoken by frightened people—but the acid of her bigotry that aroused my fury. My chart gave my birthplace as Spain; this alone was enough to trigger her poisonous prejudice. We became literally enemies and the impasse lasted until I limped out of that bloody place six months later.

So it went. When I arrived in Canada I had thought this new land would be free of confrontation, which only goes to show how naïve I was.

Perhaps my past explains why I am so convinced that unless mankind learns to negotiate reasonably and with understanding, our species will in due course destroy itself and this planet during one last, mighty disagreement. Less clear is the anger which now, on occasion, fills me when I am involved with, or am witness to, the kind of bigotry that gives rise to face-to-face clashes. When reason fails, the only way to eliminate confrontation is to avoid it, but one cannot always sidestep, one cannot always remain neutral.

The face-offs that have been taking place between whites and nonwhites in the Americas have lasted almost five hundred years, the whites essentially coming out ahead because of their numbers, technology, and organization. Dreadful things have been done by both sides—murder, rapine, and persecution—and these, too, are history. Today, there is no war, but races still have not learned to live with each other. The problems remain because they cannot be solved by angry collisions. Sadly, no primitive culture has managed to survive direct contact with European technology. This is one of the major problems facing the North American Indians. Seeking the iron tools of Europe, the guns, the horses, and the ready-made, warm clothing (not to mention alcohol!), the Indians were, and still are, willing to sacrifice their heritage in order to obtain their fair share of these "goodies." Today they talk about going back to the old ways, without realizing that they cannot, for the old ways were part of the Stone Age and *they* have entered the Space Age. They must compromise, as must the whites within our democracies. The solutions can only be found in reason and peace and understanding.

These complexities dominated my emotions as I steered the *Stella* away from the dock at Bella Bella. I was very angry. Hitherto I had never harmed a single Indian. I have an Ojibway godson; I have lived with these people and learned their ways as well as some of their language and have found much to admire in the remnants of their ancient cultures. I have noted, too, the ravages that their contacts with European civilization have caused and are still causing them. It especially saddens me to see that the majority of their solidly founded traditions and beliefs have been lost. A people who do not preserve their history in writing eventually become ignorant of their antecedents and their mythologies and creeds unless these are actively kept alive. No one can really reconstruct early Indian history, for the arrival of the Europeans created singular changes in the life-style of those natives with whom they came into contact and years were to pass—during which more changes were effected among the aboriginal's way of life—before *some* whites and *some* Indians learned enough of each other's languages to communicate clearly. But the Indian belief in *Spirit* has been preserved, at least in some groups and among individuals. This spirituality that is seen to exist in both animate and inanimate things is of paramount importance to all men everywhere, because it implies, if nothing else, that all of nature's creations have an aura that is in some way sentient and is most worthy of attention. From this stems respect for life: and if enough people respect life, peaceful coexistence will be assured. So I believe that the whites have much to learn from the Indians, and the Indians have a lot to relearn about themselves. My God! If I were an Indian, I would be so proud of my lineage. . . .

I was disgusted by what I had seen that morning. Abuse of any kind disgusts me, whether it's practiced by others or by me. I don't think there is a human living who does not on occasion overindulge in some way, but constant, assiduous abuse of one's self is degrading. Nature is never abusive. Its organisms are not given the opportunity to practice the kind of gluttony common in this day and age; they may gorge at times, death may come to wipe out communities that have become too populous for the good of the environment, but continuous self-indulgence is absent from the natural order.

As I sat at the *Stella*'s helm and Bella Bella disappeared in the distance, I sought to calm myself by looking at the wonderful world that surrounded me. Even the worsening weather was totally neutral, its elemental forces completely honest and open, offering challenge, even ready to kill those unable to meet them, but absolutely impartial.

Still, I simply could not rid myself of the effects of my stopover. Like a pendulum, my emotions continued to swing between sadness and anger and disgust. Yet none of my feelings resulted from that single experience alone; rather they came as a result of a cumulative total. The drunks of the community had merely triggered an emotional reaction at a time when I was still very vulnerable. Inevitably, Joan came into my mind. How would she have reacted? I knew the answer to that question even before I phrased it. She would have cried. Not for me, and certainly not for herself, but for the world. For a time, until the mighty Pacific rushed at us and drove my sentimentality away, I raged inwardly at the injustice that had caused Joan to die so young and yet allowed such miseries as I had witnessed to continue flourishing. Pointless self-flagellation, of course, but real enough at the time.

Then the *Stella* emerged from the relative shelter of Seaforth Channel and entered Milbanke Sound. The ocean attacked, and my being responded instantly to the challenges of survival. First came fear, then exhilaration, and fear again, and finally a determination to run this gauntlet of wind and sea. Along with this came a sense of fulfillment coupled with a feeling of pride in the *Stella*. My mind was calm again, wiped clean of destructive emotions. All that mattered was the crossing and my boat.

The *Stella* rode the seas, and I watched for dangers ahead; the swells and the currents continued to meet and joust, while the rain fell and the rocks threatened impotently. I began to enjoy myself.

Leaving Bella Bella, I had estimated that we'd have to run twelve miles before emerging from the sound to enter the Inside Passage. Now, noting that we were abeam of Vancouver Rock, which lies less than two miles west of Lady Douglas Island, I realized we had reached the halfway mark. Simultaneously, it became evident that the swells were starting to lose some of their power, although the tidal currents did not appear to be slackening their momentum. I looked at my watch and discovered that it had taken an hour and ten minutes to reach this point, despite the fact that the *Stella* was running at 1,800 RPMs. On reflection, however, I felt we had done well, for a fair proportion of the engine's power was dissipated by the rough passage. Soon after 1:00 P.M. the worst of the journey was over. Not only had the winds and rain moderated, but we were well inside the shelter of Finlayson Channel, and the tide was slackening. Because of the time, I decided to make for Klemtu, a community located on Swindle Island about thirty miles from Bella Bella. Here I would top up with fuel and lie-to for the night.

FRIENDLY WATERS

The calm after the storm is always an impressive spectacle. But never is it more so than at sea, and especially when one has emerged unscathed out of the kind of turbulence that had assailed us during our run across Milbanke Sound. The cessation of elemental successions does not occur suddenly, but rather it develops progressively, stage by stage, a hardly detectable metamorphosis that often takes an observer by surprise and may cause one to believe that some beneficent, all-powerful influence has arrived without preamble to smother the wind, banish the clouds, and make the waters still. It is easy then to dwell upon the Greek myths, to imagine that Neptune has appeared in his horse-drawn chariot and is racing over the flat ocean while the monsters of the deep rise to do him homage, to disport themselves before their sea god.

So it seemed to me on the afternoon of my hasty departure from Bella Bella. As the *Stella Maris* had coursed over the upheavals of sea and strained against the outpourings of tide, my being had run an emotional gamut from anger and fear to exhilaration. Then, for almost an hour, I had steered through Finlayson Channel without conscious awareness of the surroundings, controlling the helm automatically while my mind was in a sort of neutral lethargy, untroubled and unstimulated. But as we cleared the mouth of Oscar Passage and came abeam of Susan Island, which lay to starboard, a yellow-orange shaft of sun emerged from the breaking clouds, highlighting the sea and splashing over the shelving coast of the island, a burst of warm color that banished the monotonal gray and replaced it with vibrant hues of green and gold and silver. As though magically conjured by the spear of light, a large flock of Bonaparte's gulls swooped low from somewhere above the *Stella* and performed graceful aerobatics within the changed panorama. These swift-flying, sleek little sea birds had not yet changed from winter to summer plumage, but they were nevertheless distinctively marked: orange on feet and legs, milk-white on neck, chest, and tail, and with falconlike wings edged with jet black. In another month their heads, mostly white now, would turn a glossy ebon; and some of them were already showing irregular dark markings above the beak and on the back of the head as well as the conspicuous black spot that is characteristic in winter. The gulls performed for us, several hundred lovely creatures calling in sharp, nasal tones as they wheeled and dived and rose and fell, keeping station with the *Stella's* bow until we passed some point beyond which they seemed unwilling to venture.

Swiftly now, as though the elements had relented and were seeking to make up for the harsh treatment they had offered earlier, the clouds broke and began drifting toward the northeast, sailing before a wind that had dropped to 4 knots and was puffing from the southwest. The tide was at dead low, and there were wavelets decorated by glassine crests, translucent, placid corrugations the color of emeralds and just as sparkling. The relatively humble mountains that predominate on the islands in this area showed apple green, except for an occasional one, taller than the rest, that still preserved a halo of crusted snow on its crown; evanescent strings of creamy spume played at the feet of a cluster of islets visible fine on the starboard bow, while some nine miles ahead, Cone Island showed as a darkly verdant hump.

I stood up, admiring the magnificent transformation, while my innermost self became regenerated, charged with excitement and a joie de vivre so powerful that goose bumps arose on my entire body. I reached for a notebook that I kept handy on the chart shelf and wrote in it: "This is what I came for. It's like the end of the rainbow and the road here, no matter how rough, was well worth traveling."

I was in the act of returning the book to the shelf when with startling suddenness the water erupted all around the *Stella* and numerous black-and-white, beautifully streamlined shapes rose to keep us company, a large school of puffing, diving Dall porpoises, every one of which had burst out of the water at practically the same time and in the same formation they adopted as they surrounded the boat. Two of the larger mammals, the leaders perhaps, stationed themselves one on either side of the bow, their agile bodies half a length ahead of the boat's knifelike stem. They rose, breathed, and dived, a tireless, effortless sort of gliding that was endlessly repeated. The leaders, however, added an extra touch to their repertoires when they started slapping the hull with their broad tails, a metronomic sort of "side kick" delivered just before they dived. If I had felt excited before, I was ecstatic as I cut the *Stella*'s speed down to minimum revs, tied the wheel, and hurried forward to scramble through the hatch and stand on the bow deck, feasting my gaze on these wonderful, friendly little mammals, representatives of an order (Cetacea) that has been criminally persecuted for centuries by the human species.

My first contact with a cetacean occurred off the coast of Mallorca when I was eight years old. My brother, Jack, and I were swimming underwater in a large, well-sheltered lagoon, the sea entrance to which was only about six feet wide and less than ten feet deep. It was our favorite swimming hole in the summer of 1929, but because I was a far better swimmer than Jack, I spent a good deal more time exploring its fifteen-foot-deep bottom than did he. On this particular morning in early July, I was swimming along the sand and rock seafloor and Jack was swimming above. Suspended from a line he held was a weighted basket into which I put the seashells I was collecting. By virtue of seniority—he was six years older than I—Jack delegated to me those jobs he disliked doing himself, and collecting the shells that we later sold to vacationing English tourists was not high on his list of preferences. It was for this reason that we had come to the present arrangement. In order to collect as many specimens as possible during the ninety seconds I could remain submerged, Jack devised the line-and-basket technique. This allowed him to loll on the surface and at the same time ensured that I could collect with both hands and thus increase the margin of profits—of which, as senior partner, he obtained the lion's share.

I didn't use goggles when under the surface, so it was necessary for me to swim with my eyes no more than a foot away from the bottom, grab what shells I could see in the rather narrow periphery of vision, and then turn to dump them into the basket. It was routine, an automatic series of movements to which I had become accustomed. Jack meanwhile timed his surface swimming to match my own progress below, for the water was so clear that he could see me easily.

On this particular morning, I'd collected two handfuls of shells and had turned to put them in the basket, only to find that it wasn't there and that the water between me and the surface was considerably agitated in two places, the twin disturbances moving toward the rocky shore where we usually entered and left the lagoon. Because man's naked-eye vision underwater is poor at the best of times, I could not determine the cause of the surface commotion, nor could I see the basket that had been there only seconds earlier. Kicking off against the bottom for quick acceleration, I shot up like a cork, emerging into the sunlight within fifteen feet of a Mediterranean dolphin. I noted that Jack was streaking for the land as fast as he could swim. We had both seen many dolphins before, of course, but apparently this one had entered our swimming area and scared the stuffing out of my brother. I felt no fear of the interesting animal, perhaps because I was young enough to accept most things on trust and with interest and not yet old enough to have developed prejudices. Whatever the reason, I stayed in the water, amused by my brother's fast scramble up the rocks and greatly intrigued by our large visitor—in fact, it was a small dolphin, probably less than six feet in length and almost certainly a young animal, a member of the so-called common dolphin species (*Delphinus delphis*), abundant in the Mediterranean Sea.

At any rate, while I was treading water and watching the swift animal as it continued to swim on the surface, I became aware that it was carrying in its mouth our specimen basket, the line from which was trailing astern. I had personally made the gourd-shaped container, "remodeling" an old raffia shopping bag of my aunt's with whom we spent our school holidays, so I was not amused by the dolphin's antics. Seeking to reclaim my property, I grabbed the line as it trailed near me. Our visitor, feeling the strain, entered into the spirit of the game and began towing me around the lagoon, a thrilling ride that caused me to forget all about property rights as I abandoned myself to the pleasures of waterskiing on my stomach. Too many years have passed for me to recollect with clarity all the details of that experience, but I think my ride lasted several minutes, after which the dolphin let go of the basket, circled me twice, and then disappeared in the open sea.

Since that time, cetaceans have always exerted enormous influence on me: I studied them in the Mediterranean, and in the waters off Gibraltar, and along the north and west coasts of Africa. It may be that I have learned a few things about them during the years in between, but I am very conscious of the paucity of my knowledge. There is so much yet to learn about these wonderful creatures!

There are some seventy-seven species of cetaceans living in the world's seas. Of these, forty-seven species frequent the waters of North America. About half of the total number are known as whales, the others as dolphins and porpoises, nomenclatures that create some confusion, especially as applied to the last two animals. Generally speaking, dolphins are distinguished by a prominent snout, while porpoises have smooth, rather rounded foreheads and somewhat blunt "noses." But the order is, properly speaking, composed of two distinct suborders: toothed whales, or Odontoceti, and baleen whales, or Mysticeti. Toothed whales, including dolphins and porpoises, have rows of conical teeth and only one blowhole (which is, in fact, a breathing nostril); members of this suborder are all predatory, chasing and killing their prey above or beneath the water. Baleen whales have two blowholes and no teeth, their mouths having been shaped to function as giant scoops with which they obtain the plankton (called krill by whalers) upon which they feed almost exclusively. These cetaceans have strainers within their jaws made of baleen, a flexible, bonelike substance that allows the whale to expel the water from its mouth while retaining the minute organisms it scoops up.

Although they can hear, cetaceans do not have external

ears, and even the auricular openings themselves have been reduced to minute holes no thicker than the lead of a pencil; these may or may not transmit sound. On the other hand, evolution has modified the hearing apparatus of all cetaceans, uniting the middle and inner ears by means of a tympanic bone that is hollow and uniquely suspended from the skull by ligaments; shaped somewhat like a large conch shell, this bone is filled with a foamlike substance that is thought to increase auricular reception.

Water conducts sound at a speed five times greater than air space* and also allows sound vibrations to pass more readily through animal tissue; this circumstance enables toothed whales to, in effect, "hear" through their bodies. Thus, external ears are not required by marine animals that have developed refinements of inner-ear construction. Indeed, such appendages jutting out on either side of the head would reduce the streamlining effect of the body, would cause unwanted background noise to be made as the whale traveled at speed through the water, and might well lead to serious ear infections that would impair the sensitive echolocation equipment that evolution has given the toothed whales.

The baleen whales are not thought to be capable of echolocation, but as their auricular equipment has also been modified, it may be presumed that they can hear adequately while submerged, though whether or not they can hear while on the surface has not yet been established. In any event, hearing in the members of this species is not nearly as important as it is in all other animals. Baleen cetaceans can gather their food simply and at will by ploughing under the surface with their mouths open, and because there is so

---

*Sound travels through air at 1,100 feet per second; this rate is increased underwater to 5,500 feet, or a little more than one land mile, per second.

much krill in the ocean (it has been estimated that between 500 million and 1 billion tons of plankton are present in the seas of the world at any one time) the lives of these giant animals are generally untroubled in the absence of man.

In the matter of vision, cetaceans are again different from other mammals, for their eyeballs are fixed within the sockets. As a result, whales must move their entire bodies in order to change the angle of sight. This may have resulted from the need to protect the delicate tissue of each pupil, which could be easily irritated as it slid around in the socket, both by the salt in the water and by some of the minute, larval organisms that are constantly floating under the surface. Whatever the reason, cetacean eyes are incapable of voluntary movement and are constantly lubricated by special oils manufactured in glands within the lids, causing the whales to weep so-called greasy tears when the surplus oil leaks out. (The eyes of seals are also protected in this way and they, too, "cry" constantly.)

Some whales can dive to depths of more than three thousand feet—sonar and radio-tracking evidence suggests that sperm whales can descend to ten thousand feet—but how they manage to withstand the enormous pressure of water at such a depth is still open to speculation. So is the question of why whales don't suffer from Caisson disease, popularly known as "the bends." This condition affects divers who rise too quickly to the surface, when suddenly released pressure causes nitrogen to form bubbles in the blood. In severe cases, Caisson disease will kill a diver; even marginally fast ascents will result in nitrogen narcosis, the early stages of the disease. Moreover, any human who tried to swim as deep down as a sperm whale would be crushed to death long before he reached the three-thousand-foot level.

Toothed whales, and some seals, not only descend to great

depths without coming to harm, but they can also ascend from the deep without having to decompress. To date, the most plausible explanation offered for these phenomena relates to the fact that cetaceans and seals hold their breath during all dives, and for this reason there may not be sufficient nitrogen buildup in the bloodstream to cause serious harm. This does not, of course, explain why the animals are not crushed when they expose themselves to pressures that can build up to a thousand pounds for each square inch of body surface.

The blubber in which cetaceans are wrapped may help cushion the pressure to some extent, but this doesn't fully explain why members of this suborder are not injured during really deep dives. Blubber is principally intended to protect against the cold; rich in fat, it lies just under the skin, in some species to a depth of two feet, forming an excellent "blanket" that is much needed, for warm-blooded animals lose body heat twenty times faster in water than they do in air. Cetaceans are hairless, or at best possess about two hundred coarse hairs, so blubber is their only form of insulation.

The respiratory tract of these mammals has also been custom-designed, the air duct, or ducts, bypassing the throat and mouth and being directly connected to the enormous lungs. Were it otherwise, the animals would drown when water was forced into their breathing passages during feeding, for members of either suborder must swim actively, with their mouths open when seeking krill or when about to catch their prey. For this reason the nostrils, or blowholes, are placed on top of the head instead of on the snout and are protected by a valve that closes and opens automatically when the animals dive or rise to breathe. Contrary to some popular opinion, whales, dolphins, and porpoises do not spout water when exhaling. When they empty their lungs, especially after a deep dive, the warm, moist breath exhaled becomes immediately expanded on contact with the cool surface air, condensing much as human breath does when expelled in cold weather. The big whales, of course, exhale large amounts of stale breath and this is seen as a steamlike cloud that sometimes rises to twenty feet or more. Naturally, these geysers of breath are more visible during cold weather than at the height of summer, but they are obvious in any weather.

Can whales smell? Probably not, and certainly not while under the surface. But whales appear to have an acute sense of taste, as at least some species show marked preferences for particular kinds of food.

All of these amazing mammals are magnificent swimmers and divers, superbly designed for life beneath and on top of the sea. Some species can remain submerged for more than an hour, after which, on rising to the surface, they may breathe for ten minutes, inhaling and exhaling about seventy times during that period, literally ventilating their enormous bodies. If there is such a thing as an average stay underwater, it would be about ten to fifteen minutes for most species.

Communication is an attribute shared by all animals, but contact with individuals of the same species, with the environment, and with prey or enemy species varies considerably according to the particular characteristics of each kind of creature. Man has for thousands of years communicated verbally, placing such importance on speech that he has largely lost the ability to relate by any other means. Other animals, by contrast, use more than one kind of communicative skill. Body posture, eye contact, erection and depression of hair, olfactory recognition, and, of course, voice are some of the means by which land animals keep in touch with their environment while also advertising their feelings or intentions.

Having no vocal cords, and almost certainly lacking a sense of smell, cetaceans would appear limited in the arts of communication. Not so! These animals have been given special organs, and their bodies have undergone particular modifications that enable them to communicate most effectively while reading the "current affairs" that govern their subsurface world. Whales are attuned to vibrations and are experts in detecting and emitting sonic and ultrasonic waves. By these means they evidently can talk to one another over long distances, detect and identify their food and their enemies, and even read the shapes and contours of the ocean's floor and shore outlines. Properly speaking, the noises made by cetaceans cannot be equated with voice utterances, but I will leave it to the purists to determine the proper word to describe their articulation and shall continue to use such terms as *voice* and *speech* for the purposes of clarity.

Toothed whales can vocalize at varying scales. The lowest of these produce sounds at 20 cycles per second, which are clearly audible to human ears and remind one of the noise made by a rusty nail being pulled out of a board; at extreme frequencies, they send and receive ultrasonic messages in ranges as high as 256,000 cycles per second. Considering that these high-frequency sounds can travel 62½ miles in one minute, it is not surprising to note that whales can communicate over enormous distances. Man's voice does not begin to compare in its ability to rise and fall in frequency; his ear cannot detect sounds made at frequencies higher than 20,000 cycles per second.

Although baleen whales may be less sensitive to the sounds of their environment, they are by no means ineffective mammals, for they have been endowed with what must be the most effective digestive apparatus for "grazing" for sustenance. So they live well and wax fat on the vegetable and animal plankton they ingest. Ten species comprise the suborder, among which is the blue whale, the largest animal ever known to exist on earth. A fully adult member of this species (*Balaenoptera musculus*) is believed to consume a ton of plankton at one feeding and will measure up to a hundred feet in length and weigh in the region of two hundred tons. It is thought to eat eight tons of krill every twenty-four hours. The females produce single babies that are about twenty-three feet long at birth and may weigh two tons. They suck their mothers' thick, rich milk for seven months, by which time it has been estimated that they have gained weight at a rate of *seven pounds an hour!*

In contrast, Dall porpoises are little, toothed whales that live in the Pacific Ocean, ranging according to season from Santa Catalina Island, California, north to the Aleutian Islands, Alaska, westward to the Okhotsk Sea, U.S.S.R., and even to the Sea of Japan. Males grow to six feet in length, perhaps even a little more than that, and weigh up to about 245 pounds, being heavy of girth, while females attain a length of sixty-eight inches and a weight of 210 pounds. These animals are thought to be capable of attaining a speed of 20 knots.

The energy, agility, and obvious friendliness of the Dalls wholly captivated me, and their superb swimming skills filled me with envy. For a time I lay prone on deck, head and shoulders projecting beyond the bow so I could watch the two I considered to be the leaders. Now I was even more impressed by their speed and coordination, for they twice switched sides, spurting ahead of the *Stella* and crossing in front of the stem to alter their stations. Meanwhile, other

Dalls were surfing on the bow waves, rising on either side of the boat, swimming up to the disturbance and hanging there for about a minute, then accelerating and turning away from the hull to make room for the next pair of surfers.

It was hard at first to take note of every individual action, for there was so much going on at the same time that I couldn't help moving my eyes from one of the animals to another, my gaze lingering for a second or two before shifting to a new target. After about ten minutes, I concentrated on one of the lead porpoises, watching its movements and listening to the little puffing sounds it made with each exhalation. The animal propelled itself by swift, up-and-down strokes of its tail fluke, each thrust causing the powerful muscles on the animal's sides and back to ripple, contracting and expanding visibly while the torpedo-shaped body arched gracefully as it rose and fell rhythmically. On the rise, the Dall's body made only marginal disturbances on the water, but each time it dived, the sea splashed upward, causing smooth fans of water to rise and to release from their leading edges pearly droplets of crystalline liquid. The animal's movements and the aquatic effects they created were mesmerizing. I could have watched forever.

The Dall is mostly dark gray or jet black, decorated by a large, oval white patch on the stomach that rises on both flanks to a point about ten inches below, but slightly ahead, of the dorsal fin, which is sometimes tipped by white or light gray, causing this porpoise to resemble a small killer whale. Examination of dead Dalls has shown that they are armed with between twenty-two and twenty-seven pairs of small conical teeth in each jaw. The food of these porpoises includes hake, squid, capelin, horse mackerel, herring, and other small to medium fish.

We were doing about 6 knots when the Dalls rose to

surround the *Stella*, and now, wanting to see if they would stay with us if we maneuvered more erratically, I turned off course and put the boat into a series of figure-eight turns. The porpoises followed the helm instantly without deviating from their assumed positions. I accelerated, made the turns wider, then tighter, but my escorts kept station as easily as if they were all connected to the boat. What amazing skill!

Returning to our old course, I decided to test their speed and gradually increased power to about 16 knots. The Dalls came right along with us. I was tempted to accelerate to full power but thought better of it, fearing I might lose my fascinating escorts. Instead I reduced speed, returning to 6 knots, and continued to watch the playful animals while I wondered how they could gauge our changes of speed quickly enough to adjust without losing their stations. I cannot give a definitive answer to this question, but I believe that the animals are able to immediately detect the change in engine pitch as well as the alterations of current around the vessel that are caused by the initial acceleration. When the pitch and current remain constant, the Dalls maintain their own rate at an equal constant; but when these factors are altered, the porpoises increase or decrease speed accordingly. Similarly, through echolocation, I believe the Dalls are able to determine angles and distances, computing these instantly and thus managing to change course with the split-second timing necessary to keep station with a vessel or with their companions.

While the *Stella* and her playful escorts headed toward Klemtu, now only about five miles away, I tried to count the porpoises, deciding after several attempts that this school, or gam, consisted of between thirty-five and forty animals, a more accurate count being impossible because of the speed at which the Dalls appeared and disappeared. Additionally, from what I could see of them, I decided that all the members of the gam were adult, but I could not determine a male-female ratio. When I finished making a few quick notes, I got the camera and went forward again, shooting an entire roll of film and hoping the results would be at least passable, for it was difficult to focus on the swift bodies that were almost constantly enveloped in spray.

For an hour and twelve minutes the Dalls kept us company. Then, with Klemtu less than a mile ahead, they disappeared as quickly and uncannily as they had arrived, all of them sounding in nearly perfect unison, as though at a word of command. I was sorry to see them go.

Now I turned my attention to the chart, realizing for the first time that Klemtu was another Kwakiutl community. The thought of going there so soon after my unpleasant experience at Bella Bella was decidedly unsettling. I would be the only white within miles, and thus at the mercy of these people if they proved to be hostile. This was not a comforting thought. But there was no alternative; I *had* to put in for fuel or abandon my plans to explore these latitudes for a time, proceeding instead to Butedale. I vacillated for several minutes: Go on, or not? My eagerness to explore some of the many bays and inlets in this unpopulous region conquered my apprehension sufficiently to allow me to steer the *Stella* toward the village.

Klemtu is located on the east shore of Swindle Island within a narrow passage formed by Cone Island, which lies no more than half a mile away. Rising steeply out of the ocean, Swindle Island is an abrupt rock-bound isle that, if viewed from the air or in outline on a chart, looks somewhat like the head of a steer, the northwest horn of which juts into Laredo Sound while the northeast horn thrusts into Tolmie Channel. Its most northerly tip, Split Head, lies almost equidistant between Princess Royal and Sarah islands. The village of Klemtu is situated at the base of this headland, perched like an eagle's nest above a small, shallow bay, which at low tide reveals a horseshoe-shaped beach. The floating dock that serves the community is north of this bay, in deeper water, and connected to the height of land by a series of rather springy, precarious catwalks that rise and fall with the dock and in accordance with the movement of the tides. Running a notch above the idle, I steered the *Stella* toward the wooden dock, noting as we approached that two sullen-looking Kwakiutls were leaning on a rail fence some forty feet above, staring impassively at us.

Cutting the engine as the *Stella* nosed against the wharf, I waved at the two loungers, who did not respond. I scrambled ashore, securing the mooring lines. That done, I started walking up the steep planks, feeling sure that I was not going to be made welcome in this place, but determined to take on fuel. Impassive and unmoving, the Indians continued to stare at the boat, but as I climbed, they directed their gaze toward the open water. Some moments later, when I was only a couple of strides from them, I called out a firm "Good afternoon." At that, both heads came up and their set, taciturn faces were creased by wide smiles. In friendly tones they responded to my greeting, and I, pleasantly surprised and much relieved, asked them if they were in charge of the gasoline pump that stood nearby. No, they were just passing the time, but they gave me directions to the gas attendant's house, which was apparently located at the far end of the village. The dwelling, they said, was painted white. This was hardly news, as I had already noted that practically all of the painted houses were white, those not so decorated showing the grayness of raw wood that had never been coated with any kind of preservative.

Although the village was visible from the sea, it was entirely concealed from the landing above the dock by the bulk of an enormous, fire-blackened building, a sprawling, one-story edifice with a flat roof located just past the gas pumps. Upon inquiry, one of the loungers told me that it had been a fish cannery until recently, when it had caught fire and been gutted. The way to the village was through the building.

As I walked through the rambling ruin, I thought it would have made an ideal set for a horror movie. The walls, once white, were sooty and smoke-darkened, scorched by flames, and further defaced by cracks and fallen plaster. The cannery had been constructed without windows, a fact I found astounding, but one that was to remain unexplained. It had been lighted by locally generated electricity, but the fixtures had either been destroyed by the fire or had been ripped out afterward. What light now penetrated the gloom-laden building filtered in from a number of doorless portals, the interior having originally been partitioned into a number of large rooms from which most of the cannery's machinery had been removed, though some, twisted and scattered by the fire, still remained.

Halfway through the tortured edifice I entered a long, narrow room—perhaps it had been a passageway?—which was almost totally dark and through which I had to walk slowly, shuffling along so that my feet could feel for obstacles on the floor and my outstretched arms could ward off aboveground obstructions. Seeing an area of weak light on my right, I turned toward it, emerging presently into a large room, the ceiling of which had collapsed and lay as a pile of rubble on the floor. No doors or windows offered exits here. Instead, I saw three lean, hungry-looking sled dogs who were busy nosing around in the debris, perhaps hunting for mice. They eyed me as though I was a providentially sent meal.

I was no stranger to such dogs, and I knew that if I showed fear, they would attack. Pausing in the doorway, I waited only long enough to note that the biggest and most vicious-looking husky was sidling toward me, ears erect, tail curled into a tight spiral. The creature rather reminded me of Yukon, except this one wasn't as big and he had one blue and one amber eye, a fairly common genetic characteristic among inbred members of this species that gives the dogs a sinister appearance. True to his breed, the husky was not wasting his energies growling but was advancing stiff-legged, his lips curled back to reveal long, yellowish fangs, his entire mien telling me that he would attack if given a chance.

I am always reluctant to injure a dog, no matter how evil its intentions, and now, seeking to avoid a confrontation that might well have resulted in my having to kill the husky with my belt knife, I stooped, picked up a large lump of old plaster and threw it to the far corner of the gutted room, deliberately aiming away from the dogs because I hoped the hungry trio would rush to inspect the missile, thinking it was edible. The animal with the mismatched eyes was fast. He whirled around and streaked over the top of the debris, reaching the place where the plaster had landed a leap or two ahead of his less aggressive companions. While they were investigating, I left, retracing my way to the corridor. I soon emerged into sunlight at a place where Klemtu's single "street" began as a three-foot-wide path that threaded its way along the edge of a veritable precipice. Ahead, perhaps a hundred yards from the cannery's doorway, was a primitive and rather precarious-looking footbridge made of rough-sawed lumber. When I reached the bridge, I noted it spanned a fifteen-foot-wide chasm that descended for some sixty feet and ended at the edge of the bay; a small creek tumbled down this cleft, creating several rather picturesque cascades. The little bridge itself was furnished with handrails and was about four feet wide. In the middle of it, snoozing peacefully in the sunshine, two more huskies were lying, but they showed no hostility as I walked toward them. One lifted its head slightly to look at me, while the other merely opened its eyes. I approached the pair without looking directly at them, moving slowly, telling them in body language that I was of a mind to remain neutral but that I was not afraid of them. Peripheral vision allowed me to see that they remained prone, watching me calmly. I stepped over them and kept going.

On the pathway at the far side of the bridge I met an ancient Kwakiutl, a veritable gargoyle of a man, certainly an octogenarian but evidently still vigorous and alert. He was small and stooped, bandy-legged, his face as dark and wrinkled as a pickled walnut. Shining keenly out of the striated visage were two of the most extraordinary eyes I have ever seen. So dark brown that they were almost black, the velvety irises were surrounded by a sclera so white that it looked like fine milk glass. They were the eyes of an eagle—dignified, extremely alert, but calm and penetrating. Smiling, so that the face wrinkles traveled backward in small waves, and exposing pink, toothless gums, the old man wished me a hearty good afternoon, then told me, rather than asked me, that I was looking for the gas man. I admitted that such was my mission, whereupon the patriarch gave me fresh directions in a quiet, well-modulated voice. When we had exchanged a few pleasantries and I was about to resume my journey, he extended his right hand and we shook.

By now I had no doubt that these natives were distinctly different from those I had met at Bella Bella, remarkably so. This realization caused me to feel ashamed and guilty because I had allowed myself to become prejudiced after a single experience. The apprehension that I felt when approaching the village, seemed now to demand an apology. Later that day I was to offer it, and it was accepted with friendship and wonderful dignity.

The village itself was worthy of note. Set in a region of splendid scenery, every house was neat, even the many that had never seen a lick of paint (that status symbol so highly prized by white societies). Standing for a time at a point where I could see over the north end of Cone Island, I admired the waters of Finlayson Channel and the evergreen dressing of the nearby islands. The landscape was one about which a painter might dream. In the east and to the north, the majestic Coast Mountains of the mainland rose against the blue sky, the peaks of most of these giants still wrapped in glistening snow. Immediately below me, the blue-green ocean maintained a kaleidoscopic sparkle as a succession of gentle waves dashed themselves against the shingled beach. On the island itself, towering over the village, the land rose to form two modest mountains, through the middle of which Klemtu Creek trundled gently until it reached the chasm I had just crossed, after which the crystalline melt-waters tumbled down to unite with the salt of the Pacific. Flying, floating on the surface of the bay, or sitting on shore were groups of cormorants, gulls, and harlequin ducks, magnificently attired birds when in full summer plumage but spectacular even now, dressed in browns and decorated with white spots and flashes.

I noticed a rowboat approaching the small beach. It was manned by two youths, who waved. One of them let go of his oars long enough to cup his hands around his mouth and yell: "You lookin' for the gas man?" I yelled back an affirmative, whereupon more directions were shouted. There followed another exchange of greetings. I waved as I turned to resume my quest, which by now had been made easy by the surfeit of directions I'd been given. It was clear that my arrival was something of an event, a break in the normal routine.

Moments later I was able to identify the house I was looking for, which was located about 150 yards ahead. Not only was it the last house in the village, but it was splendidly attired in a coat of gleaming new paint. When I was halfway there, I saw another Kwakiutl who emerged from between two adjacent buildings and greeted me courteously as we passed, but I didn't stop on this occasion because I was now intent on reaching my objective.

When I knocked on the door it was quickly opened, revealing three adorable little girls, each holding on to the other for security and comfort in face of a white stranger but all smiling shyly. They ranged in age from about four to perhaps nine and were neatly dressed in colorful, simple frocks that set off their brown, plump arms and accentuated their shiny black hair. The eldest, of course, knew why I'd come. Replying to my "Hello," she explained in almost the same breath that her father had just left to go to the gas pumps.

"He saw you come. You must have passed him comin' here."

Apart from the youths in the boat, I had only seen four men on shore, the two loungers, the old gentleman, and the man I had just passed. He must have been the person I was looking for, yet he had not identified himself. Curious, I thought, as I bid the little girls good-bye and began retracing my steps.

Emerging eventually out of the cannery, I confirmed my guess as to the man's identity. He had now joined the two loungers, but when I approached the group, he smiled without speaking and began to ready the fuel hose, an enormously long tube made necessary because of the distance it had to travel from the pump to the floating dock during low tide. As he worked, I scrambled down the catwalk and received the nozzle end of the hose, in due course thrusting it into the fuel tank and signaling that I was ready. While the fuel was running, I looked all around me at the scenery and afterward, with both tanks topped up to the brim, helped the Indian withdraw the snakelike hose. After settling the bill, I asked the gas man and the loungers to join me for coffee, an invitation that was somewhat laconically accepted. The gas man merely nodded; the other two muttered a shy "Okay."

I had left the bilge pump on before helping with the hose, so now, satisfied that any fumes that might have accumulated belowdecks had been safely sucked out, I lit one of the alcohol stove's burners and busied myself with coffee-making while the three Kwakiutls looked over the *Stella*, admiring the boat even to the extent of actually feeling its smooth bulkheads and chrome appointments. The confounded, shiny wheel especially attracted them, but when I explained the problems it caused, one of the loungers turned right about and, without a word, went ashore. I wondered if I had unwittingly offended him, but a few minutes later he returned, carrying an old inner tube in one hand. Still in silence, he began to cut the rubber into inch-wide strips, working quickly with a small belt knife that must have been as sharp as a razor, judging by the ease with which it sliced through the viscous material. When he had made ribbons out of the tube, he began winding the strips around the wheel while the rest of us watched. He was careful and methodical, and he did a remarkably good job. The last end was neatly held in place with friction tape, a roll of which he dug out of a pocket. Now he stepped back, looked carefully at his work, and nodded to himself as though satisfied. At last he spoke.

"Reckon that'll make it good. No good tryin' to hold that wheel without that rubber. Like a wet fish, that wheel."

He had even wrapped the four spokes!

I thanked him, knowing enough not to insult him by offering to pay for his work, but I invited them all to sit down and I poured the coffee. They took powdered milk, mixing it in their brew, then each man put four heaping spoons of sugar into his cup. For a time we sat in companionable silence, and then I turned to the gas man.

"How come you didn't tell me you were the gas man when we passed each other?" I asked.

He took another deliberate sip from his mug, put it down, looked at me with a smile, and said, "You didn't ask me."

His reply was matter-of-fact, a straightforward statement devoid of sarcasm or any attempt at levity. He had known who I was and what I wanted and he knew that I would eventually find my way back to the pumps, so he kept his own counsel and waited for me. Such verbal economy is not unusual among people who live in isolation. They are accustomed to silence and do not find it intimidating, companionship being valued for its own, physical sake; just being with somebody is communication enough, for the minds somehow meet and are able to relate.

When the first cups of coffee had been consumed and fresh ones poured all around, I had a sparing sort of conversation with the gas man, during the course of which he told me that the tribal council had decided some years ago to ban alcohol in the community (a progressive step taken by a number of isolated Indian villages scattered along the Inside Passage). In exchange, I told him about the Bella Bella affair and apologized for my earlier apprehensions. He nodded, smiled.

"It's okay, I know. Those are bad Indians."

"Yes, and there are bad white men just like them."

Three dark heads bobbed in unison.

The loungers finished their coffee, rose, nodded their thanks, and walked off the *Stella*; the gas man, whom I gathered held a position of authority in the village, stayed and accepted a third mugful of coffee. Presently he told me that the recent cannery fire had taken the life of the previous gas attendant, whom he had replaced. After that, the Kwakiutl sat in silence, his gaze directed at the sea, his manner familiar to me and telegraphing a message: He wanted to ask me something. Often I had met this quiet preamble to a request which is common among those who live beyond the reach of civilization. I waited, fully at ease and telling him so by my own silence and relaxed posture, the while thinking that such quietude often confuses city dwellers, who seem embarrassed in the face of speechlessness. So we remained for almost ten minutes.

"We got herring eggs," said the Indian at last. "Salted. They keep long time that way."

I nodded, then watched as the Indian took a package of tobacco from his shirt pocket, opened it deliberately, removed a booklet of papers from its interior, and then took out enough tobacco to make a cigarette. Maintaining silence, he passed the makings across the table, sliding them to me. Although I don't smoke cigarettes as a general rule, I accepted the offering and began building my own shag-filled tube. The Indian, more expert, finished before I did, then dug a wooden match out of his trouser pocket. He did not strike the match until I had completed my task, at which time he rasped the head with his thumbnail, lit his smoke, and extended the flame to mine. He puffed for a while, and then, still looking out to sea, he spoke his longest sentence yet.

"Not many boats come here this time year. You first in nine weeks. The herring eggs, they gotta go north, Hartley Bay. You go to Hartley Bay?"

Yes, I told him, but not for a few weeks yet, for I was going to go to Mussel Inlet to rest and to study marine and land life. The Indian nodded, puffed again on his cigarette.

"You take herring eggs for us if no boat come meantime?"

I was more than happy to accommodate these friendly people, and I said so. The gas man then explained that the herring roe were being dispatched in trade for a supply of eulachon oil—or grease, as the Kwakiutl called it.

Klemtu is located in an area of the ocean where herring congregate by the millions during the spawning season and the villagers have traditionally traded their salted roe for an equivalent amount of eulachon oil collected by natives in areas where these smelt foregather just prior to their spawning, upriver runs. This exchange between the people of Klemtu and the people of Hartley Bay has evidently been going on since before the memory of my native friend and might have commenced in the mists of Indian prehistory.

Before we parted, the Kwakiutl surprised me by asking a few questions of his own. Where was I going? Why? Why was I planning to visit Mussel Inlet? After I explained, he said that my intended stopover was some forty miles away and was not "a good place," but when I asked him why, he shrugged, shook his head, and repeated the comment.

"Not a good place. More better you go to Green Inlet. Only twenty miles from this place an' deep in middle, but shallow by shore. An' at end is a big lake. Good drinkin' water. Nice place for big fish an' stuff."

I thanked him, promising to take his advice and to call at Klemtu before resuming my northward journey.

Studying the chart before departure late that afternoon, I

noted a well-protected cove at the north end of Roderick Island some fourteen miles from the Indian village. As dusk would be arriving within three hours, I decided to anchor there for the night rather than remain moored at the Klemtu dock.

The *Stella*, freed from her ties, set her keen nose seaward and sliced elegantly through the calm water, as if conscious of the admiring eyes that watched her departure. The two loungers again leaned on the railings, the gas man standing beside them, while the old gentleman, flanked by the teenagers who had greeted me from their rowboat, formed a small group near the burned-out cannery. None of the Kwakiutls waved, but in their own quiet way they were clearly wishing us farewell. I did wave, a short gesture made casually through the starboard screen as soon as our stern was positioned in line with the dock, for even after such a short acquaintance, these people had endeared themselves to me. Transparently honest and direct, they had made me immediately welcome. I was glad that just before leaving, I had given the gas man a package of candies, telling him they were for his little girls. He accepted the gift readily but in silence, his eyes thanking me more effectively than any words could possibly have done. How good it felt to have communed peacefully with such gentle people!

Ten miles and ninety minutes later—for we had been idling along at about 6 knots—two pods of killer whales surfaced about a half-mile to the north; they remained on the surface, swimming in our direction, three in one group, four in another, two hundred yards or so separating each gam. I tied down the wheel and went forward with camera and fieldglasses. The leading trio contained a big male—distinguishable by the length of his dorsal fin, which in this species is notably longer than that sported by the female—

and two smaller animals. Of these, the larger one appeared to be a female; the other could have been a yearling calf. The second group was evidently composed of males. When about a quarter of a mile separated us, I lowered the glasses and began setting up my camera and tripod. Suddenly, all the whales dived, the rearmost group sounding first but being quickly followed by the three up ahead. Leaving the tripod and camera, I hurried to the cockpit and put the engine in neutral, hoping that the orcas would rise again. But after waiting half an hour and with the sun already concealed behind the low mountains to the west, I decided that I had again missed my chance to photograph these intriguing animals.

We were near Goat Cove, where I planned to spend the night, so I turned the *Stella* on her new course and gave her half power. By 6:00 P.M. we were anchored and I was ready for supper.

During early evening of the second day after our departure from Klemtu, the *Stella* lay quietly in a small cove in Green Inlet, the entrance to which lies east of Graham Reach at a latitude of 52° 55′ 33″ N. It was a quiet, lovely dusk. The western sky was tinted mauve and lilac and pale peach; the water had turned a dark, almost bottle green except near the shore and close to the *Stella*, where small, golden wavelets lapped intermittently. I had eaten supper and washed the dishes, then worked on the log, bringing it up to date and noting that the temperatures had moderated considerably during the past week and that at noon that day, May 4, the thermometer had registered 72 degrees F. Evenings were still chilly, but quite bearable on deck if I wore a sweater.

Later, I sat at the bow and watched the stars emerge against a sky that was not totally dark. Now and then a fish splashed in the water near the boat and loons called occasionally, their voices cascading through the night and multiplied by echoes. The moon was between full and last quarter, a pale, gibbous orb partly concealed by the mountains and trees but casting sufficient light to enable me to see with reasonable clarity and even to observe more distant features through the field-glasses. Within Horsefly Cove, where we lay, moonlight silvered the water, creating grotesque shadows among the rocks and islets that clustered to seaward; the quiet of the night was disturbed by the buzzing of a number of mosquitoes that had become active with the coming of warmer weather.

Not long after I settled myself on the forward deck, legs dangling through the hatch, I heard movement in the water on the far side of the inlet, near the opposite shore, which was perhaps 350 yards away. The splashing noises were sporadic but vigorous, suggesting that something large was swimming on the surface. I trained my glasses on the spot. The natural restlessness of the water reflected the moonlight and changed the shapes of the shadows, making it impossible to determine whether the evanescent, dark areas were being caused by an animal, or fish, or the caprices of light. I gave up, lowered the glasses, and was content to sit, listening to the night sounds that intermittently disturbed the silence. And as so often happens, just as I had stopped looking for the maker, or makers, of the earlier sounds, their perpetrators revealed themselves.

Six northern sea lions emerged from the far shadows and began crossing the inlet, swimming toward the *Stella*, their heads seen as amorphous bumps atop the surface but their identities confirmed by the stentorian bellows that one or more of the animals began to emit soon after they came into view. We had arrived here in daylight, and it was obvious that the big seals had entered the inlet after dusk, coming in from Graham Reach, almost certainly unaware that I was in their vicinity, for these large mammals are shy of man except for those times during the breeding season when they congregate in vast numbers. Historically, sea lions have been relentlessly persecuted by humans because their gall bladders, the lips with whiskers attached, and the genitals of the massive bulls were prized in China, where they fetched high prices. The gall was used for medicinal purposes; the genitals, dried and ground up, were thought to increase male virility; and the coarse, stiff whiskers were used as ornaments and opium-pipe cleaners. This market is now almost nonexistent, but the sea lions are still hunted, their meat and blubber valued by some Asians and by native North Americans.

At the approach of winter the big seals migrate to southern California and Mexico. They head north again in late spring to breeding grounds as far away as Bogoslof Island in the Aleutians and the Pribilof Islands in the Bering Sea, after which the groups break up and begin their slow southward movement, the majority traveling and feeding in the open ocean but many of them tarrying along the coast.

The animals that I was observing reached the middle of the inlet and dived, evidently intent on feeding. They stayed submerged for almost fifteen minutes. When they rose again they were close to the *Stella* and I was able to determine that there was only one bull, a huge patriarch of evidently nasty disposition, judging by the fuss he made when a smaller animal accidentally came too close to him. It seemed that the others were females, but this was difficult to confirm because of the movement of the animals and the inadequate light. The rather bedraggled-looking bull kept edging up to one female, grunting loudly, as though ordering her to do something. But either his gruntings were as unintelligible to her as they were to me, or the lady was fully liberated, for she ignored him, adroitly avoiding his heavy shoulder each time he tried to nudge her. In the end, this aloof behavior fully enraged the lordly male and he vented his temper by roaring and ranting, making an incredible racket. I must have moved inadvertently, attracting the bull's notice, for he shut up, stared fixedly at the *Stella*, and then, cutting loose with one last defiant roar, he led the group into a fast dive. I went to bed after the show, glad to leave the chill behind and to bury myself in the down-filled sleeping bag.

7

KILLER WHALES

The next morning I awakened to a day filled with sunshine and a sea that was pancake flat. Sitting up and looking out of the starboard deadlight toward a small island that lay between us and the entrance to Green Inlet, I was delighted to see that the shore and the shallows nearby were filled with ducks and geese: wood ducks, golden-eyes, harlequin ducks, mergansers, and brant geese, hundreds of waterfowl, undoubtedly resting here before continuing their northward migration. Some swam about, feeding, while others stood one-legged and relaxed. Many of them preened, gossiping and sometimes engaging in short, ritualistic fights. The nearest were less than a hundred yards away, the farthest no more than two hundred. As I watched, a large flock of Canada geese came in to land, each bird shooting out its legs, feet-first and toes spread to make platforms out of the webs, tails held downward to act as landing flaps. At the same time, they swiveled their wings, arresting progress further and tilting their bodies backward, contacting the surface with their feet and actually waterskiing as they flapped themselves to a splashy touchdown.

I was loath to move for fear of disturbing the waterfowl, but after about half an hour my body began to demand sustenance. I got up, preparing breakfast as quietly as possible in the galley, watching the birds as I worked. And then the kettle boiled! I had bought one of those whistling kettles—not because I liked it, but because it was the only one small enough for my needs available in the Victoria ship chandler's store where I had acquired the bulk of my supplies—and now the fool thing shrieked its demented warning. Before I could remove the whistle-cap from the spout, all the birds took off, flock after flock of ducks and geese beating the water to a froth and calling loudly as they lifted, climbed higher, then circled the *Stella* before departing on a northward heading. I had hoped to photograph them, but I wasn't too disappointed, for it was a thrill to witness so many wildfowl passing low overhead.

After breakfast I went on deck to have a look around, noting that the land on the north shore rises at a slightly steeper angle than its counterpart to the south, which in some places shelves quite gradually, the incline being approximately one foot of rise for six feet of travel. Green Inlet curves slightly, its shape resembling a sausage link the sides of which have become crinkled after frying in the pan. It is about four miles long and half a mile wide at its eastern end, but in the west, at the entrance to Graham Reach, it narrows to a quarter of a mile. Six creeks tumble down along the north shore, three on the south; at the extreme northeast corner there is an opening that is raised slightly above the level of the sea through which the unnamed lake discharges its runoff into the inlet.

Strictly speaking, this body of fresh water is more like a lagoon than a lake; while it empties into the inlet during flood conditions, the ocean enters into it through the same gap during high tides. It is likely that at one time during prehistory the lake was an extension of the inlet that became almost entirely separated by an upheaval of land. This formed a curving point that today practically separates the two. Immediately below the elevated opening is an area of tidal flats a hundred feet wide and four hundred feet long, a shingle and silt bottom that is almost fully exposed during low tides. About a mile west of here on the north shore is another small bay similar to Horsefly Cove but not as deep; this one is also protected by a small island and by a knuckle of land that juts out into the water.

After surveying those parts of the surroundings visible from our position, I consulted the chart and decided that I would move the *Stella* and anchor her within the second bay, or cove, for this offered good shelter and a shelving bottom near enough shore to allow me to again tie a line to one of the evergreens growing near the edge, for safety's sake.

Making ready to leave, I started the engine, then went topsides to pull up the anchor. I could let the *Stella* drift quietly in the interim without fear of grounding because of Green Inlet's great depth—between eighty and ninety fathoms in its center. Moments later we ran out of the bay, going astern until we cleared the small island, then turning to port and running slowly alongside, but about a hundred feet from the south shore so that I could inspect the entire area before settling down for a longish stay.

At the end of the tour, I felt that my Kwakiutl friend had been right. The place was enchanting, and it had everything, including an abundance of mountain-pure drinking water. Located three miles east of the inlet's entrance and sheltered by the small cape and offshore island, the new anchorage offered excellent security, convenience, and a wonderful view. The bottom of the bay climbed relatively quickly from thirty-two fathoms to between two and four fathoms near the shore, so I could secure the *Stella* to a tree that grew close to the water's edge and still leave enough extra line to ensure that she would have room to drift and to rise and fall with the tides. The bow anchor, bought in Campbell River to replace the one lost during the De Courcy Island fracas, was a good deal heavier than the old one. Although the bottom was composed of a mixture of shale, sand, and boulders—not the best kind of holding ground—I was nonetheless satisfied that the flukes were firmly dug in, especially when they held the *Stella* against 400 RPMs of astern thrust; later I proposed to dive and make absolutely certain that the anchor would continue to hold, digging it in by hand if necessary, but for the time being I was content.

When all was secure, I tidied up and then rowed ashore, hauling the dinghy out of the water before climbing about a mile to stand on the highest point in our vicinity, a small, unnamed mountain with a rounded peak some 3,230 feet high. From this treeless knob I was able to get a good look at the surrounding region. There were three small lakes within half a mile of my lookout, located north of our position but downslope. Bathed in sunshine, the country was beautiful and fresh, a domain of rugged land, sparkling ocean, and green-blue lake that reflected the cerulean sky and the few small clouds that moved slowly across it, toward the northwest.

Alone and surrounded by seemingly endless wilderness, I at last began to feel settled, experiencing the inner calm that always suffuses my mind at such times and in such places communicating itself to my entire being. I sat down, letting my gaze wander over the scenery but not seeking to concentrate on its features, a sort of casual and restful scan of the general landscape that allowed me to absorb the beauty but did not intrude on my inner thoughts; it was rather like looking at an abstract painting executed in pastels, the tints of which are so skillfully blended that they provide the elegance and color of amorphous form without distracting the eye with intrusive details. I experience the same effect when sitting before a campfire in the stillness of the night, a mesmeric state during which there is no conscious cerebration. Time, then, has no meaning, and there is no awareness of self, simply a feeling of *being*, of existing in harmony with the total environment.

During such all-too-rare interludes, the enormous and presumptuous cortex developed by humans in the relatively recent, evolutionary past, is short-circuited and the organism is freed from the rational; as a result, it responds to the subconscious promptings of the ancient middle brain, under the guidance of which the psyche and the soma enter into a balanced relationship. Gone now are the contradictions implanted in the cortex by centuries of civilization; the being becomes fully attuned, the nervous system rests, the muscles relax. The Buddhists call this *nirvana*, believing that during this state the soul becomes emancipated and is then oblivious to passion, suffering, hatred, and delusion. I call it peace.

I was brought back to actuality by the dulcet call of a male song sparrow, his wondrous, flutelike voice issuing from a small evergreen that was downhill from my perch. Tranquilized and greatly looking forward to my stay in this place, I rose, stretched luxuriously, and began to descend, soon entering the forest where I paused often among the trees and shrubs or stooped to examine the delicate wild flowers that grew on some of the open locations.

Sitka spruce (*Picea stichensis*) dominated the lower skirts of the mountain, some trees measuring 4 and 5 feet in diameter and towering 140 feet into the air, the trunks covered in rust-colored, rather loose, thin scales. Mixed with these, in places, were white birches, most of them small but a few standing 60 feet tall; these grew either in clusters in natural clearings, or singly, fighting for space and light among the evergreen giants that would in time choke them to death. On the higher slopes, nearly all the way to the top, grew a mixture of western hemlocks (*Tsuga mertensiana*) and yellow cedar (*Chamaecsyparis nootkatensis*), both species favoring higher ground and growing almost as tall and as fat as the spruces. In slide areas, or on rocky outcrops, thick clusters of dwarf juniper (*Juniperus communis*) sprawled untidily, the spaces between each spiky shrub being covered by mosses, fungi, and small flowers. These plants, and many more, caused me to dawdle as I returned to the shoreline, so by the time I climbed back on board the *Stella* it was well past the lunch hour.

After my meal, I decided to try to catch a fish for supper, for from now on I would rely on the sea to furnish me with a continuing supply of protein and would save my canned meats and soups for those times when luck deserted me.

Using a short, heavy sea rod with a thirty-pound test line and a six-inch jigging lure, I tried for bottom fish in fifty fathoms, hoping for a red snapper, a lingcod, or a brown rockfish, any one of which would supply me with enough food for two days. Jigging requires little skill. One merely lowers the lure, or bait, to the bottom and pulls it up a yard or two, continuing to jig up and down from an anchored vessel or, as I was doing, from a drifting one, in which case the lure can be dangled over a wider area. Five minutes after I began, I got an extremely heavy strike. I let the line go slack because the fish, whatever its species, was obviously far too large for my needs. By slackening the line, I was making it easy for the creature to throw the hook. But the fish kept on running, pulling so vigorously that when I stopped the tough monofilament, the dinghy began to move. For almost twenty minutes the battle raged. I alternately gained line and then lost it as the fish ran powerfully, but eventually the deep-water creature began to tire and, yard by yard, it started to come in, though not before peeling off about four hundred feet of the total five hundred that were wound on the big reel.

When the catch was close enough to the surface to be seen, I found myself looking at a sort of piscatorial nightmare. When it broke partly out of the water and put up a last-ditch struggle for freedom, I immediately gave it more slack, for I most definitely did not want the monster, particularly within the confines of my little dinghy. The body was seven feet long, sinuous and snakelike, and covered with oval black spots superimposed on a mottled, leathery, greenish skin, but it was the head that created the greatest impression. The roundish head was about the size of a medium cantaloupe and possessed of an intimidating visage: large, black eyes stared at me balefully from above nostrils that showed as dark holes punched into a greatly foreshortened muzzle, and the lips were pronounced and fleshy. But the most impressive feature of this marine gargoyle were the murderous fangs that gleamed threateningly inside the gaping mouth. Never had I seen such daggers in the jaws of a fish! I was fascinated, but not fascinated enough to want to drag this formidable antagonist aboard the dinghy. I had seen photographs of these fish and had read about their physical characteristics and habits, but this was the first one I had seen *in vivo*, as it were; I decided that neither the pictures nor the descriptions had even remotely managed to capture the ferocious personality of this animal. It was a wolf-eel (*Anarrhicthys ocellatus*), a true fish in no way related to the eels and evidently quite common in the waters of the northern Pacific from southern California to the Gulf of Alaska. It is said to attain a maximum length of eight feet.

The question now was: What to do with it? It was not the

kind of catch that one grasps with bare hands, for its fangs were an inch long, curving inward and tapering to fine points. And by the way it was snapping, the wolf-eel had every intention of using its armament if given half a chance. I could have cut the line, but the jig would then have remained lodged in the unfortunate creature's throat, causing it to suffer a lingering death. In the end I elected to tow it back to the *Stella* without trying to remove the lure, which was hidden somewhere inside its gullet. I allowed it lots of line, hoping that the ferocious-looking fish would somehow manage to free itself on the way. Tying the handle of the rod to my left thigh so that it wouldn't be dragged into the water, I started rowing back, feeling the wolf-eel's powerful struggles. When we were near the stern ladder, the line went slack. I thought at first that the monster had finally thrown the lure, but it hadn't. It had merely darted under the *Stella's* hull. I gave it more line, tied the dinghy to the ladder, unfastened the rod from my leg, and climbed on board.

Once inside the cockpit, I reeled in line and wolf-eel, intending to get the captive into the cockpit and then wrap it in a piece of canvas to immobilize it while I removed the lure with a pair of long-nosed pliers. It *may* have been a good plan, but it was never put into effect. As soon as the sinuous body slid over the side and flopped its length on the afterdeck, it began flailing and jerking and snapping with demonic fury. There was only one way to subdue this powerful thing. With the fish club, I gave it a resounding bang on the head, killing it instantly. Looking at the formidable creature lying on the deck, I felt rather like a dog who has chased a steamroller, caught it, and then doesn't quite know what to do with it! The one thing I didn't want to do was eat it. It may have been most edible, but its appearance did not cause my gastric juices to flow. Making sure the creature was quite dead, I opened the big mouth, getting a close look at the vicious fangs for the first time: six daggerlike teeth on each jaw, strong and recurving weapons. On the lower and upper jaws the wolf-eel had actual molars, powerful grinding teeth with which the species renders edible anything from fishes to mollusks, crabs, sea urchins and, presumably, the fingers of careless fishermen. In the end, I decided that I would examine the wolf-eel in more detail, but later, after I had caught something smaller and more palatable for my supper.

Armed with a three-inch lure this time, I took the dinghy to another location, but after almost an hour I began to fear that luck had deserted me and that I might be forced to try wolf-eel steak. Then, just as I was about ready to quit, I got a strike. This one was powerful too, but it did not compare to the tug of the wolf-eel. In minutes I saw my captive, a lingcod that probably weighed about eight pounds. Satisfied, I returned to the *Stella* to find that the cockpit reeked of fish and that my earlier catch was spreading a mixture of seawater and body fluids on the afterdeck, a mess that needed to be swabbed up. But first I cleaned and dressed the lingcod, feeding the discards to a number of western gulls that had arrived the day before, soon after we anchored in Horsefly Cove, and had accompanied us to our present shelter. When I finished this job, I turned my attention to the wolf-eel, wrapping it with difficulty in two plastic garbage bags and tying up the bundle before taking it to the forward deck and covering it with canvas. Here I would dissect it later. Washing out the cockpit took longer, and I had to use half my supply of vinegar before the smell was eradicated.

At seven o'clock the next morning, soon after breakfast, I sat on deck working on the wolf-eel, first examining the contents of the stomach, in which I found the almost totally digested remains of several crabs and one twenty-three-inch whiting (*Theragra chalcogrammus*), or walleye pollack, as it is commonly called in the United States. This fish is a member of the cod family and grows up to three feet long in these waters; the individual ingested by the wolf-eel had hardly been affected by the gastric juices, which suggested that it had been caught shortly before the predator took my lure. Chopping the whiting into eight pieces, I tossed them overboard, whereupon the big gulls swooped noisily down to feast. Then I measured the wolf-eel. From its mouth to the end of its pointed tail it was 84½ inches long. I made a notebook entry. Next I jotted down details of its fins. The dorsal extended from a point just behind the head to a notch where the slender and pointed caudal, or tail fin, began. On the underside, the anal fin was also long, extending forward to end just before the anus and stomach, for about two-thirds of the creature consists of tail and the internal organs are contained in a relatively small space. There was no pelvic fin, this having been absorbed, in effect, by the long anal ridge, but the pectoral fins were wide and rounded, somewhat small for such a long fish. I was so absorbed by the study of this extraordinary animal that I quite lost track of time and surroundings until a soft but somewhat explosive sighing noise interrupted my concentration. Startled, for the sound bore rather human qualities, I looked up.

Some fifteen feet from the *Stella*'s port side, a point or two forward of midships, was the upper half of a killer whale's head in profile, the mammal's glittering right eye fixed on me and containing a look of inquisitive intelligence within which no hostility could be detected. The big whale had just exhaled. It was the sound of this spasm that had disturbed me. Even as I watched, the misty cloud of stale breath was slowly drifting upward, spreading as it traveled, and gradually losing its outline. The orca had risen quietly, disturbing the water hardly at all, but now it began to move, running parallel to the *Stella* and causing the water to roil as it fanned its great tail fluke. It inhaled with a whistling sound, then arched its great back and dived, turning on its side beneath the water and allowing me a glimpse or two of its glistening, black-and-white body as its broad tail emerged above the surface for an instant, only to disappear with a resounding slap that sent the water cascading into the air powerfully enough to douse me and the *Stella*'s bow. For perhaps three seconds I was able to follow the whale's underwater progress, its outlines growing fainter as it continued to descend. My last glimpse of him was one sudden flash of white.

I was more awed than excited as I stood on deck and scanned the water outside the bay while hoping fervently that the orca would surface again. Some minutes went by, and then, as suddenly as before, the whale rose in the middle of the inlet, about 200 yards away and broadside to me; seconds later two more orcas rose—a cow and, I was almost sure, a yearling calf. The three animals swam up the inlet, the bull leading, but after going in a straight line for about 150 yards, they all dived again. By now I was almost frantic with anxiety to see more of them; I wanted to get the camera but was afraid to leave the deck in case they reappeared while I was gone. I needn't have worried, for in less than a minute the pod rose again, having evidently reversed their course, for now the whales were closer to the *Stella*, perhaps 600 yards away, all of them facing toward us. I ran to the hatch, climbed into the cabin, and grabbed two cameras, one fitted with a 200mm lens, the other with a standard lens.

When I got back to the forward deck the bull had cut the distance in half and was moving steadily toward the *Stella*. But the cow and calf stayed away, alternately diving briefly and rising again, moving about constantly but not daring to come any closer. The bull was another matter. I took three pictures as he came toward me, tried for another, but at that point he dived, a shallow submersion during which I got a perfect view of his beautiful, torpedo-shaped body and, more especially, of the powerful tail as it paddled easily under the water. He was aimed directly at the *Stella*, and I confess to a few moments of apprehension while I wondered if he was going to charge. He appeared to be at least as long as my boat and looked so solid and powerful that I feared he would broach a hole in the hull if he elected to hit us head-on.

What a thrill it was to watch that huge, lithe shape gliding so swiftly just under the surface! Every now and then the tip of the tall dorsal fin projected above the sea, making a hissing sound as it cleaved the water, then disappeared under it as the whale arched his body and sank a little deeper. Straight ahead he came, closer and closer, but just as it seemed inevitable that he would ram us, he arched again, went deeper, and passed right under the *Stella*'s keel. I ran to the other side of the deck and got there just in time to see him resurface not more than ten feet away. I lifted the camera as he was turning seaward and almost lost my chance to photograph him when I found myself looking right down his blowhole, a pit about two inches wide that glistened with the sheen of patent leather. I recovered in time to fire the shutter and advance the film, but by now he had turned around the bow and was swimming away, his great dorsal fin bent over at the top, a flaccid organ that flopped from side to side as he moved.

He was halfway back to the cow and calf when he made a wide, sweeping circle that caused froth to appear on the disturbed water. Back he came again, and I was sure he was going to repeat his earlier maneuver. But, no—he halted about forty or fifty feet from the starboard side, again placing himself broadside to the *Stella*, his glittering eye fixed on me, a jet orb that expressed lively interest, perhaps even curiosity. Moving his pectoral fins and pumping his tail up and down slowly, he remained surfaced and more or less in one place; there was absolutely no doubt in my mind that I had become the object of his attention. I could see his milky patterns quite clearly now. On the side of his head, just above his eye, was a small, white oval patch; lower, under his chin and along his belly, though most of the latter was hidden by the water, were large areas of white, which rose up the flank, behind the big dorsal in a clublike pattern.

His mouth was closed and, where the lips met, the contrast between black and white was intense, as though he had been painted very carefully, the dark tone ending abruptly at his upper lip and the snowy shade starting at the lower. Then he opened his mouth. The great trapdoor parted to show the rows of conical teeth, sharp, yellowish, and well spaced to allow the tusks to interlock when the jaws came together. Each tooth was recurved and leaning slightly outward.

I moved closer to the rail, bending forward. The whale turned slightly to put me into better focus, for I had edged somewhat to the left. On impulse I began talking to him, uttering the first words that entered my mind in a soft voice, a nonstop monologue. Just as I was getting into vocal stride, I heard a long, shrill cry from the other whales, whom I had completely forgotten. The bull dived, turned, and disappeared, but he soon came up again, halfway between the *Stella* and the cow and calf. He called back, but his voice was different, much higher in pitch; indeed, it was so high that at least half the sounds he uttered were almost lost to my ears, registering as extremely faint whines. The bull's call had an immediate effect on the other two whales: first one, then the other dived, and as soon as they had done so the bull again approached the *Stella*. As he traveled toward us, I had an idea. My belt knife was lying near the carcass of the wolf-eel and I quickly hacked off a two-foot chunk from its tail.

When I approached the rail, the bull was again turned broadside to the *Stella Maris*, once more fixing me with that intent, intelligent eye. I spoke softly as I tossed the offering to him. The piece of wolf-eel landed a few yards ahead of the whale, but as it hit the water he moved, his broad tail thrusting him forward so quickly that he engulfed the offering before it had time to sink. I saw the flash of his teeth and the end of a thick bluish tongue before he swallowed.

I now cut the wolf-eel into five equal pieces and carried them to the rail, tossing one to the whale, but this time making sure the fish landed closer to the *Stella*. The bull began moving forward while the food was still in the air, giving me clear proof that there was nothing wrong with his vision. But I did notice that the whale viewed his immediate surroundings much as a bird will do, using only one eye. Unlike humans and most other mammals, whales do not have binocular vision. Why this obvious fact had not occurred to me before, I don't know; and inasmuch as I have not come across this observation in the literature dealing with cetaceans, it may be that other investigators have missed this point. Clearly, with eyes positioned at the sides of the head, with the enormous width of skull between them, and with pupils that cannot be swiveled at will, whales cannot focus both eyes at once on objects that are close at hand. This means that cetaceans do not enjoy three-dimensional vision, as we do; rather they see things on two planes, the way a camera lens views the subject before it.

When I threw the next piece of fish, I deliberately tossed it high in the air while keeping my gaze fixed on the animal. He obviously noted the trajectory of the food as it left my hand, and as soon as it passed from the sphere of his vision, he raised his head and turned it swiftly from right to left even as he was moving; he positioned himself beneath the falling object with mathematic precision, raising his head and chest as his mouth gaped wide. Into this maw dropped the piece of wolf-eel as accurately as if I had aimed it there. Now I got a good look at the teeth and the dark tongue, noting that the roof of the orca's mouth was also two-toned, black on the outside and decorated with a dull white splash on the inside that was broad at the back and tapered to a ragged point toward the front.

The bull slid into the water with a resounding splash, shook his head as he swallowed, and once again turned broadside to the *Stella*. Now I knew why he did that: the better to see me. I photographed him just as he exhaled, capturing his "spout" on film and noting that two sounds accompanied the exhalation: the first, an audible but soft puff; the second, a gusty low-pitched hissing not unlike a human sigh. The stale exhaust drifted toward me and I became aware that my big friend suffered from halitosis, there being a definite, rank odor to the cloud of gas.

The bull was near enough now for me to see that he was about one foot shorter than the *Stella*, which meant he was twenty-three feet long, give or take an inch or two. His dorsal fin, a recurving, triangular appendage, was about five feet tall, but, there again, I could only guess at the measurement. I noted with interest that the whale appeared able to control the rigidity of the fin, causing it to remain erect at times, then allowing it to hang flaccid, about a third of its tip curving down sloppily. When almost totally submerged, the fin remained upright, no doubt held in this position by its own buoyancy.

I threw the last piece of wolf-eel and it landed no more than eight feet from the *Stella*'s hull, but this time the bull dived as soon as he had grasped the food, submerging completely and swimming under the boat. I watched the liquid outlines of his flashing body until he surfaced again, turned, breathed, then dived anew, evidently making for the inlet. There was no sign of the other whales.

That was my first meeting with Klem, as I was later to name him in honor of Klemtu and its friendly people.

Many animals are misunderstood and maligned by man and, even in this scientific age, continue to be abused either because those who vilify them cling blindly to concepts that should have been banished during the Middle Ages, or because humans covet their meat, or their fur, or even the very food that these victims of ours must have in order to survive. Ignorance, greed, myth, and a stubborn, egotistical refusal to believe that no other species on earth but our own is worthy of consideration are, in my view, the principal reasons for such relentless persecution.

A prime example of such unwarranted persecution is the so-called killer whale, a spectacular mammal that has a reputation for evil second only to that of the shark or wolf. It is perhaps too late now to rename this whale, but it is certainly time to get our facts straight about *Orcinus orca*, as the "killer" is more properly called.

The orca belongs to the Delphinidae family, which includes the dolphins and porpoises, of which this whale is the largest member. Like all toothed whales, indeed, like all carnivorous animals, including man, *Orcinus orca* certainly kills in order to eat—it can do no less if it is to survive. Because of its size, strength, agility, and specialized physical attributes, it is an efficient hunter within its own element.

This, I know, is stating the obvious, but such things must be stressed if one is to view this mammal with the proper perspective.

The orca is highly intelligent and has acquired complex social customs, a language of its own, and emotions that allow it to feel pleasure, pain, distress, and even to form attachments for members of its own kind—what humans would no doubt call love. In more recent years some biologists have begun to study this animal, but we still know little about it or its many relatives in the seas of the world. We learned hundreds of years ago how to kill it, of course, but because of the difficulties involved in studying the orca in its natural habitat (to say nothing about the scarcity of research funds), the killer whale is still described by some authorities today as "the wolf of the seas" (an intended slur on the timber wolf as well), "a savage and bloodthirsty killer," "a merciless destroyer of life," "a gangster who preys on helpless animals." All of these quotes are taken from books published within the past thirty years; and all the books were written by biologists. Worse, the orca is also accused of eating man, the most heinous of all offenses, and has been said to leap onto ice floes in order to seize humans who stood near the water's edge. Yet, there is not one documented case to prove that the "killer" has attacked man! The opposite, in fact, holds true, for in recent times some biologists have discovered that, like the dolphins and porpoises, the orca appears to be intellectually interested in humans, toward whom it shows no hostility. My first experience with Klem certainly supported that view.

The next morning at 8:15, scanning the inlet in the hope of again sighting the whales, I was thrilled to see a large dorsal fin appear from behind the island that sheltered our bay. Cutting through the water and setting up shallow waves that fanned out triangularly, the great fin turned to port and headed toward us. Moments later Klem surfaced, slowed, turned broadside, and stopped, lying partially to one side so that his right flipper was out of the water and hanging limply against his black-and-white side. For perhaps half a minute he remained that way, exhaling in the meantime; then he righted himself and approached to within about twenty feet before making a complete circle around the *Stella* and taking station some thirty feet away, his left side toward me, his eye, glittering and inquisitive, studying me as it had done yesterday. The previous evening I had again done some angling, intent on catching several fish. Of course, I was hoping that Klem might return, and if he did I wanted to have something to offer him. Now I went to the sea-filled tub in which I had placed the dead catch. In it were three large rockfish, one big lingcod, and a three-foot-long dogfish, a small, bottom-feeding shark plentifully distributed along the west coast of North America and elsewhere throughout the world. On this occasion I did not clean or dress any of the fish.

Using the dogfish first, I spoke to Klem while holding the flaccid body over the side; then I tossed it, but its length and weight prevented me from throwing it too far out. As I had done the previous day, I kept my eyes on the whale while casting the offering. Without hesitation, Klem began to move as soon as I raised my arm for the throw; he hit the body of the small shark just as it struck the water no more than fifteen feet from the *Stella*. I watched as he clamped it between his teeth, about a quarter of the tail sticking out from between his closed jaws. Klem opened and closed his mouth once, working his jaws sideways and clearly using his thick tongue to push the meal farther into his mouth. I had been holding a stopwatch in my left hand, which I'd started as I raised the shark and stopped when I saw the prey being swallowed. It had taken fourteen seconds for Klem to travel about fifteen feet, grab the offering, maneuver it into swallowing position, and ingest it.

I picked up the smallest rockfish, which weighed perhaps four pounds, and went through the same routine, first speaking to the orca, then activating the stopwatch as I raised my arm. Closer now, Klem lunged forward immediately. He took the fish before it hit the water, rearing up his head and chest, just as he'd done the day before. Time elapsed: seven seconds. Afterward, the orca stayed near the *Stella*. Again I fed him, clocking his actions. By then I had no doubt that Klem had the intelligence to know I meant him no harm. I was almost convinced that curiosity had attracted him to the *Stella* in the first place, and now brought him back. No doubt he was pleased with the fish I gave him, but such tidbits could not on their own have induced him to return, for he had no need of them. Orcas are splendid hunters and the Pacific literally teems with food, so it hardly seemed likely that Klem would bother returning solely for the meager rations I offered. For his own reasons, the big whale had been drawn to the *Stella* and had then tarried, perhaps because I had spoken to him and fed him, but principally, I felt, because he was interested in me. I could not know if he would return again after his second visit, but whether he did or not (of course I hoped he *would!*) the thrill of our communion, the total satisfaction I felt when it became obvious that we had bridged the differences separating our two species to relate in friendship, was so great that I now look upon this experience as *the* highlight of my life as a naturalist. For twenty-six years I have studied the wild creatures of North America, but, despite my deep love for all animals, no other single contact has moved me so greatly.

That morning, May 7, Klem came right up to the *Stella*, allowed himself to sink quietly beside the hull, then rose abruptly, literally standing on his tail and reaching up to the bow rail, mouth agape. Into this cavern I dropped the last fish, the big lingcod. I saw the jaws come together, interlock on the body of the fish, and the mouth move sideways. The fleshy tongue shifted the position of the cod, and then the fish was swallowed. I didn't time this, as I was too excited to think clearly. Klem remained "standing" while he grasped and then ingested the last gift, and his right eye, which stared right into my own, was agleam with interest and, I believe, with friendship. When he stopped sculling with his tail, he sank down quietly, righted himself, and turned. He dived when about thirty yards away, ending his visit.

I was so obsessed with the whale that for the rest of the day I did little more than think about him, sitting on the sun-filled deck for most of the daylight hours, and working on my notes inside the cabin after dark. The result of all this cerebration was that I couldn't sleep that night. Trying to condition myself for slumber, I rowed ashore in the dinghy and walked up the mountain, using a flashlight to pick my way along the trail I had found three days earlier. On top of the rocky peak, I sat for a time, watching the night sky and listening to the land-sounds of the region, almost too warm in my down-filled parka. Presently I stretched flat on my back and fell asleep.

When I awakened, stiff and chilled, dawn was breaking. To warm my body, I hurried as I descended the slope, but I stopped suddenly when I noticed a sudden movement in the trees. I was just in time to see a chocolate brown pine marten, about the size of a large cat, scurry along a branch and leap excitedly to another tree, where I lost sight of it. A relative of the weasel, the bushy-tailed predator was probably heading for its den after a night of hunting.

Back on board the *Stella*, I made breakfast. Afterward, I thought I'd do some early fishing, just in case Klem came to visit again. But the whale did not come that day. I had, nevertheless, caught three dogfish and two rockfish, and when the orca hadn't shown by evening, I wondered whether to keep them or not. The rockfish would remain fresh for a couple of days if kept in a cool place, but I knew from past experience that shark flesh spoils quickly and gives off a most unpleasant odor. Nevertheless, I thought they might still be acceptable the next day if the whale returned.

I was wrong. When I awakened and went on deck, where the catch had been left in a tub of seawater, all the fish were rank, the rockfish having become tainted by the ammonia-heavy juices of the shark meat. I gave the whole lot to the gulls, rowing the mess ashore and spreading the corpses on rocks, escorted by several dozen wheeling, screaming birds. As soon as I left, the feathered gluttons descended. Within minutes, dozens of more birds had arrived from distant places, some flying in from the inlet mouth, others appearing over the top of the mountains. Leaving them to their feast, I rowed the dinghy toward the small island, where the water was almost seventy fathoms deep and where the dogfish seemed to congregate. Klem apparently liked the sharks and as these voracious predators are found in large numbers along the bottom, I felt that taking them was, if anything, beneficial to the local ecology.

I do not normally make such judgments, considering it presumptuous for man to suppose that he has the ability to improve on nature's ways, but in the case of sharks, I believe an exception can be made, for modern man has created ideal conditions for bottom-feeding members of this class. In fact, man has become an ecological force, actually changing the ecology along all the coastlines of the world. Canneries, whaling, sewage disposal, and many other sources of biological wastes that enter the shoreline waters of the world have created ideal conditions for many sharks. As a result, their numbers are increasing dramatically.

That morning, using a few aromatic pieces of "old" dogfish, I pulled six of the clan out of the water in the space of fifteen minutes. In the interim, the dinghy had drifted into the inlet and was about 150 yards away from the *Stella*. With six dead sharks in the little boat, I began rowing back, turning often to see where I was heading.

During one of these over-the-shoulder scans I got a shock when I saw Klem on the surface about a hundred yards away, just outside the entrance to our bay. To relate to a twenty-three-foot bull orca from the relative safety of a twenty-four-foot powerboat is one thing; to see the same animal while in a tiny shell of plastic was quite another! My adrenaline came in squirts! There he was, turned broadside-on to me, watching as usual with that one fixed eye. And there *I* was, wishing to be anywhere but in that situation. The island was only about fifty yards to port. Should I seek refuge on it? I turned my head again to look for the whale. He was still there, evidently in the same place.

As suddenly as the initial fear had come, it left and reason took over. Klem might well have been swimming underwater during the whole time I was fishing; he might as easily have risen right beside me, or attacked without warning from below, swamping the dinghy and, quite literally, biting my body in half. He had done none of these things. Instead he had kept his distance, watching me, but at peace. For all I knew, the orca and his family could have been underwater at any time during the last few days while I happily sculled over the surface in the ridiculous little boat; if so, they had not attempted to do me harm.

I felt ridiculous for having given way to panic, angry with myself for allowing superstition to cloud my judgment. I kept on rowing but made no attempt to call out to Klem this time because, despite everything I'd told myself to the contrary, deep inside my being fear still lingered. Klem, meanwhile, stayed where he was, moving only slightly, watching me constantly but not trying to close the distance between us.

On board the *Stella* again, I hurried to the bow deck, carrying the dogfish in a plastic pail. Klem was now within fifty or sixty feet from the *Stella*'s hull. Once more I fed him, spoke to him, and timed his movements, noting that his pod was on the surface in the middle of the inlet. I became almost certain that Klem was keeping the other whales away, ordering them to remain outside our bay. Repeatedly they called, especially the cow, and he would turn, rush halfway toward them, and call back, then return to the *Stella*. Never once did the female or the young whale seek to enter our anchorage.

During the first week of our acquaintance, Klem called on me five times, remaining for periods that varied between ten and twenty-five minutes. Then, on May 13, he came twice, once at 9:00 A.M., when he stayed for seventeen minutes, and once at 6:22 P.M., when he merely entered our bay, circled the *Stella* and left, remaining on the surface the entire time. As he was heading toward the center of the inlet, five orcas rose to the surface, breathed, and then dived before I could determine sex and age (females of the species have shorter dorsals, while young whales, naturally, are smaller overall). Klem accelerated his pace, arched, and disappeared.

By noon the next day, Klem had not arrived and since it was a beautifully warm, even hot, day, I decided to make my first dive of the trip. By now my ribs didn't hurt unless I put a lot of strain on them, so I thought I would check the anchor, then explore the bottom of the bay, where I anticipated that the water would be warmer. Accordingly, I powdered myself, struggled into the neoprene wet suit, tested mouthpiece, regulator, and tank, then shouldered the equipment. I was about to slosh the face mask in the water, to prevent fogging, when Klem arrived, rising quite suddenly about twenty yards away. As usual I had some dogfish for him. Still attired in my scuba gear, even to the ungainly flippers, I slap-padded to the rail and tossed a two-foot shark into the water. Klem ingested it, turned on his side, and opened his mouth for more. He was ten feet away. I tossed a dogfish right into his great jaws. When he had eaten all I had for him and I was waiting for him to leave, I recalled my first physical contact with Yukon, my wolf-dog, when I had willed myself to trust him fully and had placed myself at a disadvantage had he intended to bite me. I desperately wanted to know if this whale would attack if I entered the water in his presence.

Getting from the bow to the stern ladder was no easy task with the swim fins on my feet; but when I finally got there I was elated to see that Klem had followed me, keeping between fifteen and twenty feet away from the *Stella*, whose stern had turned so that it partially faced the bay opening. Slowly, speaking to the whale continuously, I stepped down the ladder. Up to the knees, the waist, the chest. It was now or never! I wet the face mask and allowed the rest of my body to enter the water. With only my head above the surface, I saw the now seemingly enormous whale arch his back and dive. So did I.

Staying under the *Stella*'s hull I looked around. I couldn't see the whale. I placed myself on a horizontal plane so I could scan the water below, noting the sunshine, a bright, deep yellow glow that picked out the bottom some three fathoms down. But I couldn't find Klem. There was just enough weight on my belt to keep me at negative buoyancy, so I allowed my legs to dangle downward again and began to turn slowly, frankly anxious, wondering where the orca was and hoping he was not even then contemplating a rush. Seconds later I saw him.

He had evidently gone into deeper water, but now he was coming back—and at frightening speed. Straight toward me! I hung there, totally helpless, taking some solace from the nearness of the *Stella*'s slimy green bottom, watching the advancing torpedo shape. I don't know how near he was when he turned—ten, twenty, thirty feet? But turn he did, with masterful ease. His marvelous body was highlighted by the sun. It flashed white, silver, at times a deep copper as the light played on his glossy tones. It was hard to keep track of movement, but he turned himself upside down, swam like that for some yards, gaining depth, then suddenly went straight up, like a rocket, fracturing the surface and creating a thousand reflections before reentering the sea, landing on his stomach, a gigantic belly flop that made the *Stella* rock violently. I too was trounced, like a straw dummy, striking my head against the hull.

Again Klem swam away, but this time I saw his wide, easy turn as he rushed back at speed, flipped onto his side when about thirty feet away, and then went belly-up, putting on the most incredible show I have ever witnessed. Now I swam out from under the hull, approaching the bull. He turned away! Several times during the next ten minutes I tried to get closer to him, but he always eluded me. Never once did he show hostility while he constantly showed off his aquabatic abilities. Four times he shot up like a rocket; twice he cleared the water altogether, each reentry convulsing the sea around me. I was tumbled head over heels at one point, finding myself almost on the bottom before I swam upward again. I was cold, but loath to leave the water while this fantastic animal was sharing his habitat with me. Then, without warning, Klem left. He simply turned away and continued into deep water. Shivering uncontrollably (the water temperature, I discovered later, was 50 degrees F.), I climbed back on board, stripped, and entered the cabin to dry off and make myself a hot drink.

Nothing I had ever done before that time, or have done since, can remotely compare to that first dive with a bull "killer" whale under the waters of Green Inlet. As a result, I have been left with an impossible dream: to spend the rest of my life getting to know *Orcinus orca*. I may, it is true, yet manage a few more periods of study, but the financial burden imposed by the kind of research I would sell my soul to make is, alas, way out of my reach. But the experience is mine until I die. It is a sustaining memory that is always fresh, that often lulls me to sleep at times when I am restless. In the darkness of my bedroom I again see Klem, dive with him, experience the inexpressible joy of living some minutes in the world of the whale.

For sixteen more days, on and off, Klem visited me. During that time we made contact on thirty-seven separate occasions for a total of forty-three hours and seven minutes; of this collective time, fifty-nine minutes were spent underwater during four dives.

After ten days had passed with no further visits from Klem, I reluctantly left Green Inlet, conscious of the fact that the man who departed on board the *Stella* had been unalterably changed by a whale called Klem.

SHARK

The *Stella* was again sailing away from Klemtu, watched as before by a small group of Kwakiutls, their faces as dour as ever but their very presence proclaiming friendship. Among them was the gas man, who, aided by the two loungers I had met during my first visit, had loaded four boxes of herring eggs into the well deck, two hundred pounds in total. Now, as we turned around a point that hid the village from sight, I gave a short blast of the horn, a farewell to the pleasant islanders. As I settled myself on the pilot's seat, I had only one fault to find with the villagers: they had neglected to tell me that salted herring roe *à la* Kwakiutl released an aroma reminiscent of spoiled caviar! The smell had already permeated the cockpit and cabin, despite the fact that I had unzipped the screens to port and starboard.

Docking at Klemtu the previous day, I'd been informed that no other suitable vessel had arrived to take the eggs to Hartley Bay, a community located at the entrance to Douglas Channel, some sixty-eight miles north. Early this morning, the four wooden boxes had been loaded, gas taken on, and then, after a chat with my Indian friends on shore, we slipped our moorings, for I was anxious to deliver the cargo as soon as possible.

It was raining, a fine, soft drizzle, but there was no wind and the day was almost unseasonably warm for early June, a circumstance that caused light fog to form at the junction between shore and water and reduced visibility to a minor extent. I hoped the conditions would improve as the sun gained height and strength above the low cloud that dominated the skies. Concerned with monitoring the weather and checking our bearings, I conned the *Stella* around Wedge Point, the northernmost tip of Cone Island, and prepared to enter Finlayson Channel on a bearing of 11 degrees magnetic. This would take us on a diagonal course, east of north, then, four miles later, we would turn on our old heading, 330 degrees, eventually passing Green Inlet to starboard soon after entering Graham Reach.

My thoughts were still centered on Klem. Would I see him again? I had told the Indians about the whale, and they had shown no surprise at the orca's behavior. In fact, they reported a number of similar encounters that had occurred in the area near Klemtu, though none had been of such long duration. The youngsters who had called to me from their rowboat on the day of our initial arrival told me that one morning they had met five orcas about a mile from shore; the whales had followed them but had shown no hostility, sounding when the boys got near land. Often, I was told, small groups of "killers" were seen on the surface between Cone and Swindle islands.

Years earlier, the gas man explained, the villagers had hunted the orcas with harpoons, using the meat for themselves and for their dogs and rendering the blubber for its oil. In more recent times they had abandoned this practice because it was easier to get their basic necessities from the supply boat that called at regular intervals. It was clear that these people felt respect, perhaps even affection, for the whales, but this was not surprising; the orcas have historically been held in high regard by all the Pacific coast Indians, as can be seen in their surviving legends as well as in their art. From Washington to Alaska, the killer-whale motif is perhaps the one most commonly found in drawings, paintings, and totem-pole carvings even to this day.

Occupied with these thoughts, I hardly noticed the passage of time and was somewhat surprised to look up at one point and find that we were already off the entrance to Green Inlet. Momentarily, I regretted that I was not again about to enter the shelter of this fascinating arm of the ocean; but then, thinking about the many miles of sea and the equally numerous bays and inlets that spread before us like toys under a Christmas tree, I gave the *Stella* more power, anxious to deliver the Indian cargo and proceed to Prince Rupert, about seventy miles north of Hartley Bay. My main reason for going to this northerly coastal town was to have the air tanks recharged, for I had been unable to afford a compressor of my own and no other community in this region offered such facilities. It was a nuisance, this two-day journey, but necessary if I was to deep-dive again. Afterward, I would travel south once more, for I wanted to spend at least another month in these latitudes before running for Alaska, which was to be our most northern heading.

Now, with the entrance to Green Inlet lying astern and the rain showing no signs of abating, I began to navigate more or less automatically, most of my attention devoted to the sea-and landscapes. We were running up Princess Royal Channel, which was subdivided by the early chartmakers into two reaches, Graham and Fraser, ending at the junctions of McKay Reach and Ursula Channel. Graham runs west-southwest and eventually leads to Grenville Channel; Fraser goes north-northwest and becomes absorbed by Devastation Channel, which leads to the town of Kitimat.

At noon, the sea continuing calm, I tied down the wheel

and prepared some lunch, carrying plate and mug to the cockpit when all was ready. As I munched a sandwich, I saw a school of Dall porpoises rise to the surface a quarter of a mile ahead, about ten or twelve animals who seemed to be greatly excited. Several of them were leaping high, jumps that took them well clear of the surface; others were dashing over the top of the water at great speed, heading north. After a few moments they dived and didn't reappear, but only about two minutes later two orcas rose, exhaled, and dived again. Feeding more power to the engine, I scanned the sea, hoping the whales would return to the surface and wondering if one of them might have been Klem. They didn't show again. I suspected that the orcas were chasing the Dalls, but as I saw no blood staining the water, I presume the prey escaped.

We reached Hartley Bay at three o'clock that afternoon, and I immediately unloaded the herring boxes and opened up the screens to air out the boat, then chatted with the two Indians who took charge of the odoriferous cargo. When I mentioned the aroma, they grinned widely and nodded, but they defended the product, saying the roe tasted "real good," when boiled. They offered to bring me a sample, but I declined the gift on the grounds that my stomach had been upset for a couple of days. That evening, as I was about to prepare supper for myself, a very gnarled, tiny Indian grandmother scrambled agilely on board bearing gifts: a recycled two-pound jam can containing a huge quantity of boiled herring eggs. The stuff looked like yellowish porridge. This, I was told, would "bloody damn soon fix your bad gut." The Good Samaritan lady showed me by her mien that there was to be no nonsense. "Sit, eat," she ordered. I asked plaintively how I should ingest the stuff, and my stupid question received the answer it deserved.

"Spoon," said the unloquacious lady, fixing me with steady black eyes.

Yes, but should I put anything on the eggs—like ketchup, or vinegar? No. I was to dig in the spoon and just eat, which I did, reluctantly. But after the first mouthful I was pleasantly surprised. The herring-egg pottage was remarkably good. Its taste was reminiscent of shrimp and crab with a dash of caviar thrown in. But I found it to be the most filling food I have ever eaten. After six or seven spoonfuls, I had to stop, telling the granny I had thoroughly enjoyed the food, thanking her profusely, and inviting her to take tea with me. She grinned for the first time, a totally toothless smile, her pleasure reflected in her dark and very alert eyes. She nodded.

Over tea that was braced by no less than six teaspoons of sugar, the matriarch chuckled a lot, now and then slapping her knee, but she spoke hardly at all. After two cups of syrupy brew, she suddenly rose, slapped my shoulder, nodded, and turned to leave. Her parting words were:

"You eat good! Eat all them eggs. Good for your bloody gut!"

My sanguinary gut at that moment felt close to bursting and, despite the agreeable taste, I had no desire to eat any more of the stuff. But the fish and crabs probably enjoyed it.

Two days later, after an overnight stay at Prince Rupert during which I slept in a hotel room for the first time in many weeks and soaked myself in a hot bath until my entire body was pink and wrinkled, I returned to Hartley Bay to refuel before continuing south. My three air tanks were full, I had bought ice for the icebox, and I had purchased two pounds of fresh shrimp from a cannery on shore. I would have felt pretty good, were it not for the weather, which had rustled up a Force 4 wind about an hour before our arrival at Hartley Bay and now, as the fuel gurgled into the tank, was turning itself into a full gale. I had intended to sail to Butedale, a community located on the northeast coast of Princess Royal Island, but it was obvious that I would have to spend the rest of the afternoon and night at our present mooring.

To kill time, I went ashore after paying for the gasoline and was intrigued to learn that all the people I met, native and white, knew about me. They didn't know *who* I was, or what I was doing in their neighborhood, but they were well aware that I had brought the herring eggs. As I was returning to the *Stella* I met Granny, who inquired after my "bloody gut." On being told that it was completely recovered, she nodded wisely before reminding me again that herring eggs are "good for bad guts." We were near the *Stella*, so I invited her aboard for tea. Side by side we approached the boat, a scruffy-looking white man accompanied by a petite Indian lady who was as spry as a squirrel and as friendly as my own grandmother had been. She really was a charming woman, a remarkable product of the wilderness. At eighty-seven, she appeared to be as healthy as a horse and her faculties were ever alert. Again she spooned enormous amounts of sugar into her tea, sipped rather noisily, and chuckled a lot, a person who found life interesting, amusing, and stimulating.

The *Stella*'s first owner had left on board a salt-and-pepper set made out of wood in the shape of twin outhouses, the sort of cheap curios one finds in souvenir shops. I didn't use them and they remained on a little shelf above the galley sink. Granny thought that these "outhouse shakers," as she referred to them, were sheer works of art. She had admired them when we first met, and she now did so again, handling them as though they were Ming dynasty porcelain treasures, smiling at them, then replacing them gently. When she was about to leave, I presented the shakers to her. I have never seen such joy reflected on a face! Holding them in one hand, she even forgot to say good-bye as she walked carefully along the dock and eventually disappeared from view.

By morning the weather had moderated and the clouds were starting to clear, so I slipped our moorings and left Hartley Bay before the sun had risen above the eastern mountains. Three hours later I was approaching the dock at Butedale, a place I had bypassed on the way up, but which I wanted to visit because I had been told that the Canadian Fishing Company Cannery located there was one of the largest in the region. An added attraction was Butedale Creek, which descended precipitously from the highlands and dropped abruptly into the ocean, creating quite a spectacular waterfall.

As we neared the dock at low tide, all that was visible from the cockpit was a sheer rock face to which was attached a narrow iron ladder that led to a landing some fifty feet above. Then I realized that apart from one rather old eighteen-foot boat, there was not another vessel tied up at the community's ample facilities. I found this unusual, but after I secured the mooring lines and looked up to the landing, the intense quiet of the place seemed even more extraordinary. It appeared as though Butedale was completely deserted. The floating dock was large, well constructed, with iron bollards and cleats, and it extended a hundred feet from water's edge to rock face. Walking to the ladder, I paused at its foot and yelled "Hallo!" When this did not produce an immediate response, I began climbing the perpendicular stairway, the handrails of which were rusty and weed-encrusted at the lower levels. It was impossible to look up during the climb, for it was not safe to lean backward; therefore, I was startled when my head cleared the landing and I found myself looking into the eyes of a large dog. The animal was not at all fierce and was clearly glad to see me. In turn, I was pleased to note that there was at least one living creature in Butedale. It wasn't until I was standing on the flat space above the dock that I saw a human, a man about thirty years old dressed in jeans and reefer jacket and wearing a floppy wide-brimmed hat. He emerged from a nearby house just as I noticed that the lights in all the houses of the village were on, even though it was full daylight.

I didn't at the time count the dwellings, but if memory serves me right, there must have been upward of fifty neat, cottage-type buildings, each with its own front garden in which blossoms were now competing with many weeds and last year's old growth, for it was obvious that no one had tended the plants for some time. When the man was halfway across the space that separated us, a small boy appeared from the same house and began running toward me. The child was perhaps seven, a thin, shabbily dressed youngster. He caught up with, then passed, the man before stopping about twenty paces from me, shyly avoiding my eyes but patting the large dog, which had immediately gone to him. The man stopped in front of me and extended his right hand. We shook. He said his name was John and asked if I needed fuel; then, without waiting for my answer, he began to talk, an endless stream of conversation during which he told me that the cannery had been closed for some time, that he was the caretaker, and that only his wife and son lived there with him. Meanwhile, the boy was swinging on an old gate, part of a fence that cordoned off a cluster of buildings in proximity to the elevated landing. The gate creaked.

I suspected that the talkative watchman was suffering from cabin fever, and when a look of utter rage suddenly filled his face and he turned and kicked his son viciously, knocking him off the fence, my suspicions were confirmed. The child, obviously in pain, hobbled toward us, rubbing his thigh; as my anger was approaching the point where I might have taken a hand in the affair, father and son embraced, the one seeking comfort, the other fondling his offspring's head, hugging him. The caretaker noted my look of astonishment.

"I didn't mean to do that, you know. It's being alone here that does it to me. Can't seem to help it. Yours is the first boat in since March. It's driving me nuts!"

That much was obvious. The man needed to get out for a time. I wondered about his wife, who hadn't so much as poked a nose outside the door of her dwelling. While he continued to talk in that fast, nervous way so common to totally isolated humans, I looked around some more. The scene resembled the set for a western movie, the kind where the lone rider enters a deserted ghost town and finds it just as the fleeing inhabitants had left it, even to abandoned personal effects, like old toys, a wheelbarrow or two, a rocker, and, on one verandah, a baby carriage. It was eerie!

I learned that the fate of Butedale was even then being debated. The caretaker said he thought it was going to be turned into a large tourist resort, but he wasn't sure. Whether this did, in fact, come to pass, I cannot now say. Certainly, the place was ideally suited for the purpose, situated as it is in one of the most scenic areas of the northwest coast. The fishing would be spectacular, the land itself a mixture of mountains and valleys plentifully supplied with lakes and creeks.

After about a half-hour, the caretaker began to slow down and I was able to answer his first question: Yes, I did want fuel. With that he unwound an extraordinarily long hose from a giant reel next to the nearby tanks. I knew the routine by now, so I started to descend the ladder. By the time I reached the dock, the nozzle was within reach and I grabbed it and dragged the hose to the *Stella*. Afterward, I chatted with the man once more and accepted his invitation to explore the deserted community with him. I spent two hours in Butedale, most of the time walking about the place while the caretaker chattered on and on. I would have stayed longer, but I could not continue to listen to the incessant monologue, or to see the sadness in the faces of both father and son. Even the unfortunate dog seemed sad and eager for company.

I was greatly cheered later, however, when I docked anew at Klemtu and was able to visit with my Kwakiutl friends, their laconic talk offering relief from the verbal barrage to which I had been treated. Once more I entertained with tea and a liberal supply of Peek Frean's biscuits purchased in Prince Rupert, such unaccustomed delicacies not forming part of the Kwakiutl diet. I had also brought three packages of licorice candies for the gas man's little girls.

During our tea party, the gas man suggested that I might like to explore Laredo Inlet, a long arm of the sea that almost bisects Princess Royal Island. I should perhaps explain that Princess Royal Island is some fifty-five miles long by about twenty miles wide, its southernmost end abutting on Swindle Island, where Klemtu is located. Indeed, seen on the chart, the two islands could easily fit together, evidence of the truth of the continental drift theory.

To reach Laredo Inlet, one must go north of Klemtu, turn to port around the island's eastern horn and go south, running between the two isles along Meyers Passage for four miles, then make an abrupt turn to starboard, still within the passage, and continue for another six miles before emerging into Laredo Sound. Laredo Inlet now lies to starboard; it is some twenty miles long and a mile or more wide. Overland, about ten miles northeast, is Butedale.

Like so many localities along the Pacific coast, the influence of Spain is conspicuous in this region of British Columbia. Curious about the name Laredo, which has been bestowed upon a sound, a channel, and an inlet in this area, that evening, after supper, I consulted some of the history books I had been able to buy in secondhand bookstores in Victoria. I found that one Lieutenant Commander Jacinto Camaño (incorrectly spelled Caamano on the charts) had sailed this way in 1792 after being ordered by the viceroy of Mexico to search for the fabled Rio de Reyes, or River of Kings, reportedly found in 1640 by Spanish Admiral Pedro Bartolome de Fonti, who claimed to have discovered a waterway that ran across North America and linked the Atlantic with the Pacific; this gentleman's outrageous lie later gave rise to the myth of the Northwest Passage. Needless to say, Camaño failed to find the River of Kings, but he did explore, chart, and name a lot of ocean and land between Washington and Alaska, including the inlet I was going to explore on the morrow.

We left Klemtu soon after sunrise the next morning under fair skies and a small wind, hardly enough to work up a few whitecaps on the green carpet of ocean. The *Stella* was making about 10 knots, dancing only a little, and I sat comfortable and relaxed, admiring the scenery. After half an hour, we were ready to turn around the east horn of Swindle Island and enter Meyers Passage. Because of this, I was paying close attention to the compass.

Without warning, the needle, which had been holding at 170 degrees magnetic, suddenly went wild, oscillating left and right and refusing to stay in its proper place. At first I thought that some steel or iron object was influencing the instrument, but after a quick check I rejected this possibility, for there was nothing near enough to account for the compass's behavior. I began to fear that the instrument had broken down, but then I remembered having seen two lines of small print on the navigational chart, placed at the end of the horn of land we had just negotiated. I foolishly hadn't bothered to read the note, because by this time I felt extreme confidence in the *Stella* and in my own knowledge of these waters. Now I checked the chart again and found that the disregarded warning said, "Magnetic disturbance is reported in the northern part of Meyers Passage." Sloppy navigation is probably the greatest cause of accidents at sea, a fact I've known all my life, and here I was guilty of such inexcusable carelessness!

The compass continued flopping about over the card until we neared the southern end of the passage, when, as suddenly as it had begun to dance, it settled down again. Fortunately, the width of this channel is less than half a mile and visual navigation is sufficient to avoid the few rocky shoals found at its northern end. Soon we turned almost due west and threaded our way between the bottom of Princess Royal Island and the top of Swindle Island, emerging into Kitawu Bay, Laredo Sound, at 11:30 A.M. Here we headed due north (01 degrees magnetic) and entered Laredo Inlet. An hour later we were anchored in a long, narrow arm on the eastern shore. I had lunch on deck, stripped to the waist. The June sun felt good on my skin. Afterward, I spent the afternoon on shore thinking about the dive that I was going to make in these waters the next morning.

The massive rock cliff dropped straight down into the water, a vertical, smooth wall of prehistoric granite bereft of caves or large crevices but festooned with seaweed and anemones of a rich brown color, which, when open, looked as though they were wearing fur collars. Crabs scuttled about, running swiftly with that sideways motion characteristic of the species, or moving more slowly, in and out of the weeds, climbing on the anemones and causing them to close up suddenly. Up and down the wall little fish darted from shelter to shelter, their gills working, their round mouths opening and shutting, sometimes becoming elongated as they ingested invisible food. The bottom itself was composed of a mixture of sand and scree, slices and slabs of rock fallen from above; it was further dotted with boulders of various sizes, also breakaways, which offered shelter to many marine organisms.

I entered the water at 10:45 A.M., dropping quietly off the stern ladder, arching, and swimming down, not wishing to create a splash. All disturbances are noted by under-the-surface life and, as on shore, the organisms usually react to them by seeking shelter. From the chart, I knew that in the immediate vicinity of the rock wall I proposed to use as a guide, the bottom was five fathoms down, so when I was some ten feet below the surface, I adjusted my air supply and swam slowly to my massive target, then followed it down headfirst. As I kicked with my fins, I kept my face turned to the rock wall, noting the life forms that scuttled about within the shelter of the weeds; on reaching bottom, I altered my buoyancy by picking up a fairly large boulder, carrying it in both hands while I walked rather awkwardly on the gently shelving seabed, stopping often to examine my immediate surroundings and sometimes glancing upward, seeing the underside of the ocean as an expanse of gold and silver. At my own level, the sea was deep blue in the farthest distance, a constantly changing environment through which an occasional fish darted like a streak of mercury.

I was within ten feet of the rock face when movement nearby, within a natural amphitheater of rocks haphazardly arranged in a rough circle, attracted my attention. A large crab, about ten inches across the shell, was working furiously with both its big claws, snipping morsels of meat from a grotesque-looking fish, a creature about a foot long with a large head and a tapered body that ended in a sharp point. The fish had huge eyes and two dorsal fins; the first one was triangular, its leading edge sporting a long, sharp, serrated spike; the second dorsal was long, undulating, and sharply grooved. The narrow tail fin was shaped like the end of a spear. This fish, a distant relative of the shark, commonly called ratfish, is a subclass of the selachians designated as Holocephali and belonging to the Chimaeridae, the term adopted from *chimera*, the mythical Greek monster who was said to have the head of a lion, the body of a goat, and the tail of a dragon. The fish have been aptly named! They have a relatively wide distribution in the seas of the world and grow to a maximum of six feet (in the northwest Pacific to a maximum of three feet, two inches). I had met them before, in other waters, so I had little difficulty recognizing the dead specimen that so absorbed the crab. The name *ratfish* (they are also called harefish) has been applied because of this creature's teeth and the shape of its snout, out of which the rodentlike dentures, fused into a single bony plate, protrude. The pectoral and abdominal fins are paddle-shaped and not unlike those found in some species of shark, and, in the males, a pair of claspers stick out behind. Males also have a fleshy, clublike outgrowth on top of the head, although the reason for this is unclear, so far as I am aware. An altogether queer fish with a cartilage skeleton and smooth, mottled silvery skin that reflects a number of metallic hues depending on the light, the ratfish is thought to have broken away from the true sharks some 400 million years ago to set up housekeeping at depths ranging from relatively shallow to as many as nine thousand feet. The one on which the crab was feasting had probably died of injuries received elsewhere, for although the members of this species are relatively slow swimmers—because of the small tail fin—they are too swift and strong for even a big crab to capture.

My arrival did not upset the armored gourmet, even when I squatted quite close to it. When I extended an inquisitive finger, the crab paused long enough to snap his powerful pincers at the intruding digit, evidencing an intention of charging if I didn't withdraw. Not wishing to disturb the feast, I returned to my ballast rock and ambled away. Soon after that I saw a twenty-inch rockfish, *Sebastodes melanops*, dart out of the shelter of a large boulder to engulf a four-inch sea perch, *Damalichthys vacca*, also called pile perch, a species abundant from southern California to Alaska. The action was too swift for the eye to follow detail, but almost immediately after the victim was ingested, a burst of small, silvery scales was ejected from the mouth and gills of the rockfish, which immediately thereafter darted back to the shelter of its boulder.

A little later I found a sea cucumber moving sluggishly over the bottom, a sinuous, warty creature with its mouthparts adorned by what looked like a feather duster. It was hard to believe that this odd, soft-bodied Holothurian belonged to the starfish (or, better, sea star) family and even stranger to view it as a delicacy, the famed *bêche-de-mer* so highly prized in some Asian countries. The cucumber was about eighteen inches long, reddish brown in color, the plumelike adornment at its head end consisting of a rosette of branched tentacles covered in sticky mucus that entraps small, free-swimming organisms. When the sluglike creature disappeared into some seaweed, I turned away. It was then that I noticed the long shadow gliding through the deeper regions near the mouth of the small inlet.

Despite the aqueous distortions and the tricks of the light, I knew it was a shark—the shape was large and too streamlined to be mistaken for anything else. It was zigzagging but swimming toward me.

I wasn't expecting to meet a shark in that latitude, but there it was, approaching in that deceptively slow manner of the clan. I felt a stab of panic that almost caused me to make a dash for the surface. This would have been the worst possible thing to do, as I well knew from past experience with sharks in other waters. Apart from inviting attack by sudden and precipitate action—which sharks interpret as the death throes of an injured fish—there was the need to decompress before rising to the surface. I was then at a depth of forty feet and thus not in mortal danger of the bends, but I knew from one injudicious rise from twenty-five feet that unpleasant side effects can result, not the least of which is a severe pain in the ears. Forcing myself to remain calm, I dropped my ballast rock and as casually as possible fin-kicked toward the granite wall, putting my back to it while watching the shark and rising at a rate slightly slower than the bubbles of air I was exhaling.

The shark came closer and I was reminded of the many fallacies that surround this incredible fish, especially the one which claims that selachians have poor eyesight. This creature had seen me, there was no doubt about it! Now that I had a closer view, I noticed it was moving its head from side to side so as to synchronize in its tiny brain the images received by its eyes, for like those of whales, the eyes of sharks are set too wide apart for three-dimensional vision. The shark appeared to be between six and eight feet long, not exactly a giant as these creatures grow, but big enough to be lethal.

When it was about twenty yards away, the shark accelerated, aiming its sharp nose in my general direction and coming fast. Sharks can't stop abruptly; their pectoral fins are placed on a horizontal plane and cannot rotate to the vertical, whereas on other fish these fins act more or less as brakes. Thus, sharks can only slow down by decreasing the rate at which they are sculling with their tail, or they can turn away to avoid collision or to suspend or avoid attack.

Seeing that the shark meant to approach me more closely, I stopped, holding on with one hand to the seaweed that covered the rock, controlling my breathing against the temptation to take quick gulps of air as adrenaline coursed through my blood, for one may hyperventilate under such conditions and the result can be fatal while below the surface. The shark, now only about twenty or thirty feet away, slowed his tail motion, but his forward momentum did not decrease until he had cut the distance in half. Then he turned and I saw ripples travel along his body, a succession of smooth movements that revealed his muscles and accentuated the suppleness of the species. Avoiding me and the wall with consummate ease, my unpredictable visitor swam lazily away, but not before I was able to positively identify him as a blue shark, *Prionace glauca*, a species that attains a length of twenty-five feet and is considered extremely voracious, although there are no records in North America to confirm that these fish actually attack man. However, inasmuch as even the small sand sharks and dogfish are capable of inflicting serious injury, no shark should ever be trusted.

Ever since I was ten years old and first began to study the small sharks I caught during the summers in rocky pools connected to the Mediterranean Sea, I have been interested in these extraordinary fish. Later, I kept foot-long specimens in an aquarium but found they could not survive in captivity. At twelve I dissected my first shark, a fourteen-inch individual that had died after three weeks in the seawater tank, refusing to feed during this time. This was the last of the species that I studied as a child. Its cadaver yielded quite a lot of information, but most of this did not become clear to me until adulthood and wider experience of the breed gave me fuller understanding.

Since then, I have studied sharks in many areas, including that region of the South Atlantic Ocean that lies off the coast of Angola. I have caught sharks with rod and line and by means of setlines dangling from floats; and I have watched them underwater. Despite such experience, the only more-or-less sure information I have gained deals with the shark's body parts and with some of the functions of these; beyond such anatomical knowledge, I have a few theories about sharks, a lot of questions, and some reasonably educated guesses. But there is one thing about which I am quite sure: *All sharks are dangerous.* Having said that, however, I would add that the average swimmer in any part of our world is more likely to die of old age than as a result of a shark attack.

Sharks *do* kill and eat people, let there be no mistake about that; and because many swimmers simply disappear without a trace, it is likely that many shark attacks, perhaps the majority, go unrecorded. Even so, the incidents are rare when compared to the many millions of people who flock to beaches all over the world throughout the year. Indeed, even those recorded incidents, when properly analyzed after the fact, tend to show that in the majority of cases the attacks have been unwittingly prompted by the swimmer—in some cases foolishly so.

When dealing with sharks, one soon learns a few simple rules of survival. The first and probably most important of these is to remain calm (easy advice to give but often hard, if not impossible, to follow). The next involves clothing and equipment. Sharks are attracted by bright colors and shiny objects: white swimsuits are more likely to command a shark's attention than dark ones; and bright belt buckles, knives, anything that flashes in the water will cause an inquisitive shark to investigate. Next, it is well to remember that sharks have superlative sensing devices that can detect agitations in the water over very long distances, so it is never a good idea to splash around violently when swimming. In shallow areas—many of the recorded attacks have taken place in only a few feet of water—where groups of bathers are having a good time and the bottom sand reduces visibility, the undersides of the feet, pale to the point of showing white under the surface, can also attract a lurking shark, so it is never a good idea to kick swiftly and violently. Bathers should immediately leave the water if they cut themselves; even a small wound will produce enough blood to alert a selachian cruising a mile or more offshore.

Blood is the lure most likely to attract a shark. For this reason, spear-fishermen who make a kill should immediately leave the water with their prey. If they are approached by a shark before gaining the surface, prudent people will drop the catch. It is better to let a shark eat your grouper than to have him dine on your backside! Lastly, it is never a good idea to get too close to a shark, and it is a very bad idea to try to grab one, even a small specimen. In general, the average swimmer or diver should leave the water calmly but immediately upon sighting a shark. The best way to prevent an attack is to forestall it.

The shark is almost certainly the most successful creature ever created. It is a superlative eating machine that has few enemies, lives a long life, and is perfectly equipped to find and secure prey. It is very hard to kill, and those who have sought to open up a shark will know that even the sharpest knife will have difficulty making the first cut, will soon become hopelessly dulled, and will need to be sharpened every few minutes. Then, too, even a fully gutted shark will not die right away and is more than capable of killing its human assailant. Indeed, sharks that have been hooked, opened up, and tossed back into the water have been seen feeding on their own entrails! I know of one case where a tiger shark was hooked, shot through the head with a 30.30 bullet, and tossed over the side, apparently dead. Within minutes the same shark took the bait a second time and did not die until a bullet fired from inches away destroyed its small brain.

If a shark has an Achilles heel, it is its internal organs, which are not suspended by ligaments and thus flop about within the abdominal cavity. When a shark is hoisted out of the sea these organs flop downward, creating an enormous bulge. Dolphins and porpoises appear to have learned this secret, for when seeking to drive away a shark that is stalking one of their young, they swim at it full bore and smash their beaks into the stomach, eventually rupturing every organ. Orcas, which also attack selachians, kill these fish more quickly, simply biting them in half. Beyond the cetaceans, however, only another bigger shark can readily destroy these voracious fish—and man, of course, but mostly from the surface, protected by a boat.

I say confidently that sharks are the most unpredictable of all life forms found on earth or in the sea. But here my certainty ends. One selachian will behave one way, while another of the same species in the same water will behave quite differently. At certain times and for absolutely no known reason, a shark may appear cowardly, scared away by seemingly ridiculous things; yet the same fish may suddenly become madly aggressive and attack anything within reach, be this edible or not. Often sharks destroy themselves by attacking a ship's propellers. They will frequently swallow anything dropped overboard, including such things as pots and pans, empty cans, paper, cloth, pieces of wood; when the indigestible load becomes too heavy, they simply throw up, ejecting the lot. Some individuals will spurn even the most tempting bait at one moment, feeding voraciously the next.

When is a shark hungry? Certainly not only when it's stomach is empty, for sharks that are gorged almost to the point of bursting may continue feeding so long as food is available. And conversely, sharks that have had to be coaxed with all manner of tempting bait before finally deigning to bite the hook have revealed stomachs that contained not so much as a sardine.

Sharks often become quite single-minded about their food, a peculiarity which has been frequently and horribly demonstrated when swimmers have been attacked and rescuers have courageously tried to save them. In case after case, the shark, or sharks, did not molest the rescuers but continued to attack the victim, often when he or she was being supported by two other swimmers.

To date, it is believed that between 250 and 300 different species of selachians inhabit the seas and oceans. One, the Lake Nicaragua shark, *Carcharinus nicaraguensis*, lives in fresh water, evidently having become landlocked during prehistoric times and adapting itself to live without salt water. But no one knows just how many sharks of all species inhabit the seas. Suffice it to say there are millions.

Despite my surprise at meeting the blue in Laredo Inlet, encountering sharks in these latitudes is not at all uncommon. I was startled because I had not been thinking about selachians, for, despite my experience with the breed, I had become accustomed to seeing them in warm waters. Selachians, it is true, are more numerous in tropical regions, but they are truly cosmopolitan, occupying all the oceans and almost any kind of marine habitat, from river estuaries and the shallows near shore to the ocean deeps and as far north as the polar seas, all of them veritable kings within their habitat.

It should not be supposed that I do not fear sharks. I most certainly do. But I am fascinated by them as well. For more than 300 million years selachians have been hunting the oceans of our world. One of these, *Carcharodon megalodon*, had teeth the size of a man's open hand, and fossil evidence suggests that this fish must have been more than a hundred feet long. Beside such a creature, a full-grown human would be dwarfed, a mere mouthful for *megalodon*. Disregarding the whale and basking shark, which are definitely inoffensive, the next largest present-day monster is the great white shark, *Carcharodon carcharias*, which attains a length of thirty-six feet or more and is armed with cruelly serrated teeth that may be over two inches long.

If for no other reason, sharks must be admired for having outlived all the creatures with whom they shared the early seas. But there is more to wonder at! Consider the shark's equipment. Its skin is covered with thousands of tiny denticles, sharp little "teeth" that will peel the skin off a man if the shark merely rubs against him. But between these abrasive spikes are pits called sensorial crypts, which can actually taste whatever the denticles rub against, the water in which the fish is swimming, and even edible particles suspended in the water. It is for this reason that a shark will often brush against a victim before attacking, evidently seeking to taste its prey before going to the trouble of charging. Most of the crypts are centered around the head, but there are enough distributed over the rest of the body to make the shark the world's best-prepared gourmet.

On the end of its sharp nose the selachian has a cluster of tiny sensors known as Lorenzini flasks, which allow it to detect differences in pressure, while its highly developed lateral lines, plentifully equipped with sensorial canals that are packed with a jellylike substance, are acutely sensitive to vibrations as well as to pressure waves. Covering its nostrils, the selachian has S-shaped Schneider folds that allow the water to filter through the olfactory tract, bringing it more messages. To breathe, the shark swims with its mouth slightly open, allowing the water to move through the gills and out of the gill slits, which are located just behind the head. Most species have five gills on each side, although some have six or seven.

A shark's teeth are retractable, folding into the jaws when the mouth is closed or only slightly open and springing upright when the creature wants to bite. And the shark never needs a dentist! It has seven layers of teeth; if one is lost from the first row, another quickly replaces it. By actual test, it has been established that the jaws of an eight-foot great white shark may exert up to eighteen tons of pressure per square inch of surface. Tests show that the teeth themselves are as hard as steel.

It was long thought that sharks must turn on their sides or on their stomachs in order to bite. This is not so. The upper jaw of a selachian is almost as mobile as its lower. The fish simply opens both gates and the teeth project forward; the end of the sharp nose, as flexible as rubber, is pushed upward on contact with the target. When the jaws are snapped shut, fixing the teeth firmly in the meat of large prey, the killer shakes its entire body from side to side and its lethal dentures slice through the victim's skin, flesh, and bone. Such bites are truly dreadful! Some years ago, Rodney Fox, a diver assisting in the filming of sharks off the coast of Australia, was bitten by a great white. He owes his life to his own courage, which prompted him to punch the attacker in the eye, causing it to release him and to the neoprene wet suit he was wearing, which literally held him together until he reached a hospital. A color picture I have in my possession shows the extent of Fox's awesome wounds. Across the upper part of the left arm and shoulder, and along the back to a point just above the hip, great gashes are visible. The bite also encompassed the upper left hip and abdomen, cutting the latter open and revealing the intestines. Eleven deep, gory punctures can be counted on the solid parts of the diver's torso, but the gaping, abdominal wound looks as though it was made by the sweep of a large and very sharp knife.

Those who believe that sharks can't see well beneath the surface may be surprised to learn that this creature's visual equipment has become extremely specialized, allowing the shark to see well in murky water and shielding the eyes when too much light would hinder vision. Such control is achieved through a series of silvery reflector plates, arranged somewhat like venetian blinds behind each eye. When visibility is poor, what light there is passes through the eye, hits the reflector plates, and is bounced back again, in this way sensitizing the retina twice. In brilliant, near-the-surface light, these plates (called tapetum) are automatically coated by dark pigment cells which block off the little mirrors. In addition, the shark does not adjust its iris in order to compensate for distance; instead, it can move the eye forward or backward to accommodate for range.

With such equipment, plus a flexible skeleton that will bend but not break, the shark is a veritable wonder of nature, a nearly perfect creation. It has acquired an evil reputation —mostly deserved, it is true, but exaggerated by man's fear of being himself eaten by anything and by the fear of being attacked in the water, where our species feels most vulnerable. As fascinated as I am by sharks, they also scare me quite a lot. But I try not to show it, as I tried that morning beneath the waters of Laredo Inlet.

As the blue shark swam away after its first rush, I felt greatly relieved, but when it was a distant, shadowy form, it turned, circled, and came toward me anew, sculling more casually now but clearly meaning to have another look. I continued to rise slowly, working my way along the wall to the place where the *Stella* was at anchor, her bottom just visible in the murky distance. The shark began zigzagging once more, drawing nearer, but still at the slow pace. When about fifteen feet from me, it turned, swam forty yards into deeper water, turned again, and aimed itself in my direction. I kept going upward and to the left, rather like a giant crab might scuttle for the safety of its rocky den. Moments later the blue charged forward, but at the last second it turned away, only ten feet from me, then swam parallel to the rock wall for about fifty yards before changing course abruptly and returning again. I was getting somewhat fed up with this beast. We were closer to the surface now, and the stronger light allowed me to note the deep shade of blue on its back, dappled in places by filtered sunshine, which altered as it moved. Despite my anxiety to be rid of this fish, I perforce had to admire its grace and sinister good looks.

The blue came closer. From ten feet away, as it faced me head-on, I had a view of its pectoral fins jutting out and stiffly held at a slightly downward angle. The high dorsal fin was a thin outline without depth of field; behind this, the stiffly erect, gently waving tail kept time with the last third of the shark's body; this was also turning from left to right, showing those silken ripples and creases. But it was the head, especially the snout and protruding eyes, that created the biggest impression. Seen from above, from below, or from the side, a shark is undoubtedly beautiful, a fluidly moving, elegantly streamlined animal vibrating with elegance; but head-on, it is ugly, sinister, and deadly looking. This one had its mouth open slightly, its rubbery lips seemingly innocent, for the teeth were folded back.

I was reasonably sure that it was more curious than hungry. Nevertheless, when it came almost within arm's length, I decided it was time to show a bit of fight. Lunging away from the wall, I smacked the blue on the end of its inquisitive nose with my balled fist, the sandpaper-rough denticles scraping my skin but, the gods be praised, not actually drawing blood.

The whole thing was ludicrous, really, for the shark turned away in such a startled manner that I *almost* chuckled. As he was veering his head toward the left, his right eye, big and round and circled in white, stared at me while his partly opened mouth, which had seemed to be grinning, closed with a snap. To encourage his departure I raised my arm and lashed at him again, whereupon he increased the movement of tail and body and shot away. It was clear that the eight-foot blue was unwilling to risk combat, at least not then; but I had no way of knowing whether or not the unpredictable creature might change his mind. By now I could determine his gender because I could see the twin claspers, extensions of the second pelvic fins found in male selachians, which are used during mating to transfer sperm when a female is ready to receive it.

The blue now kept a more respectful distance, coming a little nearer occasionally, mostly circling several yards away, following. Twice more, when he edged closer, I lunged at him, and each time he retreated. Slowly, still rising, I worked my way toward the *Stella*, eventually positioning myself fifteen feet beneath the surface and within sight of the anchor rope, which was lazily swaying up and down as the boat rocked on the surface. It was at this point that the blue turned suddenly and streaked into deep water, disappearing from view within seconds. His behavior suggested that something had frightened him. My own actions could not have produced such sudden nervousness, so I suspect that the long, curved, slowly moving anchor rope may have done the trick. Whatever his reasons for leaving, I was grateful to see the last of him.

Back on board the *Stella* after the sixteen-minute dive, I found that in retrospect I was elated by the experience, although I would not have deliberately engineered the meeting. It is certainly not advisable for a lone diver to seek the company of sharks. Indeed, it is not really advisable for a person to dive alone at any time, as I was well aware; but I was prepared to accept normal risks in this regard rather than forego the experience altogether.

Drying myself and at the same time sipping hot coffee I'd prepared and left in a thermos before my dive, I was interested to note that although I had felt some apprehension when I first entered the water in Klem's presence, my recent encounter with the much smaller blue shark caused me to feel outright fear. The matter is now purely academic, but I am sure that I felt more initially at ease in the presence of the orca because he was a mammal. The light of intellect, of reason, revealed itself in his gaze—we somehow managed to communicate. But the shark is an anachronism even in the world of fishes, a leftover from prehistory. Its eyes are cold and sinister, and its brain, lacking a cortex and by virtue of its small size and simplicity, is an organ of impulse, a cluster of neural cells that direct the creature's nervous and physiological system unburdened by rational or emotional motives. Therein, perhaps, lies the answer to the shark's unpredictability: How can one predicate the behavior of an organism whose brain is seemingly incapable of planning ahead while it apparently reacts only to the stimuli of hunger, fear, and the urge to breed?

Later that day, on the premise that the blue, or others of its ilk, might be lurking in our vicinity, I decided to try some shark fishing. It may be supposed that these fiercely carnivorous fish are easy to catch, but I knew from past experience that sharks are caught more regularly when an angler is *not* fishing for them than when he is. All too often, when trolling for conventional *pisces*, I had lost a good fish in addition to a lot of line when my catch was struck by a hungry shark; yet I have spent an entire day angling for sharks only to quit empty-handed.

On that afternoon in Laredo Inlet, I was not optimistic about my chances of hooking into the blue as I started preparing for the hunt. I didn't have any proper shark hooks, but Captain Mike had given me three halibut hooks the previous year when I went with him to the mouth of the Nass River. Halibut grow big, some weighing more than four hundred pounds, so they require large hooks. Taking two of these, I bound them tightly together with steel line, making a thick, double-pointed, single hook. I had a spare drum for the sea reel, which was loaded with seventy-two-pound test monofilament line, and to this I attached ten feet of heavy steel leader, which was in turn threaded through the two eyes of the improvised hook. After that, in the shallows and using light tackle, I caught two rockfish, each weighing about one-and-a-half pounds. Killing them, I threaded one on the hook.

I had at first intended fishing from the *Stella*, but I changed my mind when I realized that if I *did* get a strike from a big shark, it would probably break the line. I would fish from the dinghy instead, reasoning that even the largest fish would not be able to snap the monofilament under such circumstances, because the little boat would respond to the pull and move over the surface, dissipating the shark's power. When all was ready, I stacked my gear in the dinghy, being careful to include the fish club in case something nasty came up beside my frail craft. But, alas, six hours later I was sharkless. I had had a few fairly powerful strikes, and the bait fish was quite badly mauled by eager teeth, but no selachian had been fatally tempted.

The next morning I tried again, this time using a smaller hook, about half the size of the one I had fashioned. I used pieces of the second rockfish, allowing the line to go almost to the bottom and dragging it along at the mouth of the bay in which we were anchored. Twice I changed bait, throwing the mangled remains over the side. Nothing. Then, toward noon, I got a hefty strike.

The line jerked violently, the rod bent and then returned to normal as the monofilament went slack. Thinking I had lost it, I started to reel in to check the bait. The fish chose that moment to run, and I could feel that the hook was well set in its mouth. Moments later the dinghy began to move, and for some fifteen minutes we rode over the surface, heading into deeper water in the middle of Laredo Inlet. I felt sure that I had hooked a big shark, but when the dinghy stopped moving and the creature below allowed me to reel in line, coming in sluggishly, I began to be less certain. Minutes later a dorsal fin broke the surface, remained there for some seconds, and then disappeared as the fish resumed its battle. I *had* hooked a shark; it wasn't a blue but a large dogfish.

As it turned out, the sixty-seven-inch female dogfish, *Squalus suckleyi*, was shark enough. She fought like a tigress, her large mouth equipped with relatively small yet vicious teeth, opening and shutting as she sought something to bite. When I eventually killed the dogfish with the club, I dragged her on board. Because her stomach was so bulgy, I opened her immediately and to my astonishment found that she was practically ready to give birth to twelve sharklets, all of which were alive. Indeed, one of them was already occupying the birth position when I opened the female and my knife slightly nicked its back.

Leaving the young within the mother, I quickly filled the plastic tub with seawater, then took out the live infants and put them inside the container. At first they sank to the bottom, where they remained motionless but for the slow, immediate response of their gills, the slits of which moved each time the young fish sucked water into their mouths. I activated my stopwatch and noted that it took thirty-one seconds for the first sharklet to begin swimming; two more became active after thirty-four seconds had elapsed; and the fourth was one second behind its companions. The injured shark remained inactive for forty-six seconds. After that, they all swam slowly around the tub, often bumping against the sides. Would they feed? I cut up small pieces of the bait fish that was wedged in the female's mouth and sprinkled them on the surface of the water in the tub. All but the injured shark began to feed greedily.

On the spur of the moment I put six of the young dogfish into the fishnet, then took them to the stern ladder and released them one at a time. All swam away immediately, heading toward the bottom. The others I decided to keep, to study for a few days and then release. At the same time, I thought I would now try and catch a few more dogfish, thinking I might capture other females that were close to giving birth, for like most sharks, this species develops the young inside their bodies—not within a womb as placental animals do, but by retaining the eggs in two sacs, one on either side of the stomach, where the fertilized ova give rise to the embryo. Each egg is unconnected to the mother, but instead lies loose within the semitransparent sac. When birth time arrives, the young pass out through the mother's cloaca, whereupon they swim away, looking for shelter until they are strong enough to hunt, which, as I now knew, does not entail a prolonged wait.

By that evening I had caught a total of five dogfish, including the big female. Four of these were females and I was fortunate in that all contained either eggs or sharklets. Thus I obtained records of the embryonic development of sharks, from the fertilized egg, through various stages of growth, to the fully formed young ready to be born. The fifth dogfish was a male.

By morning, I found that the young shark I had accidentally cut with my knife had been eaten by its siblings. All that remained of him were a few pieces of skin, the dorsal fin, part of the tail, and one pectoral fin. The five cannibals were replete and sluggish.

Immediately after breakfast I began photographing the eggs, the embryos, and the sharklets, anxious to record all of them, but working quickly because the cockpit reeked of spoiled shark meat: I had kept the big female, wanting to use her for comparison when I photographed some of the young. I was now thinking quite clinically. I killed three of the young sharks, examined them carefully, even to taking pictures of their teeth, which, like tiny, rounded razorblades, were perfectly formed and already capable of cutting, as I found out when I introduced my finger into one mouth in order to open it wide. I used a probe for this purpose after that.

When all was cleaned up later that day, I had lunch and then devoted myself to making notes, feeling somewhat guilty for having killed so many organisms but consoling myself with the thought that sharks are expendable in these waters. Sophistry, perhaps, but it served to still my conscience and to maintain my clinical detachment.

ALASKAN WATERS

On July 24 the *Stella* was jousting with some rough water in Finlayson Channel. The tide was full, the wind was blowing at fourteen knots, but the morning was clear and sunny. Astern lay Cone Island and Klemtu, where we had put in for the fourth time to take on fuel after leaving Laredo Inlet. On this day, the *Stella* and I had been running up and down the Pacific coast for four months and nine days, but it seemed longer than that since John and I had conned the boat out of Victoria and headed her into the Strait of Juan de Fuca. It occurred to me that the passage of time had lost meaning because I had done so much and been to so many places during the 131 days that had elapsed between March 15 and now. Indeed, as I turned the *Stella* momentarily off course to avoid a floating log, it would have been easy for me to convince myself that I had *always* lived this kind of life. For the first two or three weeks the newness had caused me to recognize that I was doing something quite different, especially at those times when I felt apprehensive, but now, thoroughly at home in my boat and, more particularly, having become so familiar with the ocean that I no longer overreacted to its wild moods, I experienced a deep sense of unity with my surroundings. It was as though I *belonged* here. Withal, I now discovered that I was much better able to deal with my emotions and I recognized the fact that Joan's death had panicked me. As a result, I had run, a blind rush into the wilderness, just as a deer might make when alerted to the presence of hunting wolves.

Turning back on course when the drift log was safely astern, I visualized myself as I had been before the start of this journey, and at that moment I knew I had refused to accept the death of my wife; consciously, of course, I had realized she was gone, but deep within my mind Joan had remained alive and I had unconsciously tried to cling to the past. July 24 fell on a Monday in 1972. On that day, at 10:15 in the morning, I became aware that I was healing and ready to face reality. The process had begun before this, but it had progressed gradually, unnoticed. Unbidden, a thought came to me; it was simple and direct and, I felt, very much to the point, so I reached for the notebook and wrote it down: "Yesterday is the experience that allows a person to live today in order to be ready for tomorrow." I was now ready.

We had remained at anchor in the Laredo Inlet bay for the past two weeks, a time spent in quiet contemplation of the life that surrounded us. I had explored the land, collected marine specimens for study, and had once again encountered a school of Dall porpoises, an unforgettable experience.

Strictly speaking, the Dalls had encountered me, for I was studying the bottom in an area where the depth was about seventeen feet, when I noted a number of swift, large shadows approaching from deeper water. This was only four days after my unexpected encounter with the shark, and I at first mistook the torpedo bodies of the porpoises for the more sinister outlines of a number of blues. The bottom shelved upward, so I started to back away, but I stopped when my visitors came close enough to be identified. There were fourteen of them in this pod, and what a sight they were as they sped through the clear water! The time was just noon and the sun beamed straight down, reaching the bottom around me and creating a sort of marine fairyland, its light obviously hurtful to some of the small bottom organisms, especially the chitons, but helpful to others, who were actively hunting. Ugly little sculpins were darting about everywhere, gulping down minute bits of life that were too indistinct for me to recognize; crabs were also active, scuttling sideways, some burying themselves in the sandy bottom after capturing a morsel of food. Minutes earlier I had disturbed a small octopus, a creature about eighteen inches long; it darted away, propelled swiftly backward by its water jet, its gray, bulbous body inflated, the protuberant, intelligent eyes, so like a goat's, fixed on me while it scooted away to hide itself within a bed of kelp.

Into this enchanting world came a gam of Dalls, but at first they made me nervous, for they were all aimed straight at me and their rate of travel was tremendous. I stood still, conscious only of the approaching black-and-white squadron and of the bubbles I was discharging, which rushed upward audibly. Would the porpoises smash into me? If they did, these would be my last conscious moments of life. But my apprehension was needless. When the lead animal was about ten feet away, it veered right with incredible swiftness and was instantly followed by the others, a procession of magnificently beautiful and supple beings that returned to deeper water, completed a wide circle, and came hurtling back, repeating the same maneuver three times in quick succession, an impromptu troupe of shiny black-and-white circus performers whose corpulence contrasted with the agility displayed by each animal. I swam toward them as they were making a fourth run, and they changed tactics. First one, then the others rolled onto their backs as they traveled, altering course slightly to pass beside me, no more than five feet from where I floated. In a matter of seconds the school was returning, but on this occasion they turned on their sides, facing me, the turbulence created by their swift passage causing me to dance in the water. The line swept by almost nose to tail, and as each porpoise passed me, it turned, heading into deep water. I was too elated by the show to bemoan their departure, and before I had time to swim back to the place where I had seen the octopus disappear, the gam returned.

They arrived in a bunch, but when they were still about thirty feet from me, the leaders dashed ahead, aiming for the surface, their big tails paddling furiously. Up, up, and out of the water they went, three animals in quick succession, and before they fell back into the ocean a second or two later, the rest of the gam followed. The action was swift and confused, the surface whipped to a froth and attended by waves and currents that traveled downward, tossing me around as though I were weightless. For some moments I became disoriented. When I'd found my bearings again, the last two Dalls were already plunging back down.

My clearest impression of the performance was obtained when the first three porpoises leaped up together. I saw that each was trailing a stream of silvery bubbles beginning midway along their bodies and falling away to the sides, liquid sequins that lost their form as the porpoises gained distance. I saw the three heads break out of the water, then the bodies were through, and lastly the furiously pumping tails emerged. For an instant I saw simultaneously the outline of the flying porpoises above the surface as well as the implosive dimples made when a rain of sea fell downward. The waves and currents came immediately after this, and events became too confused for me to follow. To the best of my knowledge, each Dall jumped only once and those porpoises that reentered the sea first began immediately to swim toward deeper water. How long did the show last? A minute, maybe less—I really don't know.

Topside, divesting myself of my equipment and wet suit, I looked in vain for the porpoises on the surface. They had disappeared and did not come again while we remained in the bay. Checking my last tank, I found that there was hardly any air left in it, and this ended my diving for the time being.

About a week later, listening to the weather station, I was startled to hear the date. I had underestimated our stay by eight days! It was Saturday, July 22. The next afternoon the *Stella* headed out of Laredo Inlet and retraced her course through Meyers Channel, again experiencing the magnetic interference that set the compass needle dancing.

Now the *Stella*'s bow was resolutely set toward the north. We were Alaska-bound at last, our route planned to take in Hartley Bay, a fuel stopover, then Prince Rupert, for the same reason and also to have the air tanks filled. From there we would run through Chatham Sound before entering U.S. waters as we headed for Revillagigedo Channel. Up to this point, I was still hoping to reach Ketchikan by Wednesday afternoon, but not long after twelve o'clock it appeared that the weather was going to conspire against us. The wind freshened, the sky started to cloud over, and when I switched on the radio I was told that a low front was sweeping in from the west, bringing increased winds and heavy rain.

Nearing Butedale several hours later I was tempted to seek the shelter of its harbor, but because the wind remained steady at 17 knots and the skies, though heavily overcast, had not yet begun to drop the promised rain, I decided to take a chance and head for Hartley Bay, which was only thirty-five miles distant (a four-hour trip at our present rate of speed). It was 3:00 P.M., so I wasn't worried about running into darkness before arrival, for in those latitudes at that time of year the light does not fade until about 11:00 P.M.

At five o'clock, more or less at the point of no return, the rain came. It arrived with a thunderous fanfare and great, orange forks of lightning; the clouds ruptured and the water whipped against the *Stella*, drumming on the deck and on the canvas screen and beating against the windshield so that the wipers were nearly useless. Visibility was almost instantly reduced to half a mile, and the angry sea tossed spindrift high over the bow. Wind velocity increased to 20 knots. But the game *Stella Maris* took the elements in her stride, as she had always done. I wasn't worried. Rather, I found myself enjoying the storm. Its primordial aspect released within me a sense of turbulence that was exciting and challenging, a blend of raw fear and elation that caused me to become very much aware of my own mortality and yet at the same time made me feel vibrantly alive. I was familiar with this contradiction: I had encountered it more than a few times in moments of war.

I stood before the wheel and kicked my shoes off, wanting to feel every vibration and bounce of the *Stella*, seeking to experience the storm as intensely as my boat was doing. The thunder roared in the distance; near strikes cracked like gunfire and vividly illuminated our surroundings as the sea rose and fell, rose and fell.

I was almost sorry to reach the shelter of Hartley Bay at 7:30 that evening, for I was still enjoying my adrenaline "high." A white man on the dock helped me moor the *Stella*. He must have thought I was drunk because I couldn't help chuckling as I talked rapidly. In truth, I suppose I *was* drunk, but with elation, with a sense of good purpose, and a feeling of utter contentment.

Aware of the ocean underneath my body, that night I slept

like a man drugged—until the mewing of the gulls accompanied by the sound of a boat's motor woke me. Sitting up, I saw that a tug was tying up nearby. I noted also that the weather had worsened.

At breakfast, the radio announced that the wind was then at Force 10 (48 to 55 miles per hour) and was whipping up thirty-foot waves. Again I was pleased. We were snug in harbor after bulling our way through the turbulence and keeping ahead of the present storm, an upheaval that would surely have destroyed the *Stella*.

For two days the gale lashed the coast, a battering, wet force that kept all vessels in harbor. During this time I was content, occupying myself by completing the notes I had started in Laredo Inlet and examining about a dozen specimens I had killed with fresh water. (Most small marine organisms react to fresh water much as they might to a drug if the water is poured in a little at a time so that it slowly dilutes the sea's constituents. In this way, such things as chitons, which would normally curl up if killed more quickly, retain their original shape, dying relaxed.)

During the evening of the second day, I made two plankton nets, fashioning each out of a pair of nylon pantyhose, three pairs of which I had bought during our earlier trip to Prince Rupert. As I worked, I smiled at the memory of the saleswoman's expression when I had asked for the dainty wear! Unshaven, wearing a blue, woolen toque, and dressed in jeans and sweater, I obviously didn't look like her average customer. When she asked me what size and I said it didn't matter, her eyebrows went up. Still puzzled, she then asked if I wanted them all the same size and color and when I again said that this wasn't important but that I preferred all the same color, the poor girl became quite confused. As I was about to leave the store, I realized that she had only charged me for one pair, so I returned to her counter to adjust matters. Her back was turned to me and she was chatting with another girl. As I approached, I heard her say ". . . *weird*. He didn't know her size!" The unfortunate girl turned scarlet when she saw me and became even more confused when she realized her error.

Although I wasn't sure that my idea would work, I thought that the fine mesh of the nylon would stand up to the pull of the ocean, at least long enough to allow me to collect some samples. I cannot now remember the exact price for those three pairs of pantyhose, but I know it was under three dollars, certainly cheaper than what I would have had to pay for just one manufactured plankton net.

Designing my net as I went along, I first tied a knot in each leg, just below the place a wearer's knee would have reached; then I cut off the feet and ankles. After that, I stitched the waist to a wide strip of canvas, cut on the bias and doubled over a circle of heavy-gauge wire to act as a frame, and then four lengths of strong nylon line were fastened equidistantly to the wire and knotted together two feet from the net; to this the towing line would be secured. The completed structure looked more like an inverted beehive with twin spires than it did a cone. But as I was to discover later, it worked.

On the morning of our fourth day at Hartley Bay the weather cleared and the wind was stilled. Under blue skies and in the face of a light breeze we left our harbor, entered Wright Sound, and soon afterward headed into Grenville Channel, a narrow, thirty-five-mile-long waterway squeezed between Pitt Island and the mainland. By three o'clock that afternoon, still navigating under clear skies in warm, placid conditions, we passed the little community of Oona River on Porcher Island. To starboard lay the estuary of the Skeena River. At eight that evening we were moored in Prince

Rupert, at the public boat harbor. An hour later the *Stella* was refueled, and I had been fortunate enough to get the air tanks recharged just minutes before the attendant closed up for the day. This was a relief, because the distance between Prince Rupert and Ketchikan is approximately a hundred miles and thus the journey would take between nine and twelve hours, depending on sea conditions. For this reason I wanted to get away very early in the morning, giving myself plenty of time to arrive in Ketchikan with daylight to spare.

On July 30, as the unseen sun was bloodying the tops of the mainland mountains, the *Stella* slipped her moorings and nosed away from Prince Rupert, encountering a relatively flat sea that was almost bubbling with life. Within two hours of departure, while we were crossing Chatham Sound at low tide, two groups of Dall porpoises rose to the surface. One was only half a mile away and contained seven animals; the other, about a mile astern, was larger but I could not count its numbers because of the distance. Already we had sighted numerous groups of harbor seals, some of the animals sunning themselves on rocks, others swimming and diving, evidently feeding and often calling when they popped up to the surface. There were birds in the skies, of course; no stretch of the Pacific coast is ever quite free of birds, although during bad weather even the hardy gulls tend to sit out the storms on rocky ledges. Chasing us, a mixed flock of gulls screeched and wheeled, most of them staying astern but several flying overhead and depositing their limy droppings on the clean deck. Cormorants abounded in the water and in the air and twice I saw bald eagles, wings outstretched and almost immobile as they used the updrafts to glide parallel to the mainland coast.

I cut back the revs at this point and put a plankton net out, allowing it to drag about a hundred feet astern for an hour. On retrieving it, I was delighted to find that my impromptu rig had worked well and that, except for a few runs, had withstood the test admirably. Inside I found almost nine ounces of planktonic organisms mixed with bits of seaweed and a few small pieces of assorted debris. Much of the stuff resembled jelly, and it was difficult to determine whether it was made up of animal or plant life. Some ova could be clearly seen, as could tiny jellyfish; there were also some minute larval organisms that I was unable to identify, except in a most general way—minute, bug-eyed creatures, clearly fish, whose internal organs could just be discerned through semitransparent stomach sacs. But the prize of prizes was a two-inch veiled anglemouth (*Cyclothone microdon*), a deep-water fish that had rows of luminous dots distributed along both sides of the stomach as well as shorter rows on either side, in positions that would have coincided with the lateral lines had I been able to find these sensors. Unfortunately, the fish was dead.

Because of its condition, I estimated that the fish had been dead for at least a day; its photophores were no longer luminescent, but I was delighted to have its body to examine. Adults are said to reach a maximum of three inches, although this is clearly guesswork. The species has been collected in tow nets in the mid-Pacific and brought up from great depths, but larger specimens may exist at deeper levels. The specimen I was examining was dark gray, almost black, its body resembling that of a smelt, but having large dorsal and pelvic fins. The abdominal fin was short and ragged, a seemingly useless appendage, while the pectoral fins were also relatively undeveloped. The eyes were quite small, the mouth fairly large and well filled with needlelike teeth.

Soon after my somewhat hasty examination of the plankton, we crossed the Canada–U.S. boundary, which in this region is located at 54° 38′ 40″, as nearly as I was able to determine. The *Stella* was about two miles to port of Lord Rocks, a cluster of granite fangs lying just south of Cape Fox, and as I raised the fieldglasses to get my first glimpse of the Alaskan coast, I noticed that the water between the reef and the cape was agitated. The sea was otherwise calm, so I focused the glasses on this place and was puzzled to see a number of dark, indistinct shapes rising to the surface and swimming on top of the water at a great rate, then diving again. I turned the *Stella* off course and increased power, keeping well clear of Lord Rocks.

When we had traveled about a mile I was able to see that a dozen or more northern sea lions were responsible for the furious commotion. At first the animals appeared to be heading for Nakat Inlet, but they suddenly turned right around and dashed toward the rocks I was passing. Then I saw the dorsal of a killer whale. It broke through the surface, traveled about a hundred yards immediately behind the last seal, and disappeared again. Slowing the *Stella* to just above the idle, I tied down the wheel and craned out of the starboard screen, glasses to my eyes. Now I saw red patches on the water. As I concentrated on the rearmost sea lions, the gaping jaws of a whale appeared and closed on the body of a female. A second or two later the seal was dragged down and the water was stained crimson. Including the one that had just been killed, there were twenty-nine sea lions in evidence. By now the leaders had reached the safety of Lord Rocks, two of them, a bull and a cow, bleeding from indeterminate wounds. When the last survivor had climbed out of the water, the bulls in the herd began roaring, a tremendous row that I could still hear when the *Stella* was about a mile away. I saw no more whales and could not determine how many sea lions had been taken. But it was a sobering experience. The clinically trained part of my mind found it of absorbing interest, but my emotional nature was saddened, not quite able to reconcile the carnage with my memory of Klem, who had been so friendly and docile. I am sure that if I had witnessed the sea-lion hunt before meeting Klem, I would not have risked myself in the water with him. After the fact, I felt that I could still do so with impunity should I meet him again, just as I had continued to trust Matta and Wa*, the two wolves I raised, after watching them bring down and kill a deer.

Revillagigedo Island lies just off the mainland of southern Alaska, tucked neatly inside a pocket formed by the rugged coastline. Seen on a chart, the island resembles a piece of jigsaw puzzle that had not quite been fitted into place, its contour accented by a blue, horseshoe-shaped ribbon on which are printed in several places the words *Behm Canal*. This is a natural saltwater channel, which sweeps northward at the outset, turns eastward, then veers sharply south to join the waters of Revillagigedo Channel at a point almost opposite the southeast coast of Annette Island. From its upper entrance to its end, the Behm Canal is more than a hundred miles long, but because it is interrupted by so many small islands, inlets, and bays, an exploring vessel could navigate three or four hundred miles and still fail to visit every part of the waterway.

On the west face of Revillagigedo Island, the town of

*See: *Secret Go the Wolves* by R. D. Lawrence, Holt, Rinehart and Winston, New York, 1980.

Ketchikan is located, a community of some seven thousand people (the population in 1972). It lies 680 miles north of Seattle, Washington, and 225 miles south of Juneau, Alaska. Apart from being known for its fishing, logging, and pulp-processing endeavors, Ketchikan's touristic fame stems from its location, which offers sport fishermen a plethora of things to kill, and for its totem poles, billed as the "world's largest" collection, a rather exuberant claim in that totem poles originated in only one region, the west coast of North America. Nevertheless, the totem logs are worth seeing.

What it is like to visit Ketchikan in the winter I do not know, but the hustle and bustle I encountered there in August caused me to suffer culture shock! Tourists were everywhere, having come by air, on board their own power-boats and sailboats, and, just ahead of the *Stella*, aboard a giant, sleek ferry, the *MV Columbia*, flagship of the Alaska Marine Highway fleet. This quite beautiful but monstrous-sized vessel caught up with and passed us while we were running between Ham Island and Hog Rocks, which are located at the western entrance to Revillagigedo Channel. The *Columbia*, of course, was steaming in midchannel a mile or more to the east of us; even so, her wake caught up with the *Stella* and bounced her around.

This encounter took place during the early afternoon of August 1, when we were about fifteen miles away from Ketchikan and making good time under bright blue skies and in positively subtropical heat, the thermometer having reached 86 degrees F. at noon. At four o'clock we were tied up at the Thomas Basin boat harbor, located beside Stedman Street, the *Stella* occupying one of the last three remaining berths. A short time after that, having paid for and thus secured our place for the night, I conned the *Stella* to the fuel wharf and had the tanks filled and the oil checked, immediately thereafter returning to our berth. I cleaned myself up and donned some town attire, then locked up the *Stella* and went ashore to a little local sightseeing and to have a decent dinner.

By eight o'clock the next morning we were passing Point Higgins to starboard, having cleared Tongass Narrows; soon after that we made a sharp turn to starboard and entered the channel between Betton and Revillagigedo islands. From here, passing between a cluster of four small islands, we turned north, the Cleveland Peninsula lying abeam to port. At noon, having run thirty-three miles, I turned off course to enter Yes Bay and to refuel at the little community of Yes that lies snug on the north shore, three miles from the entrance.

With the advantage of midnight sun, I did not stop here overnight, but turned right around and reentered the Behm Canal, setting the engine at low power so I could admire the magnificent scenery.

If one stands on an elevated place, and if the weather is clear, snow-clad peaks on the mainlands of Alaska and Canada sparkle in the sunshine and remain highlighted until near midnight. Against this background of distant peaks lies a domain of sprawling mountains, dense evergreen forests, and blue-green ocean. Bald eagles cry shrilly as they circle and glide in a constant search for prey, their voices mingling with the restless murmur of the Pacific and the strident cries of the gulls. Land animals come to the very edge of the sea, even lap its waters when they need salt; and marine animals visit the very edge of the land. As two nations meet and merge with one another, so do ocean and terrestrial life forms come together. Here lies a region of bigness and splendor, a corner of our continent so blessed with scenery that an observer is tempted to describe it in superlatives using words like *grandiose, magnificent, breathtaking*. But although all of these terms apply, they cannot, either individually or collectively, do justice to the Alaska–British Columbia milieu.

Such were my thoughts that evening as the *Stella* arrived at the point where the Behm Canal swoops to starboard and heads on south. Immediately ahead was Burroughs Bay, on the mainland coast; separated from the bay by a short, narrow neck of land was Fitzgibbon Cove. A mile and a half deep, this little wrinkle between land and sea offered ideal anchorage, having thirteen fathoms of water at its end and a mud bottom that promised excellent anchorage. I had already noted from the chart that Burroughs Bay becomes shallow five miles from its mouth (for the bottom is obstructed by sand and gravel washed down the Unuk River), and thus decided that Fitzgibbon Cove would serve as my main shelter while I remained in these latitudes. Coming abeam of Point Whaley, on Revillagigedo Island, I saw the mouth of the cove about three miles away.

I put the *Stella* in neutral, selected a medium-sized spoon, which I attached to my fishing line and cast astern, immediately engaging the gears and allowing the boat to go ahead at trolling speed. We were not yet halfway to our destination when I reeled in a small salmon for my supper. After that, we entered the cove and anchored and I was pleased to note that three creeks tumbled down gentle slopes into the cove, assuring me a plentiful supply of fresh water.

Alaska's weather was kind to us during the time we spent there. Typically, as I learned when I awakened the next morning, the skies were cerulean, the temperatures hot, and the seas calm. As I breakfasted on deck, basking in the sunshine and dressed only in shorts, movement on the west shore attracted my attention. From out of the evergreens strolled a she grizzly and two fat cubs, each about the size of a plump malamute, but shorter. One was the color of buckwheat honey, the other a medium brown, more like its mother. They were no more than a hundred yards away and obviously unconcerned by our presence in their domain. The mother raised herself on her hind legs, standing by the water's edge like a shaggy totem pole, staring at the *Stella*; her cubs, meanwhile, obedient to some unheard command, remained near the forest. But when the she dropped back to all fours and uttered a short grunt, the young ones trotted to her side. Now the three bears strolled toward the end of the cove, the cubs playing, dashing ahead of their mother, the sow appearing to check the shallows, perhaps searching for fish. Presently they left as they had come, entering the forest and disappearing inside its green maw.

When I finished my meal, I went for a quick swim, finding the water too cold to endure for more than five minutes but feeling refreshed by the dip. On board again, I consulted a calendar and decided that I could only allow myself three weeks in Alaska if I was to return to Victoria before the ocean turned angry and cold and rain became almost daily events. Monday, August 21, was the day I chose to begin my southward journey. With this decision made, I put the matter out of my mind and began loading some supplies and equipment into the dinghy, for I was going to leave the *Stella* in the cove and journey upriver, crossing into British Columbia if this was possible.

Taking enough field rations to last me a week, a light rod and a selection of lures, the tent, axe, .22 rifle, and some other essentials, I scrambled into the plastic shell and started rowing. After one day, however, I changed my mind. How I wished I had been able to bring a canoe with me! The pygmy boat was an impossible craft in which to negotiate thirty miles of flowing water. Not that the current was swift at this time of year; it was simply that the flat bottom of the squarish craft acted as a brake. I camped on a spit of sand the first night, having managed to travel about ten miles at the expense of blisters on both hands occasioned by the oars— and my hands had been protected by rows of calluses before I started! The next morning I allowed the orange bubble to drift slowly downriver, returning to my starting point in about a quarter of the time it had taken me to reach the camping site. I was disappointed but not greatly so, for there was much to see and do in the vicinity of the *Stella*.

As it turned out, it was a good thing I'd decided to turn back, for the only rain that fell over that part of Alaska during the duration of my stay began the same afternoon, soon after I had returned to the *Stella*. The downpour was fine, steady, and lasted almost forty-eight hours, keeping me close to home, except for a couple of fishing trips. But, as though to make up in some measure for this inclemency, the heat, pregnant with humidity, became intense.

The following morning I spent two hours watching four adult bald eagles as they fished in our cove. On three occasions individual birds caught fish that were too large to lift out of the water and were forced to "row" themselves ashore with their wings, as I had seen other eagles do on the shores of the Skeena River.

Two days later I went diving, selecting an area midway along Fitzgibbon Point, the spit of land that sheltered the cove, and submerging near shore in three fathoms. The bottom here was a mixture of rock, mud, and shell, with numerous grottos and shallow caves, all bearing collections of seaweeds, anemones, small crabs and fish, and many more tiny creatures, most of which were unidentifiable.

When I was still about six feet from the bottom and some

ten feet from the undersea shore rocks, I saw my second wolf-eel, but this one was only about four feet long. It detached itself from a cluster of rocks below but slightly ahead of me and darted away into deeper water, almost certainly frightened by my proximity. I recalled its relative's mouth and teeth and was pleased to see it leave. Soon after that, I saw a small school of Pacific barracuda, a fish that are thinner than their warm-water relatives but almost as vicious-looking. Resembling pike, but with infinitely more danger-ous teeth, these barracuda have not been known to attack divers, as their relatives do on occasion. The dozen or so that I watched were only about two feet in length and were swimming in a ragged, loose line about five feet from the bottom and near the sloping undershore, presumably hunt-ing. They were not disturbed by my presence but continued their systematic search of the seafloor, moving in a leisurely way and occasionally snapping at some unseen prey.

When I was down on the bottom, I noticed a number of common sea stars, purple, five-lobed organisms that are in no way related to fish but *are* related to sea urchins, sand dollars, sea cucumbers, and other allied organisms. These stars are plentiful from California to as far north as Sitka, but for all their familiarity, they are quite fascinating animals. This species, *Pisaster ochraceus*, is commonly purple but can also be brown or yellow. The sea star travels on thousands of minute tubelike feet, which it also uses to adhere to rocks and to its shellfish prey so tightly that to dislodge a specimen one must literally pry it off with a knife or small crowbar. If they lose some of their feet—which remain stuck to the rock for some time after their owner has been removed—they will grow replacements within a couple of days. In addition, their upper surface, which is seen to be covered by shallow craters among hard, whitish ridges, is, in effect, equipped with extremely tiny clawlike mechanisms, known as *pedicellaraie*. If you hold the star upside down against the tender skin of leg, arm, or stomach and leave it there for a couple of minutes before pulling it away, you'll notice a whole series of minute, slightly painful nips, for the star and its relations use their body "claws" to cling to the skin. If left for long, they begin to rasp and grind; this is how they rid themselves of parasites, such as the larva of barnacles and other shellfish, countless thousands of which are always floating in the sea, seeking a place to cling to while they complete development. All these creatures get short shrift when they land on *Pisaster*; they are ground to death! A simple experiment will quickly show a curious observer just how effective the star's tiny pincers are. If one crumbles a piece of ordinary blackboard chalk and sprinkles the flakes and crumbs on top of a sea star, in no time at all the animal's pincers will grind the chalk to a fine powder, right before the watcher's eyes. When it comes to eating, the sea star is hardly a gourmet. It will eat anything it can reach with its stomach, for it can turn this organ virtually inside out, placing it on top of or around its prey and feeding by this means, as the sea star has no mouth as such. In this way it will tug with thousands of its tiny sucker feet at the shells of mussels or clams, or any of their relatives, until it has opened up a crack between the two shells; into this it slides its inside-out stomach and begins to "munch," in effect digesting its meal outside of its own body! The sea star eats whatever kinds of shellfish happen to be available within its wide-ranging habitat. The ones I observed in Alaska varied in size from a few inches across the body to about fourteen inches, but I have encountered sea stars twenty inches across in Canadian waters.

Feeling the chill of the water, despite the wet suit, I had decided to give myself one more minute, then rise, when I noticed movement within a narrow cavity located on the vertical rock face, at a point where the bottom began to slope rapidly. Descending and stretching myself prone on the seafloor, I peered into the two-inch crack, but it was too dark inside to see whatever it was that had attracted my attention. I was about to start ascending, when I noticed that some organism had built itself a little wall at the mouth of a small cave, closing it with small stones, pieces of shell, and even a badly rusted piece of iron about two inches long and an inch or so thick, roughly round, which I guessed was part of a large bolt. The wall was thicker at the bottom than at the top and was mostly covered in weed except at the lip of the crack, where the coming and going of the den's occupant had rubbed off the growth. Only one creature that I knew of could have accomplished that little feat of engineering: an octopus.

As a child I had gotten to know these cephalopods very well indeed, netting small ones and keeping them in seawater aquaria and capturing three-foot-long specimens and moving them to rock pools that were ten to twelve feet deep and at least that wide, connected to the Mediterranean Sea by a shallow entrance. I used to select pools with entrances that could be readily blocked with stones, leaving spaces between so that the sea could still flow into the pools but making the barrier high enough to keep my specimens inside. There I could study them from above through the clear water, or, skin-diving, get acquainted with them in their own world for periods that varied between sixty and ninety seconds—and it is amazing how much one can see during one-and-a-half minutes if one looks hard enough!

Now, on the floor of the Pacific, I had found the den of what promised to be a good-sized octopus, for the cave was evidently deep and the wall that the animal had built was eighteen inches wide and fourteen high. The entrance crack itself proved, when measured on my next dive, to be two-and-three-eighths inches wide. The uninitiated may think that only a small cephalopod could use this narrow gap as a portal, but I had seen these plastic creatures flatten themselves and virtually flow through extraordinarily small openings, their ability to elongate and compress their bodies being nothing less than spectacular. But I needed a light in order to take a look at this specimen, and since I was already chilled to the danger point, I rose to the surface.

Two hours later I descended again, this time carrying a powerful, waterproof flashlight in one hand and some pieces of raw fish in one of the pantyhose nets, which I had kept, for they also make useful little bags. The octopus was inside its den and began to turn pink with emotion as soon as the light played on it. I had trouble guessing its size, but the creature was quite large, judging by its eyes and tentacles. Two sucker discs larger than all the others, one on each of two arms, identified this specimen as a male. Inside his shelter, his eight arms curled around his baglike body and his yellow eyes with their black pupils looking at me fixedly, the octopus remained still, its only change the pinkish hue that slowly spread over body and arms. Having made friends with many octopuses in my youth, I knew enough not to push this first acquaintance. Satisfied that he would still be there tomorrow, I slipped half a dozen pieces of fish into his den, switched off the light, and ascended, wanting to preserve my air for as long as possible.

At 11:00 A.M. the next day I was outside the den, this time carrying two dead whitespotted greenlings, each about eleven inches long. Slowly, taking care not to focus the light directly into the den, I offered one of the fish, noting that the octopus began to move in its lair and was not on this occasion showing signs of emotional distress but was instead retaining its camouflage hue, a mottled, slate tone that mimicked its surroundings. Cephalopods, rather like chameleons, can change color at will, blending cleverly within any habitat regardless of shade. Introducing the fish into the small cave, I let go of it and backed away, holding the light so that it would give just enough illumination to see by. Almost at once, a tentacle emerged, hesitated, then felt carefully for the greenling; curling around the fish, the arm was withdrawn. Already the octopus knew that I meant him no harm, recognizing me as a source of food. That was enough for this experiment. I rose, leaving him alone.

In the afternoon I repeated the same performance, using the second greenling. This time the tentacle came out of the den mouth and curled around the fish before I had let go of it. Success! I knew now that on my next trip, or at the next after that, Soopla*, as I decided to call him, would either come out of his cave or at least send his entire arm through the doorway to meet me halfway.

The second trip next day brought good results. As soon as the light began to shine in Soopla's direction, he came into view, sliding like foam through the crack and propelling himself backward, then stopping and descending to the bottom, resting on his upcurled arms. I approached to within about three feet of him, seeing his eyes as they fixed themselves on my body, and I extended an eight-inch herring. He quickly took it and spread himself over it, opening the mantle that connects the arms, like a solid web,

---

*Mac, one of John Steinbeck's central characters in both *Cannery Row* and *Sweet Thursday*, referred to cephalopods as sooplapods when talking with Doc at one point in the second of these two delightful stories. Being a great admirer of the author as well as of his books, I could do no less than pay homage by conferring the mispronounced term on the Alaskan octopus.

tapering along each tentacle until it ends halfway along the arm. Soopla had begun to feed on the spot.

Patience is essential when one seeks to become acquainted with any animal. Never is this more true than when dealing with octopuses, but not because they are dangerous or likely to attack—except in such imaginative horror stories as those written by Jules Verne. In real life, even the largest specimens are gentle and docile and want nothing more than to be left alone. I knew from past experience that sudden movement, or a premature approach, would panic the sensitive, highly nervous animal and undo all the work that had gone before. For this reason, I stayed down four minutes, then left Soopla to his meal.

In all, I made twelve dives with the scuba gear before I ran out of air; during the last five, Soopla always came to meet me, allowed himself to be stroked, and often felt my face and body with his tentacles. Once he actually wrapped himself gently around my head, covering my face mask. He was just about three feet long (by judgment, not measurement) from the top of his round body to the tips of his arms and, as I have said, gentle; but because he could accidentally pull out my mouthpiece, I raised my hands and lifted him up as high over my head as I could reach, releasing him soon after. Soopla seemed to resent that, for he dashed home, shooting a squirt of ink as he left. This cloud, which simply serves to put a barrier between an octopus and an enemy, soon disperses, but the cephalopods move so quickly when in "high gear" that while the sepia fog is still clearing, the octopus is already hidden in some new place.

My friendship with Soopla turned out to be a major highlight of my time in Alaska. Not for more than thirty years had I had the opportunity to renew my acquaintance with these fascinating and highly intelligent sea creatures. I counted myself amply rewarded for the time and trouble I had taken to develop our relationship, even though the oxygen I used up in this pursuit made more far-ranging underwater explorations impossible.

During the morning of August 20, the day before we were due to leave, I made one last, quick dive, taking several ten- and twelve-inch fish to Soopla. Without scuba equipment, I could only stay down half a minute (my breath-holding capacity had been *much* better when I was twelve!), but this was long enough to meet Soopla, stroke him once gently, and allow him to take from my hand the pantyhose bag with all the food in it.

At seven the next morning the *Stella* stuck her nose out of the Fitzgibbon Cove and began to retrace her course. We were to stop for fuel at Yes, then press on to Ketchikan, from where we would return to Canadian waters.

VISITORS FROM THE DEEP

Running at low speed at a time of high-water slack—the period of zero current preceding an ebb tide—the *Stella* nosed into the entrance of Foch Lagoon on a heading of 256 degrees during early afternoon on our fourth day out of Ketchikan. The weather was fine and warm, the sea flat —calm, ideal conditions under any circumstances but especially welcome just now, for the narrow passage that leads into the lagoon is only two fathoms deep in the center of its fairway, which is lined on both sides with jagged rocks that protrude from the water like fangs in some giant, gaping mouth. Overall, this corridor is only about six hundred feet long and two hundred feet wide, but it is far from straight and ends in an area of shoals that must be carefully negotiated.

Located at a latitude of 53° 46′ N., on the west side of the Douglas Channel and about twenty-four miles north of Hartley Bay, Foch Lagoon had intrigued me from the very moment I noticed it on the chart. Crooked as a dog's hind leg, this secluded, oceanic pool starts out by running almost due west, turns abruptly on a west-northwest course, then swings again to aim at true north. Overall, it is six miles long from its mouth to its terminus and a little more than one mile across at its widest point. It is contoured somewhat like a deep, irregularly shaped dish that has had a small chip broken out of one edge of its lip, the chip forming the entrance to the lagoon. The bottom immediately outside the lagoon, in Drumlummon Bay, is covered by thirty-six fathoms of water at its deepest point, but from there it begins to climb quite steeply to meet the shallow gateway. At the end of the twelve-foot-deep fairway the seabed is covered by sixty feet of water; three miles inside the pool, 136 fathoms, or 816 feet, of ocean lie beneath the keel of a vessel, from which location the floor rises once more, but gradually, until it shelves at the end, where a large creek tumbles down from the adjacent mountains and creates a small, sandy estuary.

This nearly landlocked inlet is not too dissimilar to a great many others found along the coast between northern Washington and Alaska, except for two unusual circumstances. The first involves the fact that the lagoon is connected to the Douglas Channel, and more particularly that this arm of the ocean is subject to abnormal wind and current fluctuations. Tides can rise as high as twenty-four feet; ebb currents predominate, but northern winds reduce, or may eliminate altogether, the force of flood streams, while southerly winds increase their strength and duration. As a result, it is dangerous to try to enter Foch Lagoon during an outflow, for the amount of water that pours through the gateway is enormous and travels at considerable speed. When an exceptionally high tide ebbs, no vessel can breast the boiling race during the peak of the flow.

The second peculiarity of the lagoon also relates in part to the narrow entrance and to the rise and fall of the tides but has to do with the fact that no less than twenty-three creeks empty into the firth. At least twice daily, significant volumes of ocean run in from Douglas Channel and are flushed out again during the ebb. At the same time, the surrounding creeks are continuously discharging fresh water into the pool.

These factors cause temperature and salinity levels to alter constantly, circumstances that create an aquatic habitat that is different from the one outside the entranceway. Just how greatly it differs is not currently known. Without some extremely elegant research, it is impossible to foretell the magnitude of the changes that occur, or even to time the frequency and duration of the occurrences. The major components of seawater are common salt, magnesium chloride, magnesium sulphate, and calcium sulphate, which are found in varying concentrations but each in unvarying proportion to the others, a bit of natural chemistry not yet fully understood. Compounds that contain potassium, iodine, bromine, as well as a variety of other elements are also found in the sea. For these reasons, in areas where rivers and ocean meet and mix at periodic or constant intervals, the amounts and kinds of salts and elements found in the ocean will vary, such variance having some effect—negative or positive—on the life forms within the habitat. This applies to all ocean coast biomes to a greater or lesser extent, the norm—that is to say, the average proportions of dissolved materials found in seawater—being calculated at 3½ percent of volume, or 3½ pounds of salts and compounds for every hundred pounds of water, but whether or not such "ideal" concentrations *ever* occur in coastal environments is a debatable issue.

Once we were safely anchored in a small bay on the southwest side of Foch and a little more than two miles from the entrance, I regretted that I had not allowed myself enough time to study this biologically fascinating ecosystem, but on reflection, I realized that any serious investigation would require more time, equipment, and specialized knowledge than I possessed; so, I stopped thinking in clinical terms and told myself that I should look upon my stay here as a holiday, a few days in which to relax while enjoying my surroundings. It was now August 24; I planned to leave on the morning of the thirty-first.

Eating a late lunch on deck, I became intrigued by a large herring gull that landed on top of the dinghy, paused to look at me, then flapped down to perch on the bow rail. I threw it a piece of bread, expecting the bird to rise and catch it in midair, but it remained passive until the food landed on the deck within a couple of feet of the rail; now it hopped down, strode forward, and ingested the offering. I shared my meal with the gull, then got up and entered the cabin through the hatch; the bird again perched on the rail. When I returned a little later and started to unlash the dinghy (for I was going to row ashore, climb one of the many medium mountains that ringed the lagoon, and take a good look at the surrounding country), the herring gull was still on board, now preening its feathers and altogether ignoring my presence. The bird was fully adult and appeared to be in good health, yet it was unusual for a member of this species to remain in such close proximity to a human, especially in these sparsely peopled regions. As I lowered the dinghy into the water with a clatter that did not disturb my visitor, I decided that the gull was tired and had elected to have a rest on board the *Stella*.

Beaching the dinghy on a fairly wide crescent of shingle in the center of which a lazy stream emptied itself, I started to climb the relatively easy flanks of the southernmost mountain, a tor that rose 3,260 feet and overlooked the Douglas Channel as well as the lagoon and the surrounding country to the north, east, and west. The land was predominantly dressed in lodgepole pines, arrow-straight trees with slender trunks, which rose from fifty to a hundred feet in height and looked rather like giant paintbrushes because the branches of this species usually fan out from a point about three-quarters of the way up. In other parts of the lower slopes grew clusters of Sitka spruces, some of which were even taller than the pines, their branches running out horizontally from the scaly barked trunks.

When after an hour's leisurely climb I reached the peak of the mountain, I found that the southern aspects of it were so densely treed that the water of the Douglas Channel was no longer visible; the view of the lagoon and its surrounding country was not, however, obstructed. From my position, I was able to count fourteen mountain peaks that virtually encircled Foch Lagoon, some of them a thousand or more feet taller than the one on which I stood, others lower. From my vantage I also counted seven bald eagles, each big bird flying a good distance from the others as it hunted for fish.

During the climb I had seen several Steller's jays, the western counterpart of the blue jay, and a number of varied thrushes, cousins of the robin. In addition, the calls of song sparrows filled the wooded slopes and on higher ground golden-crowned sparrows were in evidence, the male of this species made distinctive by its light gray front and neck and more particularly by the black bands on the sides of its head, in the center of which is a wedge-shaped splash of golden yellow. Nuthatches and chickadees were, of course, abundant in the area.

When I returned to the *Stella* in late afternoon, the gull was still sitting on the rail but now occupying a position fine on the port bow, closer to the hatch opening. There it stayed when I climbed on board, as nonchalant as before, but eyeing me expectantly, as though willing me to find some food for it. Responding to this silent plea, I cut some pieces off the rockfish that was going to be my supper and returned to the deck, tossing the food at the bird, who responded by hopping off the rail and feeding greedily.

Panhandling is a common characteristic of gulls, but this

one surpassed any of its fellows in the art! Significantly, it was the only herring gull in our vicinity, and whenever mew and glaucous-winged gulls came near, it scolded them noisily. Members of this species, *Larus argentatus*, usually breed inland in this region, although they range from the Atlantic right across Canada and into Alaska. For this reason they are not commonly seen on the west coast, especially during the summer. Perhaps this one had gone astray. Because only the gulls themselves are able to distinguish between males and females of the species, I could not determine the sex of my visitor, but I got into the habit of thinking of it as a female. After she had been my uninvited guest for two entire days, I christened her Emelia, the name of a small island in Douglas Channel a mile or so north of Drumlummon Bay.

Apart from those insults she screamed at her cousins when they dared to approach us, Emelia was companionably quiet. She preferred the bow section of the *Stella* but alternated occasionally by perching on the cabin top, content to hop or take short flaps when she needed to rise a foot or two above the deck. Had I not seen her fly when she first landed on the boat, I would have been tempted to assume that there was something wrong with her wings, for she was the most reluctant aviatrix I have ever met. Of course, I spoiled her, making sure that she always had enough to eat; but after five days during which she gulped down every bit of fish and bread I gave her but did no more than hop-fly from the rail to the cabin top, I decided she needed some encouragement. First I tried to chase her off the *Stella*, but she wouldn't go; she hopped around a great deal but did not take to the air. By this time I could approach her closely and she would take food from my fingers, but she would not allow me to touch her. Like all gulls, she suffered from a continuous nasal drip, which is the means by which these birds rid their systems of the large amounts of salt that they ingest; this is concentrated in solution within nasal glands and discharged slowly through the nostrils, running down the bill and dripping off its end.

Since she would not allow herself to be chased into flight, I decided to put her on short rations, feeding her lightly that evening. The next morning I refused to meet her accusing, hungry eyes when I left in the dinghy to row into the center of the lagoon, where the water was 116 fathoms deep, and where I planned to test the bottom for fish. For this purpose, I had fastened a piece of rockfish to a weighted hook that was tied to twenty feet of thirty-pound-test steel leader; this in turn was secured to a hand-winch (known in British Columbia as a hand gurdy) that contained a thousand yards of strong nylon cord, for none of my orthodox fishing reels could hold enough line to reach down almost seven hundred feet.

The hand reel was bolted to a piece of two-by-six-inch spruce board that was twenty-four inches long. On board the *Stella*, I would clamp this to the transom, but in the dinghy I secured it by sitting on one end of the board, the reel protruding between my thighs. To date, I had only used this method of fishing on four occasions, and on three of them I had failed to catch anything. The fourth attempt produced a halibut that appeared to be about six feet long when it came to the surface after putting up a scrap that lasted forty-eight minutes and then, only about ten feet from the *Stella*, gave one convulsive heave and straightened out the hook, freeing itself. I stopped using the heavy gear after that one experience because it seemed pointless to catch large fish only to throw them back again in a weakened or injured condition. But now I was overwhelmingly tempted to try the deeps of the Foch Lagoon, driven by insistent curiosity. Alas, after an hour all I'd gotten for my pains was a three-foot dogfish, which I released after netting it, the ungrateful little shark cutting the net in four places before swimming away. Disappointed, I quit, returning to the *Stella* to find that Emelia was no longer on board.

Occupied with the dogfish, I had not seen the gull fly from the boat to the north shore of our bay, but now I located her; she was sitting on a rock, preening and taking the sun. Just then she took to the air, circled once over the *Stella*, and then swooped down, aiming at the water some yards away and dropping low enough to pick up something from the surface. Holding the prize, she rose, turned, and headed straight for the *Stella*, landing in her usual place on the bow rail. I was standing by the hatchway and I noticed that she was carrying a little fish in her beak, holding it by the tail. Now she attempted to turn it, so she could swallow it headfirst, but the tiny, slippery thing fell on the deck, landing about a yard from me. Curious about the identity of Emelia's prize, I made a grab for it before she could hop down. It was such a strange fishlet that I purloined it, wanting to at least identify it before returning it to its rightful owner. Emelia squawked at me, indignant, but I assured her that she would get her prize back. To make it up to her, I went into the cabin and returned with some bread. That satisfied her.

Inside, I examined the small fish. It had obviously been dead for at least a day but, apart from being somewhat mangled by Emelia's beak, was in good condition. It was one-and-one-sixteenth of an inch long by seven-eighths of an inch deep, and its dorsal and anal fins were tall and narrow, the former sticking straight up, the latter projecting straight down. The caudal, or tail fin, was wide but exceptionally short and wavy in outline, while the tiny pectoral fins looked more like small leaves than fins. Instead of the usual gills seen in other fish, this one had a hole in front of its pectoral fins, an aperture that looked remarkably like an ear hole. In truth, it was a grotesque little fish. It had an upturned nose and a rather gaping mouth whose lower lip came to a stiff point and whose teeth were shaped rather like tiny grindstones. Consulting several books, I eventually identified it as an ocean sunfish, a creature of tropical waters that occasionally turns up in these latitudes. Adults of this species, *Mola mola*, grow up to nine feet in length and about eight feet in depth, and it is because of this extraordinary, almost round shape that the creature is often called a headfish. I would have liked to preserve it, but it was too badly damaged, which was a pity, for I felt it was rather unusual to come across such a small specimen of the breed. Females of the species are incredibly prolific, releasing an estimated 300 million eggs into the water from two ovaries. From the information I was able to glean after spending an hour with the literature, it is supposed that these sunfish breed in tropical seas, yet Emelia had captured a veritable baby here in Foch Lagoon. Headfish periodically range as far north as Alaska and are thought to feed on crustaceans, mollusks, sea stars, and fish. The Latin word, *mola*, means grindstone. When I gave the fish back to Emelia, she was not a bit interested in its rarity, merely in its edibility; in a blink, she swallowed it. Soon after that experience, she left us, circling twice overhead before disappearing toward the east.

We headed out of Foch Lagoon during low-water slack on August 31, running upchannel to the town of Kitimat, where we took on fuel after getting stuck in the river estuary, a mishap that necessitated my going over the side and pushing the *Stella* off the sandbar. Here we did not tarry, but because

I had worked for an hour to push and rock the boat off the bar, and because we hadn't left Foch Lagoon until late morning in order to wait for calm water to prevail in the exit fairway, it was almost one o'clock before we headed southward again. We went very slowly to avoid repeating the earlier experience, for the Kitimat River dumps a lot of silt into its estuary and this causes new sandbars to form on a regular basis, certainly faster than they can be charted.

Some twenty miles south of the river estuary, the Douglas Channel is split by a number of islands. The largest of these, Hawkesbury, and next largest, Maitland, combine to form two additional channels, Loretta and Devastation, the former eventually rejoining Douglas, the latter sweeping southward and ending in three arms; one leading to Verney Passage, another to Ursula Channel, the third to Alan Reach. Having a choice, I decided to return along Devastation Channel, then enter Ursula in order to stop for a day in Bishop's Bay, where there are some natural hot springs. But as I came abeam of the southern end of Loretta Island at about three o'clock that afternoon, an attractive little bay lured me into its shelter and I decided to stay the night. Deep and well protected, according to the chart it was a good anchorage. Here we stopped and I spent a pleasant afternoon and evening sunning myself, catching a three-pound salmon, and collecting some tide pool and shoreline specimens, which I studied and classified that night after a large supper of fried salmon dipped in white wine and accented with oregano, a little garlic powder, and a touch of paprika. Since I had needed to open the bottle of wine for the fish, it followed that the meal should be enlivened by its consumption, and while I was attending to the culinary preparations, the Chablis, recorked, was dangled over the side and allowed to chill in the water. Later, replete and content, I worked for an hour on the specimens I had collected, then turned in, meaning to get an early start the next day.

At 12:32 A.M. I was awakened by the sound of movement in the water and I immediately climbed out of the bunk, believing at first that a wind had sprung up and was disturbing the surface. But as I was putting on jeans, I realized that the *Stella* was moving only slightly, a gentle rocking that belied the presence of a blow. I paused to listen, realizing immediately that there was more sound than movement, a noise rather like that made by water swirling over a reef, a continuous susurrus that appeared to be surrounding the boat. I finished dressing, then took the five-cell flashlight and went on deck, going through the hatch to stand on the bow.

The night was clear, a half-moon illuminating the water and coastline. By this light I was astonished to see that the surface of the entire bay, which is three-quarters of a mile long by about half a mile wide, was moving with a persistent, undulating motion similar to that which might be noted in a pot of gently boiling water. The upheavals were rhythmic, the pulsations caused by unseen forces beneath the surface that sometimes appeared as swells similar to but gentler than those experienced on the open ocean and at other times showed as domes of sea rising perhaps three feet only to dissolve as quietly as they had arrived. Although the entire bay was affected, the movement was not uniform; sporadic upthrusts occurred in different places at different times, leaving large areas of still water in some localities and frothy patches, like whitecaps, in others.

I had not expected to encounter such a disturbance twenty-five miles inside an arm of the Pacific, but I recognized it for what it was, a phenomenon occasioned by the movement of sea along coastline, when relatively cold water comes in from the deeps and the warmer surface water is pushed seaward by the capricious currents that dominate along the Pacific coast. These exchanges, known as upwells, are of particular benefit to the coastal ecology because the water from the deeps that is forced upward and shoreward brings with it nitrates, phosphates, and other substances that have been used up in the more shallow waters by the living things found there in such great abundance. The occurrence is common all over the coastlines of the world, but it occurs with regular frequency along the Pacific shores of North America, especially during the summer.

These stirrings of ocean often bring with them life forms not usually found in local waters. In addition, they frequently trigger great activity among the organisms that dwell within the spheres of their influence because large numbers of planktonic life forms move with them.

I shone the light into the water, aiming the powerful beam at a place within a dozen feet of the bow. Captured within the brilliant cone, literally thousands of minute, darting organisms of various shapes were revealed within inches of the surface. Below these, somewhat larger creatures darted and lunged, evidently feeding on the upper layer; beneath the second echelon, still bigger fish could be seen as they entered and left the sphere of light. Moving the beam slowly, I saw hundreds of fish, some measuring only about six inches, others three and four feet long. It was a display the like of which I had never before witnessed, a free-for-all, Lucullan orgy during which everybody seemed to be eating everybody else, except, of course, for the unfortunate plankton, the appetizers at the head of the menu.

I was instantly filled with piscatorial zeal. I did not need food, but I could not resist the urge to dip a lure into that melee. Since I didn't want to kill anything, I used a red salmon fly about two inches long from the hook of which I had filed off the barb some weeks earlier; this allowed a fish an excellent opportunity of regaining its freedom, thus offering a greater challenge to the fisherman. If any fish *were* landed, however, they could easily be freed without risk of serious injury.

The artificial fly had hardly touched the water when it was struck powerfully by a fish, the indistinct outlines of which could not be identified. It was heavy and struggled fiercely, but as I was using thirty-pound-test line, I had it on board a short time later, whereupon it wriggled free of the hook and began flailing on the deck. Incautiously, because I was anxious to identify it, I made a grab and closed my right hand around the end of its body, between dorsal fin and tail, while trying to grip it behind the gills with my left hand—and it bit me. The stab delivered to the end of my index finger hurt a lot, but in the excitement of the moment I ignored it as I fought to immobilize the creature in order to examine it. The light was dim, so it was not until I had wrapped a cloth around the body, thus allowing me to get a good grip on it, that I managed to switch on the flashlight. By the beam I found myself staring at an extraordinary fish, the mouth of which bristled with shining fangs. About three feet long, the fish had a slim, tapering body surmounted on the back by an enormous dorsal fin, somewhat like a sailfish's, but not as tall and proportionately longer, beginning just behind the head and ending at a point midway above the anal fin; behind the dorsal was a small, fleshy, adipose fin, similar to those of salmon and trout. The eyes were large, the black pupils surrounded by a relatively wide, yellowish circle. I recognized this specimen from photographs I had seen; it was a Pacific lancetfish, *Alepisaurus borealis*, which can grow up to six feet in length and is found along the shores of the ocean from southern California to the Bering Sea. It was an ugly-looking customer, its sharp snout shaped so that the lower jaw projected beyond the upper.

I looked at my finger to find that it was bleeding profusely from a deep cut, three-eighths of an inch long, which ran slantwise between the nail and the first knuckle. When I picked up the strange visitor to throw it back into the water, I noticed that the enormous dorsal fin was able to fold itself out of sight, disappearing into a deep groove that ran along the back.

After a hasty trip to the cabin to dress my injury, I returned to the bow and in quick succession caught a large coho salmon, two vermilion rockfish about twenty-four inches long, and a quillback rockfish, *Sebastodes maliger*, that was about the same size but was so armed with spines that I allowed it to shake itself off the hook without seeking to touch it. Now I stopped fishing but continued to watch the display that surrounded us. Some time later, I used the pantyhose net to scoop some of the tiny planktonic creatures from the water and then spent almost an hour watching what seemed like millions of minute, translucent, red larvae that drifted in after the water around the *Stella* had remained quiet for a time. They were surrounded by a dense school of herring, which were feeding on them. I was unable to identify these half-inch creatures. They looked somewhat like salmon fry, but this was clearly only a superficial resemblance, for salmon spawn inland and their fry do not venture into the ocean until they are at least completing their first year of growth.

By morning the sea had returned to normal, except that the surface of the bay was dotted with dead fish, most of them small but a few measuring a foot in length; the gulls were having a feast, as were many small, live fish. I went out in the dinghy to look at some of the dead specimens, and after examining more than a dozen and finding them fairly normal representatives of these waters, I noted a very small, unusual fish, the most striking features of which were eyes housed in barrellike containers, their sight being directed upward.

On board, I searched the literature, comparing the specimen's characteristics as I read about a species known as barreleyes, *Macropinna microstoma*, a "large" specimen of which grows only to one-and-three-quarters inches in length. The one I discovered was "medium-sized," measuring one-and-a-half inches. Barreleyes are the kind of organism that appear to have been put together during a haphazard experiment! The body is deep, measuring nearly half its length; the dorsal and anal fins are large and wide; and the tail is also relatively big, resembling that of a goldfish. There is a salmonlike adipose fin between dorsal and tail, the abdominal fins are exceptionally long, and the pectorals are big and fan-shaped. The head looks like a series of bony plates put together with glue; the snout is similar to a duck's bill, projecting forward and flat; and there are no teeth in the jaws. But it is the arrangement of this creature's eyes that are most astonishing. These staring orbs are placed at the end of twin containers, the bases of which are somewhat wider than the tops and turned into smooth flanges that adhere to the head, being so marked as to appear to have been riveted in place. The eyes, quite large for so small a fish, can only look up—unless the fish swims on its side or upside down! The cornea projects above the rim of the barrel in which the orb is housed, and the lens protrudes farther still, like a piece of convex crystal. What this creature lives on or how it hunts was not mentioned in any of the books I read. So I opened its stomach. The gut was crammed with minute larvae, but without more specialized experience I could not identify the seemingly different types of organisms that had been compacted and turned into a loose mass of jellylike material in which a few hair-thin bones were evident. I received the impression that the barreleye earns its keep by browsing along the bottom, using its eyes to look for dangers from above rather than for food. The stomach contents and absence of teeth suggested that the fish sucks up tiny, soft-bodied animals that can be swallowed without mastication, organisms such as the larvae and ova of fish, or the larvae of barnacles and other members of the Mollusca phylum. Records show that these fish have been captured at depths varying from forty-eight to five hundred fathoms, a spread which suggests that barreleyes can adapt to a wide variety of habitats. The greatest depth in Loretta Bay is given on the chart as twenty-four fathoms, but the waters outside vary from thirty-six to almost two hundred fathoms.

If I had not run out of formaldehyde, I would have sought to preserve the specimen; as it was, I threw the fish back into the water after making a rough drawing of it and noting all its details.

Before noon that day the *Stella* was lying at anchor in Bishop's Bay and I was soaking in good, hot water in the springs that bubble out of the ground near the shoreline, spilling their overflow into the sea. This area is also of biological interest and merits investigation. Perhaps one day I may be able to return to Foch Lagoon and Bishop's Bay with enough time and equipment to do thorough studies of these fascinating marine ecosystems.

11

THE SPIRITS DANCE

Namu lay five miles astern when the five orcas appeared on the surface about half a mile ahead of the *Stella*. We were making 6 knots, heading south through Fitz Hugh Sound on September 12, my birthday, while enjoying fine, clear weather and a sea that was only marginally agitated. I was about to increase power and close the distance between us and the whales when the pod sounded. Hasty observation of the dorsal fins left me with the impression that the group was composed of one large male and four females of various lengths.

Seven minutes later, with Hakai Passage in sight to starboard, the group rose again, this time about four hundred yards ahead. Now I accelerated to full power, soon cutting the distance in half, then adjusting the controls to match the whales' speed. Through the glasses I was able to confirm my earlier supposition. The bull was at least twenty feet long, the largest of the four cows almost that size, and the smallest about fourteen feet in length. The *Stella* was now making 12 knots and so were the whales. The distance between us remained constant.

Eight days previously we had left Bishop's Bay under cloudy skies, but with calm seas. The temperature by this time was chilly, advertising the approach of autumn and the coming of gales and rain, but despite the inclement prospects, I found myself reluctant to hurry, unwilling to bring our journey to an end. Nearly six months had passed since the day I took possession of the *Stella*, and during this period my attachment to the small boat had grown strong; the prospects of terminating our relationship and selling the vessel were far from appealing. Then, too, I didn't know what I was going to do afterward, for with every sea mile traveled, I had given no thought to the future. Now, as the moment of decision loomed closer I found that I was still unable to plan ahead. Procrastinating, I elected to live one day at a time while enjoying the scenery and observing the animals and birds we encountered as we ran south in easy stages. Until today, except for some rough going when we crossed Milbanke Sound, our voyage had been relatively uneventful. We had docked at Klemtu for the last time four days ago and had lounged there for two entire days. Then, perhaps because I needed to understand the influences that had caused me to leave Bella Bella so hurriedly on our way north, I spent twenty-four hours in that community, departing from it without having formed conclusions that differed to any great extent from my initial impressions.

The previous night we had spent moored at Namu; this morning, my birthday arrived unnoticed, until I set down the date in the log. It was then noon and we were still tied up at the float, so after the entry was completed and I had eaten some lunch, I made coffee and celebrated my arrival into the world by adding a measure of brandy to the brew. With a second cup of the same perched on the chart shelf, we headed away from land and reentered Fitz Hugh Sound. About an hour later the orcas arose for the first time.

Watching the gam through the fieldglasses, I noticed that the bull was swimming rather erratically, going from left to right, sometimes dashing ahead and as often lagging behind.

Then, while he was in the center of the group, he began to roll, turning right around so that his white markings flashed with each maneuver. This slowed the group, for the cows, perhaps admiring the bull's antics, matched their pace to his. After I had observed this behavior for several minutes, I brought the *Stella* to within a hundred yards of the gam and reached for the camera. Alas, it was at this moment that the bull completed his last roll and dived, followed immediately by his harem. They didn't surface again.

We reached Port Hardy, on Vancouver Island, in late evening, making our last approach with the running lights on. The next morning, we made for Kelsey Bay, farther down the east coast of the big island, crossing over fairly rough water in rain that began at first light. By the time we reached the shelter of our next port, a gale had started, and by next morning it was blowing at Force 8. The *Stella* remained moored and I, dressed in a rain suit, decided to go ashore to explore some of the country in the vicinity of the town. I packed a lunch and a flask of coffee.

The Adam River runs down from the mountains and passes Kelsey Bay at a distance of about five miles, flowing in a northerly direction east of the community and eventually emptying itself into Johnstone Strait. The valley through which this waterway courses is long and fairly wide, flanked along its entire route by majestic mountains, which are for the most part covered in densely packed timber; those mountains that lie south of the river are taller, their peaks snow clad for most of the year; those located north of the stream are green all the way to their tops. It was into this region that I walked that morning, setting a brisk pace at first, then, hindered by the evergreens, walking more slowly and allowing myself time to observe the life forms that periodically drew themselves to my attention.

After lunch on the west bank of the fast-flowing river, while I was drinking coffee, a small flock of band-tailed pigeons alighted in the lower branches of an enormous Douglas fir, their owllike voices filling the wet forest with soft, rather mournful notes. This species, *Columba fasciata*, is found in Canada only along a thin, coastal belt of the British Columbia mainland and on Vancouver Island, then southward to Utah, northcentral Colorado, in all of the Pacific states and the Rocky Mountains, and southward to Central America. Its common name derives from a pale, broad band that extends across its fanlike tail. It is a sturdily built bird with yellow feet and a buttercup-hued bill with a black tip. The lower back and upper tail coverts are a bluish gray, and the upper parts of the wings and the back are slate gray; the light green neck shines metallically and is further enhanced by a white crescent just behind the base of the skull. The head, throat, and chest are a beautiful shade of mauve, delicately laced with pink streaks in certain light.

The flock numbered seven birds, all moving restlessly, either hopping from branch to branch or, more occasionally, flying down to feed on the berries of a shrubby cascara, *Rhamnus purshiana*. From this tree is derived the laxative, *cascara sagrada*, which used to be prescribed extensively by the medical profession to relieve cases of chronic constipation. This medicine is obtained from the bark of the tree. The berries, presumably, do not have laxative properties, else the pigeons would not have indulged themselves quite so freely!

By midafternoon, an estimated eight miles from Kelsey Bay, I was walking along a height of land that overlooked the river and a relatively wide area of open land, when movement on the edge of the shrubby clearing attracted my notice. I stopped, concealed by the thick trunk of a fir, and lifted the glasses to scan the place, which was about 100 feet downhill and about 150 yards away from my position. At first only tree trunks and brush rewarded me, but a moment or two later I saw the head and shoulders of a cougar, a tawny statue that was evidently checking the more open country before venturing across it.

This subspecies of mountain lion is found throughout the entire forested range of Vancouver Island and has been classified as *Felis concolor vancouverensis*. These cats are somewhat smaller and darker than their relatives elsewhere in North America, being fourteen to twenty inches shorter in overall length and thirty to forty pounds lighter, though weight is a variable in all subspecies.

As I watched, the puma stepped confidently into the open, allowing me to see that it was soaking wet and somewhat thin, which suggested that it had not been hunting success-fully in recent weeks. I judged its weight at about a hundred pounds and its length at about seven feet, including a tail that was probably thirty inches long. Flicking this sinuous ap-pendage as though irritated, the cat marched resolutely across the opening, paused for a moment to examine the treeline from which it had emerged, then moved swiftly into the forest with graceful, easy bounds. No more than a couple of minutes elapsed between the time I had first spotted the cougar's movement in the undergrowth and the instant the cat was again swallowed by the forest, but I was able to note that it was a male. Its coat was the color of toffee made darker in places where the wet had caused the hairs to adhere to the body. Contrasting with the tawny coat were milk white blazes around the mouth, chin, and chest.

Brief though the sighting was, it immediately suggested a new venture, one that I could devote myself to after this journey was completed. I had studied cougars in the past, but never over a period of time; rather my observations had been sporadic and limited to individual animals in a number of locations. When wintering in the Kootenay region of British Columbia with Yukon, I had left him behind occasionally while I sought to track mountain lions, a pursuit that yielded few sightings but during the course of which I had learned a great deal about the animals by studying the marks of their passage. On one grim occasion I was persuaded to accompany a local hunter (exterminator would be a better word) during a chase on foot accompanied by trained cougar hounds. That gruesome experience would not soon be forgotten, because it was my gun that directed a bullet into the cat's brain. I had been forced to shoot when the overweight hunter lagged so far behind me and the dogs that he was nowhere in evidence when the mountain lion turned to attack.

Now, as the cougar disappeared in the forest, I thought it would be interesting to attempt to study mountain lions during the coming winter and spring, working in one specific location, perhaps the mountains of southeastern British Columbia, a region that Yukon and I had visited before undertaking our voyage up the Nass River. Although I made no definite plans then and there, the idea had appeal, partly because of a deep sense of nostalgia but mostly because it provided me with a new goal. Retracing my path to Kelsey Bay, I played with the notion; then, in sight of the town, I tucked it into the back of my mind, where it could simmer quietly until the time was right.

I slept soundly that night, rocked by the motion of the *Stella* and soothed by the rhythmic drumming of the rain. When I awakened at dawn the weather had settled down. The wind was now at Force 3, a strength that did not inconvenience us, and although there were clouds overhead, big white ones that now and then obscured the sun, they were sailing toward the northeast, for the light blow was fanning up from warmer latitudes.

Kelsey Bay was still slumbering when we slipped our moorings and made for Race Passage. As a result of this early start, we arrived at Campbell River just before 11:00 A.M. Here I had the gas tanks filled, then turned around and settled the *Stella* on a bearing that would take us across the Strait of Georgia to Powell River, on the mainland, for I had concluded that even though I had left my car in a garage in Victoria—and would thus have to cross to the island by ferry to collect it again—I would almost certainly sell the *Stella Maris* more quickly in the big city.

To this end, after spending the night in Powell River, we started early the next day and completed an uneventful passage down the west coast of British Columbia. At 4:17 P.M. on September 16, we tied up at a marina in West Vancouver.

My camp was located within the shelter of some young alpine firs that intruded into a small valley about two thousand feet up the south flank of Mount Toby, a 10,537-foot white-top that forms part of the Purcell Range in the East Kootenay region of British Columbia. Before me, a good campfire was boiling water for tea while flushing the front part of my body with heat; at my back, a small lean-to shelter made of dead poles and thatched with evergreen branches contained my packsack and sleeping bag, which I had spread over a "mattress" of short boughs. It was late afternoon and while I waited for the tea water to boil, I sat on the ground, my back against a fir trunk and the *Stella*'s log propped on my knees, for I was making a final, retrospective entry that would complete the record of our voyage. I suppose that the conclusion of such a narrative should have been undertaken at the coast, instead of more than five hundred miles inland, but I had neglected the task in order to make arrangements for the sale of the boat and because I had become anxious to leave the crowded streets of Vancouver. After half a year away from civilization, I was intimidated by the clattering, roaring traffic and the many hurrying humans that seemed determined to elbow me off the sidewalks, and I had the feeling that I was traveling in an alien world dominated by mindless animus. Vancouver is a beautiful and prosperous city. Backdropped by tall mountains and lapped by the ocean, it had always, hitherto, made me feel welcome and at ease, but now this was no longer so. The city, of course, had not changed. *I* had, and I well knew it.

It had been too late to make the sale arrangements with a boat dealer the evening I arrived, so I slept on the *Stella* for the last time, rose early, and, aided by the Yellow Pages and the telephone, made the preliminary contact. An hour or so later a sales representative arrived dockside and we negotiated a price. Later yet, at the salesroom, I signed the necessary papers and returned to the *Stella* to pack my belongings, belatedly discovering that I had a lot of gear to haul away and that I could surely have used the station wagon. I called a taxi, loaded up my packsacks and bundles, and gave the cabbie the address of the Devonshire Hotel, a hostelry that I had often used in the past as a pied-à-terre in the city. There, from lunchtime to the dinner hour, I rested while trying to find solace on the television screen, but apart from catching up with the more negative aspects of the current news situation, I could find little there to interest me. By evening, I knew I had made a mistake; instead of feeling rested, I found I had become angry, irritated by the banalities so profusely broadcast and depressed by the irrationality of the world as seen through the eyes of dispassionate newscasters. I showered, dressed in city togs, and went downstairs to the dining room. There I began to relax, lulled into tranquillity by a young woman piano player who coaxed classical music from the instrument. Amidst the kind of seedy-genteel elegance that I prefer above all other, in a quiet atmosphere where the dining-room staff moved and talked softly, I found myself again enjoying the grace of civilization.

The next day another taxicab carried me and my baggage to a ferry that took me to Victoria, after which I collected the car, put my belongings inside it, and then drove north to Kelsey Bay, where I boarded the Prince Rupert ferry.

That night I was on deck when we began the crossing of Milbanke Sound and I leaned over the stern rail and watched the ocean, luminous and sparkling, under the light of a full, yellow moon. Phosphorescent plankton tumbling in our wake looked like a meteorite shower passing swiftly and incandescently through the atmosphere, while off in the distance the moon and stars were reflected on the sizeable Pacific swells. Milbanke Sound had the power to bounce the huge vessel that carried me over its restless surface. Occasionally there came a clanging thump, evidence that the ferry had encountered a runaway log; the impact of wood against metal reminded me vividly of the first trip made by the *Stella* over this expanse of turbulent sea.

Later, lying in a comfortable bunk within a cabin that was tiny by big-ship standards, yet luxurious and spacious compared to the *Stella*'s modest quarters, I slept intermittently, in part because I was restless but mostly because I wanted to savor the crossing, which might well be my last experience of the Inside Passage. Accustomed to awakening with the rising of the sun, I was on deck when the east began to glow. The ferry was then entering Wright Sound, the Douglas Channel lying to starboard. I remembered the *Stella* with too much nostalgia, so I went below and became the first customer for breakfast in the saloon.

We docked at Prince Rupert at about 9:30 A.M. An hour or so after I drove off the ferry, the station wagon was running on the Yellowhead Highway in that area where the road clings to the skirts of the mountains and lies above the Skeena River. Coming to a place where there was room to park, I stopped the car and got out, noting that early ice already coated the shore waters, thin panes that glistened in the sunlight. Now I felt that I had come full circle. Here I'd begun my small odyssey on a spring morning, driving this same car after coming off the same ferry. The ice had been retreating then; now my return coincided with the new ice of autumn.

It was at this point that I concluded the *Stella*'s log, closing the travel-stained book and securing it with an elastic band. Rising, I went to the packsack and put away the record, then took out a new book, this one intended to serve as a land journal. Herein I noted that after leaving the ferry terminal I had driven virtually nonstop for thirty hours, following the Yellowhead route, then turning south to pass through Quesnel, Williams Lake, Kamloops, and Princeton, from where I swung east on the old road through the mountains I had first traveled with Yukon. This took me through the town of Trail via a series of loops, climbs, and drops until I reached the West Kootenay region of British Columbia, at Salmo. From here I followed Highway 3 to Creston and Cranbrook, in East Kootenay, where I stopped, checked into a motel, and fell asleep at one o'clock in the afternoon. I woke up at six the following morning, September 22, and checked out immediately after breakfast. I drove northward through Kimberley, soon afterward turning off the main highway to follow a secondary route that runs west of Windermere Lake. Between the communities of Inveremere and Athalmer, another somewhat rough road plunges into the forested mountains and runs through a valley. This road ends abruptly where the wilderness begins. Above it is Mount Toby.

Leaving the car, I set out into the bushland, following my nose. My backpack contained enough food for two days, an axe, one mug, one frying pan, and one saucepan in addition to a change of clothes and my sleeping bag. To this day I am not quite sure why I decided on this course of action, though it may be that I felt in need of a quiet period during which I could contemplate my life and perhaps firm up plans for the future. In any event, after climbing gradually upward for about two thousand feet, I found a small alpine valley at one end of which a rivulet of icy water cascaded to form a small, ice-bound pool. Here I made camp.

Now, the first part of my new journal completed, I put the notebook away and made tea, then replenished the fire and cooked my supper. Afterward I sat at peace as evening came, weakened, and was eventually banished by night. Frost was in the air, but I was warm and comfortable, swathed in a goose-down parka, a fur hat on my head, and the heat of the fire bathing the front of my body. My eyes roved between the mesmeric flames and the equally hypnotic stars as they emerged one by one until the sky was filled with phosphoric lights. Not a wisp of cloud intruded between the forest and the infinity of space. The moon, made gibbous by the wane, hung over Mount Findlay, its distorted lower edge seeming almost to touch the darkened peak. In that star-hung firmament the blackness of space was not noticeable, the backdrop appearing as a glowing, deep blue.

From the valley I had an undisturbed view of the northern sky. Around me the evergreens whispered, for there was the merest hint of a breeze stirring the gentle needles, causing them to rub companionably against one another. At this time the forest was quiet for the most part, though now and then I heard the rustle made by mice as they scampered through tunnels dug beneath the thick carpet of dead needles that covered the ground. Earlier a distant pack of wolves had howled suddenly, but only once. Within the shelter of some of the trees in my vicinity roosting birds chirped sleepily on occasion, and sometimes this small note was followed by a nearly imperceptible sound, which was made as the caller changed its stance among the needles.

When I first noticed the Aurora Borealis it must have been about midnight; I had momentarily mistaken the first pulses of the lights for stray reflections of moonlight, but then the full intensity of the green-blue refulgence became unmistakable.

As I watched the celestial display, recollection of the stellar reflections seen in the waters of Milbanke Sound from the stern rail of the ferry caused me to compare the remembered image with the actual spectacle, but as I continued to stare into space, I had a vision of the surface of Foch Lagoon and saw again the dancing, shimmering plankton that had come so mysteriously when the deeps yawned and caused the ocean to pulse. My light probing at the water had created an Auroral effect; the luminescent little creatures beneath the surface had reflected it and glittered like the stars now sparkling over my head.

With the heat of the fire flushing my face, I noted how the northern lights contracted into themselves, going from sweeping waves into individual shafts that, like searchlights, put a fluorescent blush on the distant treetops and caused the snow that sheathed the mountain peaks to take on a mild, pink hue for fractions of a second, until the lights again expanded and swept over the universal plane.

It occurred to me that the lights were like music—mind music, appreciated through the eyes rather than the ears, a kaleidoscopic, mute sonata that stimulated the imagination and conjured visions of beautiful things. A sense of peace and well-being came to me and there was room in my mind only for good memories. A Cree Indian had once told me that he could see right inside himself while he watched the lights, adding that all of him was then "just good, like sweet berries on a bush." He'd said of the lights: "*Chepuyuk nemehitowuk*," which means, "The spirits are dancing." Good spirits, he insisted, for they give light and allow a man to look at the truth that lies in his own heart. I had not fully understood my friend's meaning at the time, but now I could sense at least a part of it. Since earliest times the northern lights have lightened the hearts of those men who crouch contemplatively before an open fire while at peace with their wilderness environment. So they did for me that night, for I was ready to believe in the dancing spirits of the Cree.

Fantasy, of course! As explained by science, the northern lights are a natural phenomenon that occurs when tiny particles break away from the sun and, traveling at high speed toward the earth, collide with one another, and undergo ionization. This is undoubtedly true, and yet it is so much more satisfying to view the Aurora Borealis as the Cree see it, to think of the lights as dancing, well-intentioned spirits bent upon offering solace to the mortals who look upon them!

As I contemplated those gentle pastels glowing in the September sky, the explanations of science were of no consequence as the Stone Age being each of us carries deep within his subconscious responded to the display. I had begun my journey to this place feeling an irrational guilt for abandoning the *Stella Maris* and turning my back on her. She had become a companion and had carried me bravely over more than sixteen hundred miles of Pacific waters. Even though I told myself that the little boat was an insentient object crafted for pleasure-seekers who wished to romp over protected, offshore seas, I couldn't help feeling that I had betrayed her, just as I had once felt I'd betrayed my wolf-dog Yukon when I took him out of the wilderness and into the city of Winnipeg—and, if the truth be known, just as I felt that I had betrayed Joan in some way when the tiny balloon that inflated inside her head burst and killed her.

Now, soothed by the motile patterns of the marching lights, I was no longer troubled. I realized that my feelings of guilt had been evoked by egotism, that exaggerated sense of one's own importance that has so much trouble dealing with personal loss. Yukon and I had shared life together and we had each derived benefit from our relationship; he had taught me much about himself, and I had given him the trust, love, and understanding he'd so desperately needed when he came to me. Joan and I had entered into a rich and rewarding partnership, sharing a deep understanding of each other in an atmosphere of tranquil, mutual love. Her death had *not* diminished me. I knew that she had contributed to my growth and had left me a part of herself that will continue to exist within me until I, too, have run my course. I had done battle with negative emotional forces, and I had won, helped by Yukon and by Joan, and by the *Stella Maris*, and no less so by the wide-sweeping and turbulent Pacific Ocean. And though I had now left the sea, I still had the wilderness and my inherent determination to learn from it, and to share my experiences with others.

I felt elated, looking forward to the future, whatever it might bring. Waiting until the fire died down to twinkling, ashen coals, I turned in. As I lay relaxed inside my sleeping bag, the distant howling of the wolves reached me again, a medley that began low, climbed the scales until it reached the highest pitch, then slowly faded.